VITTORE'S
SECRET

K.N. Cipriani

abbott press®
A DIVISION OF WRITER'S DIGEST

Vittore's Secret

ISBN: 978-1-4582-0495-0 (sc)
ISBN: 978-1-4582-0496-7 (e)
ISBN: 978-1-4582-0497-4 (hc)

Library of Congress Control Number: 2012912639

Abbott Press books may be ordered through booksellers or by contacting:

Abbott Press
1663 Liberty Drive
Bloomington, IN 47403
www.abbottpress.com
Phone: 1-866-697-5310

Printed in the United States of America

Abbott Press rev. date: 01/28/13

CHAPTER ONE

Cara exited the quiet little Italian side street where Caffè Greco was located and entered Piazza di Spagna. Ahead of her, atop the Spanish Steps, loomed the 16th century church Trinità dei Monti whose Baroque majesty set the tone for what this area would become today, one of the most famous fashion districts in the world.

Tourists proudly carried bags from the couture houses of Valentino, Bruno Magli, Giorgio Armani, Salvatore Ferragamo, and Gucci. She herself had the red signature bag of the world famous jeweler, Cartier and it held the most expensive gift she had and would no doubt ever purchase.

Cara had arrived at the Leonardo Di Vinci International Airport ten days earlier and the moment her feet hit the ground her life had been a whirlwind of emotions; love, hate, betrayal, fear and joy, pure unadulterated joy. She had cried more, smiled more and had made love more since landing in Italy than she had in the past five years. Now in two days she was headed back to New York City to rebuild her life. For while in Roma her old one had crumbled and nothing in her world would be the same again.

A commotion on the other side of the Piazza drew Cara's attention. Two men stopped their cars and were standing in the street shouting insults as the drivers around them blared their horns impatiently. She smiled. That is exactly how she entered The Eternal City, with angry drivers cursing her and her driver, Romano. Dear pudgy, toothless Romano. Who knew he and his stinky, rusted out Fiat would have lead Cara to such an incredible vacation?

Cara drank in her surroundings listening to the insanity in the street. *Italians were definitely passionate people.*

Ten Days Earlier

The flight from New York City to Roma had been uneventful; the trip, however, was not. Cara had begun her journey in the coach section of the huge Boeing 777-200, row 24, fourth seat in a row of five. Now she was in first class with her feet curled up under her, sipping a martini. The average person would have called the chain of events that led to this new seating arrangement proof of divine intervention. Cara took it in stride and added it to the long list of occurrences that had interwoven themselves in her life.

Her father told her she always managed to "land in it". He said she could get herself into more trouble than any one person he had ever known, yet she somehow managed to come out smelling like a rose. She smiled thinking of what her father would say to this turn of events.

She had been sitting next to a woman with two children, a boy around two years old and a girl about five. They were an hour into the flight and Cara noticed a man pacing in the aisle next to the woman. The woman reached out her hand to make him stop and shook her head. He put his arms up in frustration and the woman finally stood and moved to the front of the plane as the man took her seat.

"Daddy, where did Mommy go?" asked the little girl sitting in the center seat next to Cara.

"She is with your brother, James. He isn't feeling well; Mommy went to take care of him." The little girls' father replied.

"I want Mommy!"

Oh, oh, here we go!, thought Cara. She actually loved kids, but when she saw that she was seated next to two children and one parent coupled with an eight and a half hour flight, she knew somewhere along the route there would be tears.

"Bethie, Mommy will be right back. Where is your coloring book?" He asked, not really expecting her to know because he was already digging through a tote tucked under the seat in front of him.

"I want Jimmie and Mommy to sit with us!"

"They can't Bethie. We told you there were not enough seats together." "Daddy" found the coloring book reached across a sleeping little boy and handed it to Bethie, who promptly threw it on the floor, spilling her drink onto her tray. Bethie began to cry waking her baby brother, who began crying, also.

Cara quickly grabbed her little cocktail napkin trying to stop the liquid from spreading towards her. She wasn't just trying to be helpful but grape juice was quickly heading her way. The napkin was completely ineffective in stopping the flow.

"Bethie stop crying!" "Daddy's" tone was not calming Bethie down.

Cara was beginning to wonder if "Daddy" was going to help with the mess his daughter made. "Excuse me do you have any napkins over there?" Cara was trying to direct his attention to her plight, but he was obviously out of his element. His eyes were in panic mode.

A flight attendant stopped to see what was causing the disturbance and found two crying children and a grown woman trying to hold back a tidal wave of purple dye.

"Can I help you sir?" she asked.

"Get my wife; she is up in business class with our son who is not feeling well."

The flight attendant finally directed her attention to Cara, "I will send someone with a towel."

"Thanks!" Cara had her hands on top of the tray to create a dam.

Bethie snapped her head around and looked at Cara noticing for the first time that someone was seated next to her. Then she saw the empty seat to Cara's left.

"Daddy, tell this lady to move so Jimmie and Mommy can sit with us!" Bethie gave Cara a challenging look.

Cara did a double take. *Was this kid really only five?*

A towel arrived, "Let me help." Cara caught the delicious fragrance of his cologne before she saw his deep blue eyes. Her heart stopped. *Damn, this guy's handsome!*

A male flight attendant leaned over her shoulder and began cleaning up the tray to Cara's right. They were a tangle of arms and hands; hers to hold the liquid back, his mopping it up between her hands. His chest pressed into her back, it was rock hard. Cara melted a little.

"There, I think you're safe to move now." His breath was hot against her neck; his cologne was like an aphrodisiac. Cara's heart raced.

Damn it! She hated it when a man made her remember how long it had been since...*since what Cara, since you've been in bed with one?*

"Daddy, tell her to move!" Her reverie was shattered.

The attendant looked across to "Daddy", "Is there a problem I can help you with sir?" He continued to wipe up the mess and handed Cara a clean towel for her hands, perfect hands with really long fingers. *Doesn't that indicate something?* Cara smiled as she quickly glanced at his hips. Indeed it did! *Damn!*

"My wife and I couldn't get seats together." "Daddy" sounded more than a little pissed.

"Would you like me see what I could do?"

"Please." Ah, finally relief in the man's voice.

"Where is your wife sitting?"

"Business class, she's with our son."

"I see. I will not be able to get all of you into Business Class, will that be all right?"

Cara watched Mr. Yummy and "Daddy", who wasn't such a bad looking guy either.

"Anything, just don't leave me alone with the kids." He sounded so desperate Cara almost volunteered to be his Au Pair for the remainder of the flight. Then she looked at Bethie and changed her mind.

"I could move to another seat and they can have mine. No one is sitting next to me." Cara was more than willing to flee from Bethie and company, although "Daddy" could join her if he wanted.

"Would that help you out, sir?" the attendant asked the overly stressed father.

"Yes!" the fathers' voice boomed. Cara couldn't blame him. Bethie could eat him alive; he needed backup. Cara glanced down to see the now quiet Bethie, arms crossed with a smug little look on her face, well aware that she just accomplished her goal.

Was this really a child or a demon spawn?

Cara began collecting her things. The sooner she was away the happier she would be.

"Thank you, Ms?" the attendant asked.

"McGuire, Cara McGuire."

"Thank you, Ms. McGuire, allow me, and I will locate another seat for you."

When they were safely away Cara asked him, "Do you guys get combat pay? Bethie is quite a challenge!"

"Fortunately, Bethie is coach's worry."

They arrived at the bulk head that separated coach from business class. "Wait here please, Ms. McGuire," he directed her to the planes mid-galley, "I will move the wife and child from business class to coach. Then I will take care of you."

A huge butterfly hit the inside of Cara's stomach silently hoping he would take real good care of her.

Cara studied his long torso and broad shoulders. He fit into his clothes like he were wearing an Armani suit rather than a standard issue American Airline uniform; couple that with his perfect complexion, brown hair, blue eyes and the brilliantly white teeth and he could have been a model for the airline rather than a purser.

"Thank you…?"

"Ian."

"Ian," Cara repeated his name as he stepped past her to attend to Bethie's family reunion.

Cara waited ten minutes before Ian returned. She picked up her tote and purse and turned to go towards the back of the plane.

He touched her elbow softly, "Ms. McGuire, you deserve the combat pay, please follow me." He then turned, walking her straight through business class to first class.

He glided his hand towards an empty seat. "Here you are. Now is there anything I can do for you Ms. McGuire?"

"I think you already have! This will certainly be a memorable flight!"

"I can always find ways to make your trip more memorable." He was leaning in very close to Cara's ear and a shiver went down her spine.

Yikes! Cara's face reddened.

Ian smiled pleased with himself that he was making her blush. "At least let me get you a dirty martini," he hesitated and leered at her like a hungry predator, "or maybe you like it filthy?"

Double yikes! This could be fun.

"How filthy do you suggest?"

Ian raked his eyes over Cara starting at the top of her wavy auburn hair, taking in her emerald green eyes and stopping at her chest and letting his eye move down the opening of her blouse to her deep cleavage. He smiled.

"I think you would like it very filthy, Ms. McGuire."

E Gads!

Cara settled herself into her new seat as she waited for her martini. She pulled out her tour book, stuffing it into the seat pouch in front of her, got her iPod from her purse so she could listen to her music and then began taking off her boots. Cara loved to go barefoot and that wasn't going to change just because she was 35,000 feet in the air.

Cara had her skirt pulled up to her knees. She was wearing a caramel colored lace skirt that fell about mid-calf. She bought it for the trip and decided to wear it on the plane. She knew it would have made more sense to have worn warm-ups but she was going to Roma for god's sake. In the city of romance and fashion, warm-ups would have been so American!

With her left boot off she was leaning over to remove the other when she heard, "Scusate."

She saw a pair of long muscular legs covered in denim standing a few inches from her. She looked up and BAM! Her mouth dropped open as she looked at the most gorgeous man she had ever laid eyes on. His jeans fit tight in all the right places and the thin silk tee stretched snuggly across a six-pack abs. His hands were large and his arms rock hard. He was built like an athlete. His jaw was strong; then she saw the darkest brown eyes she had ever seen gazing down on her.

"Huh?" *Intelligent reply Cara, You've wowed him now!*

"Scusi, my seat is next to you." He motioned to the empty seat by the window. "Per favore?"

"Oh, sure." Cara stood, her skirt falling around her legs. She glanced at the man who seemed to enjoy watching it drape around her before meeting her eyes and smiling.

Cara made a move to get out of the way so he could get to his seat, but he moved in the same direction. Cara quickly moved in the other direction, as did he. By the fourth attempt to let him by he took matters into his own hands, literally. He placed his hands on her waist and lifted her slightly while he moved her to one side as he stepped to the other. His eyes were kind and smiling.

"We dance well, Bella." His mouth was beautiful. His lips were amazing. Cara gnawed on her lower lip knowing the slight pain would keep her mind focused.

He took his seat and Cara sat as well and began trying to get her right boot off. Her hands were shaking. *Get a grip Cara, jeeze!* She really needed to get to Roma and meet up with her fiancé. She had begun envisioning every man she met naked. It was sexual tension on steroids and it was driving her nuts!

"Scusate?"

Oh god, now what? "Yes?"

"May I help you remove your boot? It is very difficult to do in such a small space." His smile set butterflies off inside her.

"Thank you."

"Place your foot here."

Cara angled herself in the seat and placed the heel of her right boot on his knee as directed. He looked at her foot for a second then turned and smiled at her as his hand slowly pushed the hem of her skirt up past her knee. Then he let his fingertips tickle down the inside of her leg on their way to the zipper of her boot.

Ohmigod.

Cara let out a squeak. He turned his head from her boot to her eyes and smiled. She felt the boot slowly being removed from her foot.

What the hell are you doing! Damn you are going to get yourself into so much trouble.

He leaned over and placed her boot on the floor than sat up reaching between her legs took the hem of her skirt and brought it down over her knees, then touched her leg softly, "Finé!"

Cara was close to passing out when she heard, "Ms. McGuire, I have your martini."

Cara grabbed it and took a huge gulp!

And that was how she ended up in First Class with a filthy martin. She "landed in it".

CHAPTER TWO

The reason for her trip to Italy was to meet her fiancé, Bryan, who had been there for the last three months working on a project for his father's law firm. And although flirting was fun, Cara knew she'd never act on any of it; nope, she was loyal, stupidly loyal.

Cara sipped her martini thinking about her and Bryan. When he left in June, things had been a bit uncertain. They rarely saw each other over the past year and when they did it was disappointingly unromantic. And because of the abstinence, Cara had begun to imagine what every man she encountered would be like in bed.

She was fairly certain neither she nor Bryan would survive their first night in Italy together, at least she hoped they would not because if she *did* she would have to seriously reconsider this "until death do us part" promise she was so eager to commit to. She never realized how pent up sexual energy could influence every aspect of her waking day.

Cara pushed some errant curls of hair out of her eyes.

She thought back to last Friday night when she met her sister, Katherine and her friend Jenna at the Boathouse Grill in Central Park. Cara loved it there. It was always serene. At least it was until that Friday night, when her long working hours and lack of sex was the topic of discussion.

Cara replayed the evenings' events over in her mind.

She arrived thirty minutes late, as usual. She was so predictably late that neither her friends nor family ever arrived early, knowing that she would not be on time. Cara rushed into the restaurant and saw Katherine and Jenna at the bar, laughing uncontrollably. Poking her head in between the two women she gave them each a quick kiss on the cheek, "Share with me, what's so funny."

Cara's eyes wide in expectation needing a good laugh, she hoisted herself on to a bar stool. The two of them looked at each other and broke out in laughter again. "What gives, come on share!"

A guilty expression crept over Katherine's face, "Oh, Cara! I am so sorry!" She was trying to keep a straight face and her struggle sent Jenna into tears of laughter. Katherine worked so hard at suppressing her laugh it actually exploded out of her throat like a sonic boom. Both women nearly fell off their stools and every time either of them glanced at Cara, they went hysterical again. It was maddening because Cara had the distinct impression she was the source of their hilarity.

"OK, what did I do now?"

"Oh honey, it's not you," Katherine tried to sound sympathetic, "its Bryan." She glanced at Jenna again, both women trying to get themselves under control.

"Come on you two, we're not going there again are we? I know neither of you likes Bryan, but he is my fiancé." They had trolled this piece of real estate so often there wasn't a particle of soil left unturned.

"Ah huh, like we should leave him alone because of all the

consideration he gives you? I'd have kicked his sorry ass out when he started expecting me to work to pay for his law degree!" Jenna put the stir straw in her mouth and rolled it around with her tongue giving her that look saying, "You know that I'm right!"

"OK, OK!" Cara held her hands over her head acquiescing. "I need a good laugh even if it is at Bryan's expense. Come on give." Cara motioned to the bartender for a glass of Sangiovise wine.

Jenna placed her drink on the bar and leaned forward into the two women, making it obvious to Cara who the traitor was.

"Cara don't get pissed at me for telling your sister about this, but since you told me, I can't get the image out of my head!"

Cara shared much of her life with Jenna so it was difficult to imagine which incident she was talking about. Cara started doing a mental inventory of what she could have told Jenna that created this much amusement. She was not prepared for what came next. Jenna reached over and took a quick sip of her drink, her eyes dancing with laughter.

"Remember about a year ago, you were telling me how Bryan's sex drive had hit an all time low, even for him!" She hunched closer bursting with anticipation of telling the story again. "She got the apartment all romantic," Jenna's hands waived in the air as if magically constructing the scene for her audience, "bought candles, Kuma Sutra oils, a Fredrick's of Hollywood Bustier, put on mood music, hoping to kick their sex life up notch."

Cara dropped her head into her hand. She knew exactly the night Jenna was talking about, the most humiliating evening of her life! She peeked up at Jenna knowing she was enjoying this too much and there was no way to stop her once she was on a roll. Cara glanced at Katherine sitting on the edge of her seat, listening, waiting, even though Cara knew she had heard the story only moments before.

"Bryan never disappoints does he Cara? You decided to give him a lesson in sex 101, thinking all that would bring out the beast in him."

Jenna was telling the story with such familiarity Cara suddenly wondered how many times she had actually told it. Great! Now all of New York is in on her "life's most embarrassing moment" Cara moaned. "Jenna."

"She got him to bed, taking the lead, thinking that taking the dominant role would spice things up a bit. Am I right?"

"God, Jenna, you've turned this into a short story, I don't remember telling you about this in exactly the same way." Cara looked at her friend who gave her a wave of her hand.

"My way's better." Jenna continued, "There she was on top, eyes closed, head thrown back. Her body getting carried away, and she heard him, snore! Snore! Can you believe it! Bryan fell asleep under her while she was making love to him! He fell asleep, I can't believe it. Can you imagine looking down at the man you're in the middle making love to and he's fallen asleep!"

Katherine chuckled, "Cara, I can't even imagine what that would do to your ego! You do know it's his problem and not yours."

"Cara," Jenna looked at her and lowered her voice to a whisper, "he couldn't even have been in the game if you know what I mean, he was asleep! Snoring! Has it been so

long since anyone has made real love to you, you don't even know what it supposed to feel like?"

Katherine snorted a laugh. It was so damn funny but with Cara sitting right there; she didn't know whether to laugh or cry.

Cara hung her head, then slowly a laugh began in the pit of her stomach. Jenna was right. The image was hilarious. Cara started laughing and Katherine and Jenna joined in. She caught Jenna doing some type of movement with her arms, apparently simulating the futile motion of her sexual efforts. Cara let out a roar, laughing so hard tears came to her eyes.

Then she heard a few people around her laughing too, but not at their own private jokes but at hers! The bartender stood there in front of them shaking his head and said to her, "You need to get another boyfriend."

"That's what we've been telling her, kick him to the curb!" Jenna punctuated her comment by stabbing the stir straw from her drink into her mouth, "Get rid of the man, Cara! Go out and find a guy that knows what to do with what he's got, what to do with you! Don't you guys agree!?" Jenna flicked her hands above her head as if she was trying to gather all the strangers around them to assist in some sort of intervention.

A guy a few seats down from them leaned over so he could be seen by Cara, "Lady, you are way too pretty to put up with that crap! I'm with your friends, dump the jerk." Voices of agreement rose up around them. She just loved sharing her most intimate moments with strangers, but the good thing about New York City, she'd never see one of them again. So she lifted her glass and saluted them and thanked them all for their opinion.

"OK, I promise if he screws up while we're in Italy, he's gone, all right?" Cara looked at both of them waiting for approval.

Jenna piped up, "Oh he's going to screw up. The only question is how bad?" She pulled on the stir straw in her drink glass again, "You can take that to the bank!" punctuating her point by raising both her eyebrows.

Cara looked around the First Class cabin. Surely her love life wasn't the only one screwed up! She thought of Bethie and her "Daddy" and Mom. They didn't look like they enjoy a lot of playtime in the bedroom. Mom looked frazzled and "Daddy" looked like he was more comfortable sitting across a boardroom table scrapping it out with adults than relaxing with his wife and kids.

And there! She eyed a young stylish couple a few seats ahead of her in the center aisle. The woman was way too young to be wearing a St. John's suit and the guy looked as if he just walked out of a pant press. If they were as uptight in bed as they were in their appearance there is not much going on in their bedroom either.

Cara rethought that statement. What about her, what did she scream to the world? She glanced down at her outfit. A crisp white feminine shirt, caramel colored lace skirt, soft and sexy, and riding boots. It was a statement in contrasts. Much like Cara saw herself. She was intelligent, but funny; sexy, but cute and impatient but damn near celibate!

Ok, maybe she could have worn a blouse that didn't reveal quite so much cleavage. But that was her body, the only thing that didn't reveal cleavage on her was a turtleneck. Plus there were a few things Cara really, really liked about herself, her eyes, her smile and the "girls". So she put her best foot forward. She glanced down at her cleavage again and a little smile crossed her lips.

"Bella, do you see something you like?"

Damn!

Cara blushed, how the hell do you respond to that? "I thought I spilled my drink." *Oh there's an image for him to keep in his head, a dribbling alcoholic.*

"Let me see." He leaned his head towards her and moved the edge of her blouse to the side brushing his finger gently along the curve of her breast. "I do not think you spilled anything. Should I look lower?"

Holy Crap!

Cara sat there frozen. She couldn't believe she was letting this total stranger fondle her. What the hell was she doing! Why didn't she slap this guy or at least tell him to keep his hands off!

"I'm meeting my fiancé." The words whipped out of her mouth like a sword challenging him to a duel. Cara groaned inwardly, what else could she possibly do to make a fool of herself?

Stand back Adonis, I am spoken for!

The statement was no deterrent and he made no attempt at disguising his lustful gaze, he moistened his lips as his eyes returned to her face.

Yikes! Be careful, Cara. This guy is no amateur.

"You have beautiful eyes, Bella" again his gaze shifted looking not only at her chest but lowering them even further and stopping at her hips, before reversing the path meeting her eyes, "In fact you are beautiful, Bella." His smile sent rockets off inside her.

Wow! Cara glanced down to check if she was still dressed. For the first time in her life she understood the statement, "he undressed her with his eyes".

Cara was speechless. All she could do was look at this guy. He was dark, just like she liked her men; dark thick hair that hung below his collar; dark brown eyes bordering on black and dark complexion. And his lips, *ohmigod,* she had never seen anyone's lips that lush and smooth. Cara absentmindedly touched her fingers to her lips, *yep not that smooth!*

"You should not be embarrassed by the attention you receive, Bella, you are about to land in the most romantic city in the world." Even his voice was perfect! "Italian men will not ignore you." He lifted her hand to his lips and kissed it. Then she felt the warm, soft, velvet tip of his tongue lick softly between her ring finger and her middle finger.

The intake of her breath was loud and ragged. A warm flow of heat escaped her and she shivered. Her pulse quickened so fast the veins on her neck beat out of control and she felt faint. *What the hell?*

"I am sorry, Bella." He had a very wicked smile on his face that revealed a lot of things but sorry was not one of them. "You are tired from the trip and I play too hard. Shall I order you some food, so you can regain your energy?"

She couldn't speak. Her mouth opened, but no words came out. Cara just looked at him, she couldn't look away even though she felt like an idiot. *I am hypnotized. He has hypnotized me! I can't move!*

"Ian, per favore, Ms. McGuire needs a light snack. Cheese and fruit should do. Grazie."

He turned his attention back to Cara, "I saw Ian whispering in your ear. I do not know your sexual preference but *he* is bi."

Cara looked at him a bit bewildered and shook her head, "Who the hell are you?" *What a time to get her voice back!*

He laughed, "Vittore Falco. I heard Ian call you Ms. McGuire, may I know your first name?"

She felt like she was slogging through mud her senses were so numb. "Cara."

"Ah, Cara Bella! It is pretty, no?" He brushed a strand of hair from her face, "This fiancé you travel to meet, he has been away from you for a long time?"

"Yes, he has. Mr. Falco..."

"Vittore, per favore!"

"Vittore," *Does this guy have any idea how horny she was! His life could be in peril.* "I didn't mean to give you the wrong impression. I really am not interested in..."

"Oh but Cara, I believe you are." He smiled broadly at her. "But I will stop making you uncomfortable. You will find Italy has very passionate people, it is something you will get used to." He reached out a hand to stroke her chin; Cara finally got control of herself and jerked her head to the side.

"Look," she paused briefly, "if we are going to sit beside each other for the next six hours, we are going to have to set some ground rules."

"You mean playground rules?"

"See, that is the first rule, no more innuendos."

"I am sorry, Cara. I have made you mad."

"No, it's just a little nerve racking. Can we have a real conversation?"

"Si, what would you like to discuss?"

Cara sat back relaxing. Her body had been coiled for the last ten minutes. *This guy was dangerous!* "Where do you live in Italy?"

"Ah, see Cara, I give you the world to discuss and you want to discuss me." He saw her ire flame and he laughed, "I live in a small village in Umbria but I work in Roma. And you Cara, where do you live?"

"I am from Arizona but I've lived in New York City for ten years. I moved for my job, you know, "if I can make it there I'll make it anywhere".

"I have been to Arizona; it is the Wild West, no?"

"Well, I don't know how wild it is; sometimes I think New York is wilder than anything I've ever seen in Arizona!" She was enjoying the easy conversation. No thoughts of throwing him in the aisle and ravishing him. She was making progress.

"This job that took you away from the west, what is it?"

"I'm a curator for the American Wing of The Metropolitan Museum of Art. I'm a gemologist." Vittore raised his eyebrows, apparently impressed. "It is mostly researching and cataloguing, pretty exciting stuff." She smiled as she sipped more of her martini.

"From Arizona to New York City studying gems; how is that Bella?"

"Put that way it sounds unusual, but actually Arizona

has some of the largest mines in the United States for semi-precious stones, turquoise, peridot, amethyst and garnet." She was enjoying his interest; she hadn't talked about her passion for gems with anyone in ages.

"If it were not for Arizona's mines, I would never have become a gemologist."

"And why is that, Cara?"

"When I was a child my father and I were riding and I wandered away from him when we stopped to rest the horses and I fell into an old mine. It wasn't that deep but I broke my leg and hurt my wrist."

"It sounds dangerous, Cara, did your father find you quickly?"

"Pretty fast, although it would have been hard not to find me, I was screaming at the top of my lungs." Her mouth tugged at the corner, remembering her father's panic when he found her battered and crying.

"He pulled me out with a rope attached to the horse and hoisted me up. I was only seven, but that was the day I discovered my passion. I came up out of the mine with my pockets stuffed with "pretty stones". My Dad said from that day forward, "Cara, you always manage to land in it!"

"It is a phrase I do not know, but I think I understand the meaning." Vittore glanced up and nodded to Ian who stood waiting with her snack.

"Oh, sorry, here." Cara put the tray table down and Ian placed a plate of crackers, cheese and fruit on it. He leaned over and his cologne wafted over her again, *So, he is bi? How did Vittore know that?*

"Ms. McGuire, Signore Falco," Ian leaned in further

towards Vittore, "my offer still stands." He shifted his eyes to Cara, "It would be exciting."

"Ian, you have wasted your talent for persistence on being a flight attendant but I *only* bed woman and then *only* alone. Cara however will need to make her own decisions."

"What!?" Cara sat open mouthed staring at Vittore.

"Ian has not shared with you his desire? Ian, do not tell me you have become timid on me?"

"Signore Falco, I can only dream."

"What!?' repeated Cara.

"Ian and I play this game on every flight. You, however, Cara are a new little mouse for this cat to play with. You must be careful. Ian has designs on the three of us sharing a bed." Vittore never removed his gaze from Ian's face, not angry, but definitely not happy.

"What!?" *How many times has she said that now? Well here I go again!* "What the hell are you talking about! I'm not going to bed with either of you much less both of you!"

Cara blushed when she noticed half of First Class was staring at the three of them. *Damn!*

"Ian I think we should not upset Cara any further. I do not think it is a game she will enjoy playing."

"Damn right I won't!"

Ian shrugged his shoulders ever so slightly and walked away.

"Did that really happen? Did we both get hit on by the same guy?"

"Si, Cara." Vittore again looked at her briefly, "and your rejection of me may drive me into his arms."

"What!?"

Vittore laughed as he reclined his seat and made ready to take a nap. "Oh Cara, you are so easy to rouse."

CHAPTER THREE

Vittore felt a stirring next to him and woke to find Cara trying to look out the airplanes' window. The plane was descending and they would soon be landing in Roma.

"Would you like to change seats for the approach? I have seen the city from the air many times. It is bellisimo."

"Would you mind?"

Vittore raised his seat up and placed the pillow into the front seat pocket. "Did you not rest at all, Bella?"

"Silly I know but I was too excited. I've been reading my tour book and taking a cram course in Italian." Cara rose from her seat to let Vittore out. After maneuvering around each other in the aisle Cara then took his seat.

"May I point some things out to you as we approach?"

"Please, per favore." She smiled jokingly at him over her shoulder, "Mensa member, you impressed?"

"Cara you impressed me the moment I laid eyes on you!" Vittore laughed softly and nodded his head towards the window. "That is Corsica and Sardinia."

"I had no idea they were so close together it looks like one big island." She pressed her face closer to the window to get a better view. "The water is so blue! Will we be able to see the Coliseum from here or Vatican City?"

"Possibly Vatican City depending on the runway we must land on. The dome of St. Peters Basilica will catch the sunlight and become a beacon. We will watch for it."

Cara waited anxiously hoping to catch a glimpse of the Eternal City from the air. She was excited. *Roma the root word of romance,* She grinned at Vittore a Roman - *the reason for the word romance.* She made a plea to God to let this be the most romantic trip of her life.

They descended rapidly and it was time to prepare for landing. The buildings below went by so fast Cara couldn't identify any of them. What was unmistakable though was how tightly packed the city was. Unlike New York City where the skyscrapers blocked the view of the streets, the buildings in Roma allowed you to see into them making it clear you were entering an ancient city, one of the most ancient in the world.

As the plane taxied to the gate Vittore undid his seatbelt and slipped his hand into his jean pocket, "Cara, I would like you to keep this if you need any assistance while in Roma." Finally producing a business card and handed it to Cara, the card was still warm with his body heat, "It is your first visit to Roma and I would be happy to tell you of some of the most beautiful places that thankfully have never made their way into a tourist guidebook."

"Thank you, that is very kind. But I think my fiancé has planned out our trip." Cara held the card looking at it for the first time, it held only his name and phone number.

Vittore stood and began removing luggage from the overhead bin, "Si, I understand Bella," he closed the overhead and leaned his forearms against it and looked down on Cara who had moved to her original seat to begin gathering her things. "If you should change your mind, I can show you a few areas you may enjoy."

Cara lifted her head to reply and looked straight into his hips, *oh god! I see an area right now I would enjoy!* Cara flushed as she pulled her eyes away to look up into his face. He winked at her. *This guy is a numero uno European playboy! I'll bet he's never gone to bed alone.* A squeak escaped Cara's throat.

"Cara it was a pleasure meeting you. I hope you keep my card and call me either while you are here in Roma or in New York. I am there often. I would enjoy seeing you again." Vittore lifted his Louis Vitton satchel and turned to leave.

"You're in New York often? What is it you do Vittore?"

He turned to tweak her nose, "I watch," he began walking towards the exit then turned and took a few steps backwards, looking at her he shouted and waived, "Ciao, Bella."

Cara lingered after landing allowing Vittore to get well ahead of her, she wasn't sure she could walk behind him without gaping at him and embarrassing herself further. She imagined the movement of his hips as he walked through the airport, her body shivered in pleasure at just the thought. *Oh yeah, good plan hanging back.*

She strolled down the gateway and emerged into a disorienting cacophony of sights and sounds. A few yards behind her she was still in the U.S., but now the murmuring around her was in a language unfamiliar to her and the few hours of studying Italian she did on the flight over, she quickly noted, had been an effort of futility.

After clearing customs, Cara shouldered her tote and looking around she spotted a few people that were on her flight and followed them, hoping they too were on their way to baggage claim. Along the way she began studying the signage hoping to become familiar with the language. Bagagli-Baggage; di sotto-down; Bagno-Bathroom. She was musing about how the uninitiated could easily mistake Bagno for Bagagli and didn't notice the women in front of her come to a complete stop causing Cara to topple her over, crashing her unbecomingly to the ground.

"Ohmigod, I didn't see you stop. I am so sorry!" Cara dropped all her bags to run to the women's aide, only to be pushed aside roughly by a man reaching for the fallen woman first.

"Stupido! Idioto togliti dia piedi!*" he shouted as he glared at Cara. "Mia Bella stare attento amore mio."

She got the stupid/idiot no problem and she heard Vittore use Bella, and assumed it at least was not a curse word. Oh yeah, she'll master this language in no time, if she doesn't die of mortification first. Cara collected her dropped luggage and tote and made her way to baggage claim.

Bryan told her he hired a limo to take her to the hotel and that she should look for a driver holding a placard with her name on it. Instead she heard her name being bellowed out by a short stout little Italian man, "Cara McGuire! Cara McGuire!"

She pushed her way through the crowd around the baggage carousel, "I'm Cara."

The man gave her a quick look and placed his hand on his chest, "Romano" he flashed his most alluring toothless grin. Again he pounded his chest "Romano, L' autista."

Cara just gave him a blank stare, she had no idea what he was saying, something about autism?

"L' autista". Romano held up his hands in the universal sign of steering a wheel.

Cara smiled, "You're my driver! Autista-driver!"

"Si! Si!" Romano replied, "Bagagli?" he said glancing at the carousel.

"Yes, my claim tickets. I have them right here." Cara dug through her tote and triumphantly produced three baggage claim checks. Romano sauntered to the carousel and began inspecting each bag against the ticket as Cara watched to assure no error was made.

Gathering her three bags into a manageable heap, Romano shot off for the exit, glancing over his shoulder at Cara waiving her forward all the while shouting, "Sbrigarsi! Sbrigarsi!"

Where the hell's the fire! Cara dodged her way around travelers in an attempt to keep Romano reasonably happy.

Romano dropped her luggage beside a rusted out Fiat and popped the trunk as Cara stared in amazement at Bryans' idea of a Limo. She climbed into the back seat and one whiff of the cars' interior sent her diving for a window to get fresh air. The car smelled of body odor and cigarettes. Cara continued to gulp air praying that fresh air would blow through this foul smelling car as they drove. She didn't look forward to driving through the streets of Roma with her head hanging out the car window like a dog.

Romano started the car and at the same time stuck his arm out the driver's side window and pulled into traffic without a glance. Horns blared, shouts rang out, fists pumped and Romano was oblivious to it all. He moved forward chewing on an old used cigar. Cara thought she was going to get sick!

They traveled along the streets of Italy apparently pissing every driver off they encountered.

Romano suddenly swerved into a left hand lane causing a red Bugatti Veyron to jerk its wheels to the left to avoid a collision and almost careening it into a barrier wall dividing the traffic lanes.

The driver of the Bugatti lifted his body up out of the seat and made all kinds of hand gestures and shouts towards Romano. Cara sunk low in the back seat as the man in the leather coat and sunglasses kept pace with Romano demanding an apology. *Dear God, just get me to the hotel in one piece.* Finally the Bugatti driver lurched forward leaving the rusty Fiat in its wake, but not before more arm and fist pumping.

Cara peaked up over the driver's seat. Romano had on an Italian opera and was singing at the top of his lungs, a fact that went entirely unnoticed by her due to the drama out the left side of the car. Romano stuck the cigar in his mouth, turned his head towards Cara, smiled and blew out a cloud of foul smelling smoke right into her face. *Agh, I'm gonna be sick!*

After another twenty minutes they arrived at the St. George Hotel. Romano pulled into the covered portico and almost came to a complete stop before speeding around the drive and shooting back into traffic, tires screeching and Cara went flying across the seat. Cara pounded on Romano's shoulder shouting over the opera. "What the hell! That was my hotel, take me back!"

"Mi scusi la signorina. Fare una deviazione."

Cara tried to remember 'deviazione' her latin,.. Diviazione what is the root? *Division, no that isn't right, deviation, that's it he needed to make a deviation! A detour, it was detour!* "No

Diviazione! Hotel adesso. I don't care about any detour. Take me to my hotel NOW!"

After a lot of shouting and hand waiving by Romano he returned to the portico and Cara then saw the red Bugatti sitting in front of the entrance of the hotel. As Cara climbed out of the Fiat she shot a look at Romano and said "Coward!" hoping it translated the same in Italian.

A bellman helped Romano get her luggage out of the trunk as she dug through her tote looking for money for a tip for a job well done, *right*! But when she looked up, Romano had already jumped into his car and was weaving in and out of traffic leaving in his wake horns blowing and angry drivers.

Cara looked at the bellman and just shook her head and smiled, "Idioto." Might as well start using what she had learned.

Cara turned to enter the doors leading to the lobby of the St. George Hotel. To Cara's surprise the hotel was quite small having no more than five floors. She assumed it was not a part of a chain like Hilton or Marriott, she just hoped it was nice. The lobby was intimate and well designed. It reminded Cara of a tailored suit. Lots of texture, little pattern, all neutral and clean lines.

She scoped out the room and saw the man in the leather coat that had been driving the Bugatti, his elbows resting on the dividers that separated the desk clerks from the guests. He was on the phone and his voice was tense and loud, this man was mad!

"It is non importante. It could have been handled in a week or two." Pause as the person on the other end of conversation spoke. "It is your decisione. Si, Si. It would have been fine with me to have waited." Pause, "Si, call me when you get it done."

The man snapped his cell phone shut rather angrily and turned. Yep it was him, leather coat, sunglasses, hair tied back hopefully he didn't get a glimpse of her in the back of Romano's Fiat, or she'd be the one catching his wrath!

She diverted her eyes quickly hoping she'd become invisible. Damn! Men's shoe tips one o'clock only inches from her own. I am going to track Romano down and kill him myself.

"Are you stalking me, Bella?" Cara looked up in surprise into Vittore's face. With the sunglasses, hair tied back and the coat covering his perfect body, she hadn't recognized him. Not that she saw beyond his mouth and eyes and...*Get a grip, Cara!*

"What are you doing here?" Cara demand. Processing if he could have followed her but of course she was behind him. So it would appear as if she had followed him.

"I always stay here when I am in Roma and you, how did you select this hotel?'

"My fiancé selected it." Cara felt like she was in the scene from Casablanca where Rick says, *"Of all the gin joints in all the towns in all the world, she walks into mine."*

"Do you believe in divine appointments, Bella?" Vittore tilted her chin back gently with his knuckle and looked deeply into her eyes. "If not, I think you should begin giving it some consideration. Falling into mines and into my life may indeed be an act of God." He smiled broadly then returned to the registration desk and spoke to the man behind the counter who replied very seriously, "Capisco il, Signore Falco, Si, Si!"

Vittore motioned to a bellman to collect Cara's luggage, handing him a keycard.

"Cara, you will be well looked after. Enjoy your stay." He leaned over her hand and kissed her knuckles, she waited, holding her breath, to see if he would run his tongue between her fingers again. He lingered, a huge smile creeping across his lips, then he lifted his head just to her eye level and winked. Vittore stood and strolled towards the elevator.

Why did everything this man do cause her knees to buckle!

"Scusi, Signore Falco." A woman came out of an office adjoining the registration desk trying to hand Vittore a piece of paper. He put up his hands and backed away shaking his head as he entered the elevator. Turning around to face the doors and as they drew closed, he blew the woman a kiss.

Yep she nailed him, an Italian flirt! A very sexy flirt but definitely a flirt!

Cara was escorted to a small suite on the fourth floor and since there were only five she figured Bryan had gotten them a room with one of the best views the hotel had to offer. She looked out the window at the twisting warren of small side streets alive with people going about their days' business. She wasn't sure she was going to forgive Bryan for laying Romano on her, but this, this more than made up for stinky Fiats and chubby toothless drivers.

She did a very quick tour of the suite but could not concentrate on doing a thorough investigation; she was tired and felt dirty. So she stripped and jumped in the shower after calling room service for pasta and a salad. The beating of the hot water eased all the tension from her body. Cara laid her head against the marble of the shower letting the water beat down on her head and neck. She was so tired, she wasn't sure she'd even be able to eat. Cara decided to just give in to her jet lag, eat what she could and go to bed.

CHAPTER FOUR

The next day Cara woke to the sound of someone gently knocking on her door.

Bryan? Maybe he got here early!

She wrapped herself in the big fluffy robe provided by the hotel and opened the door. A waiter stood in front of her with a cart filled with dome covered plates, a coffee carafe, a pitcher of orange juice and not a single rose, but a huge bouquet of at least two dozen cream colored roses.

"I didn't order this." She looked quizzically at the waiter.

He smiled and bowed his head, "Complemento." He said as he guided the cart into her room to prepare the dining table for her breakfast.

The fragrance of the roses filled the room; she took a deep breath and smiled.

Now this was a vacation!

She had been so tired when she arrived yesterday she really hadn't looked around the suite, while the waiter laid out linen and silverware; Cara explored the suite of rooms.

The entry of the suite led to a sitting room whose upholstery was covered in soft gold damask and the sofa was filled with pillows of various patterns and hues of aqua and gold. The tones were as clean and fresh as the Aegean Sea whispering serenity and calm. The ceilings were 12 feet giving the rooms a majestic feel and there were fireplaces in the sitting room and bedroom both ornately carved marble with curves and scrolls that begged to be touched and stroked.

Cara took a deep breath and looked around the suite again, the rooms were sensual; it might be hard leaving the rooms and actually seeing Roma! Cara smiled and then let out a little sigh as she returned to the dining room.

The waiter was putting the finishing touches on the table setting. Cara watched in lazy silence as he finished his ministrations. Stepping back looking over his creation, he turned to her and said, "Perfecto!" sweeping his arms wide.

"Perfecto!" she smiled back.

He crossed the room to where she was standing and lifted her hand to his lips. He didn't kiss her hand as Vittore had, but rather brushed his lips across the back of her hand. He then stood, bowed and said, "Ciao, Bella!"

Cara laughed, "All this "Bella" stuff could go to a girls head!" He looked at her questioningly, "Grazia" she motioned towards the table, "Grazia."

"Ciao", he replied pushing the cart out of the suite. Cara gazed at the table, the room, the view and whispered, "Perfecto." Thinking Bryan got it right!

After breakfast Cara made her way to the lobby of the hotel in search of the Spa. According to Conde Nast magazine the Spa at St. George was an unexpected oasis of pampering and indulgence; made more decadent in that it was located directly across the Tiber River from the Vatican. The Spa also was the salon for Edwardo, one of the most noted stylists in Roma. Cara had requested an appointment with him prior to leaving New York City but was unable to secure one. So when a note arrived that morning saying Edwardo had a cancelation and since she was staying at the St. George, he could fit her in, she was thrilled.

Cara was anxious to see what Edwardo could do for her often out of control thick curly head of hair. Her hair could go from looking like she was a mad scientist to a sophisticated Diva; she was hoping he could give it less of a duel personality.

Cara had booked a 10AM appointment for the Spa at the St. George Hotel. Since Bryan was still in France handling a few last minute details and would join her at seven that evening, it was Cara's plan to be buffed, puffed, oiled and massaged all day. First because she loved massages but more importantly it would help rid her body jetlag.

Cara entered through a set of frosted glass doors that had *The Spa at St. George*, etched into them. At the far end of the entrance was an archway that framed a wall of aqua and blue glass tiles that had water cascading over them and falling into a pool lit from below. The sound of the water was relaxing and tranquil.

Cara went to the reception desk and gave her name, "Buon giorno! Sono io Cara McGuire." She touched her chest lightly and smiled hoping she was conveying enough information for the woman to understand she was there for an appointment.

"Signorina McGuire, we have been awaiting your arrival. Your trip to Italy was good?" The woman was dressed in cream dress pants and had a cool aqua cashmere sweater that bore the logo of the Spa. She looked fresh and clean and was a relief from all the black that is worn at so many salons in the U.S.

"Si, Grazie. My trip over was amazing. But this," Cara

looked around the Spa, "this is what I have been waiting for, being pampered like I was a princess." Cara beamed.

"We will take good care of you Signorina. Follow me per favore." The woman walked around the counter and escorted Cara into a room containing a locker, dressing table and chair. The room had the cool aqua and cream colors of the entry. The overstuffed chair was done in a brocade pattern of swirls that was almost hypnotic. All the woodwork was dark mahogany giving a relaxing contrast to the cool tones of the aqua.

"Signorina, remove your clothing and place them in the locker along with any valuables." She opened the door of the locker to reveal the interior, "A robe and slippers are provided while you are visiting us today in the Spa." Then she nodded towards the dressing table, "and over here are a few amenities you may find useful." She indicated a glass tray filled with personal hygiene items and off to the side a blow dryer, brushes and gel.

She reached over and handed Cara an envelope made of expensive cardstock, "This is your itinerary for the day." She moved towards the door, "When you are finished undressing please go into the sitting room opposite your locker and be seated. We will come for you."

Cara slipped out of her jeans and tee shirt and stood naked in front of the mirror attached to the inside of the locker door. She scrutinized her body as she ran her hands up her hips, along her torso and touched her breasts softly. She smiled.

There is nothing wrong with this body Cara. If Bryan doesn't throw you down and make passionate love, you're going to see Italy without your fiancé!

Be careful Bryan…be very careful.

She slipped into the robe and slippers and opened the envelope and checked her scheduled.

First on the list was an appointment with Edwardo. Then her manicure, pedicure, full body massage and facial and finishing the day off was again Edwardo to style her hair. The day included champagne, hors dourves and bottled water, lots of bottled water.

After changing, Cara moved to the sitting room as instructed. The receptionist came in shortly after and escorted Cara to Edwardo's salon.

Edwardo stood looking at Cara in the mirror and ran his fingers through her thick curly mass of hair. Cara watched his mind whirl as he assessed what he was going to do with the length, curls and color. He smiled broadly and nodded his head once and said confidently, "Buon."

He then called for his assistant and thus it began, Cara turning her hair over to a man who couldn't speak English or explain what he was doing, she just trusted like she had never trusted in her life.

Edwardo highlighted her hair, cut it and then put some type of treatment on it before turning Cara back over to the Spa receptionist.

Cara's head was wrapped in a cotton cloth bound tightly, "Excuse me? Am I suppose to leave this on?" she asked the receptionist.

"Si, Edwardo has put a curl relaxer on your hair and it will need to sit for an hour or more. When you are done here in the spa, I will take you back to Edwardo and he will wash and style your hair. Do not worry Ms. McGuire; we will take very good care of you." She smiled sweetly as she led Cara back into the sitting room she had been in earlier.

Cara sat down and a woman came in and wrapped her feet and legs with warm towels and put heated mittens on Cara's hands.

"Ms. McGuire, allow me to lay the chair back so you are comfortable. You will rest for a few minutes before we begin the massage." She gently tilted the chair back just slightly. The music was soothing the warmth of the towels felt fabulous; Cara began drifting off to sleep.

She felt a hand gently touch her shoulder. "Come sta? Mi chiamo Stefano." He knelt in front of her and removed the leg warps and the mittens. "Mi segua." He stood and beckoned Cara to follow him. She scuffed along behind him as he took her into a dimly lit room, filled with the scent of pomegranates.

"Togliersi abbigliameto, per favore." He turned and pointed to a hook on which she could hang her robe.

"Si."

The man turned and closed the door and Cara removed her robe and slipped under the sheet. The massage table had a heating pad under a thick cotton blanket that immediately eased her back muscles.

Oh Cara, you are about to enter heaven.

For the next six hours Cara was completely in the care of the Spa employees. Every inch of her was exfoliated, massaged, steamed and moisturized. She was so relaxed, she felt like rubber. She wanted someone to put her on a gurney and wheel her into her suite and just leave her there. Cara did not want to exert one muscle.

Edwardo had worked a miracle; she still had a head of long curls but he managed to discipline them into a shape that she knew she would be able to maintain. The blonde highlights toned down her auburn color and the relaxer softened the texture. She decided it was a good thing he didn't speak English, he had free reign and apparently got the bid for top stylist in Roma for a reason.

In the elevator on her way up to her room, she was trying to decide what to wear tonight, or maybe she'd indulge herself even further and purchase a new dress, she still had a little bit of time.

She opened the door to her suite, the room smelled of the roses sent up with breakfast and in the background ever so softly she heard music. She knew she hadn't left a radio on and went in search of the source.

Poking her head into the bedroom her breath caught in her throat. Lying on the bed was a dress of dark blue satin and beside it was a pair of shoes whose straps were of delicate silk and perched in the weaving of the straps were stones as blue as sapphires. She rushed over and picked up the shoes, only then seeing an evening bag that matched, made of silk and adorned with the same blue stones, she gazed at the shoes, they were the most beautiful things she had ever seen. She peered more closely at the stones, *No Way!* A shiver went down her spine, they were REAL Sapphires! She snapped up the purse, REAL! Her heart was doing somersaults. Nestled into the neck of the dress was a note, "A beautiful dress for a beautiful woman."

O my God, maybe Bryan spending three months in Europe was having an effect on him. In the five years they had been together he hadn't popped for so much as a dinner out. He made tightwads look generous. Now a suite and this, she stroked the satin of the dark blue fabric lovingly. Tears came to her eyes, not only had he surprised her with this gift, but he actually got it right! The dark blue of the dress would set off her green eyes and auburn hair; how did he know that, he sure learned a lot while he had been away!

Cara picked up the dress and turned it around. The dress was cut so low in the back she wondered how she would keep it on her shoulders. She stripped off her jeans and top and pulled the dress up over her hips. All that kept the dress attached to her body was the small strip of fabric that curved around the arm holes and trailed gracefully down the back where the curve of the fabric ended just below her waist.

Well no bra tonight!

It was without a doubt the sexiest most alluring dress she had ever seen. She slid into the shoes and gasped; never had anything this beautiful been on her foot! She was pleased that she had chosen a French manicure and pedicure; any sort of color would have been sacrilegious.

Cara twirled around the room, and stopped in front of the full length mirror and stared. She was beautiful, "Belisomo," she whispered.

Oh Bryan is going to have his hands full tonight. She couldn't wait.

She checked the clock, just enough time to apply her makeup. Cara slipped out of the dress and lay it lovingly on the bed. She bent to pick up the note and kissed it, "Thank you." she whispered then turned towards the bath.

At five minutes to seven Cara slipped the dress back on checking herself out on all sides in the mirror, she wanted everything perfect, "perfecto"! She noticed the black lace of her panties ever so slightly peeking above the bottom of the dress where it ended at just below her waist. She frantically dug through her dresser praying she had something that was low enough.

She could be pretty daring but going without a stitch of underwear, even caused her to blush. Way in the back she found a red thong. *Err*! Why didn't she check this out earlier! She slipped out of the black lace panties and replaced them with the red thong. She looked at her back; no tell-tale exposure of red peeking through. She gazed at herself in the mirror, she was breathtaking. She smiled mischievously; maybe the red thong would be just the thing to add fire to the night.

She leaned over and slipped on her shoes and grabbed her bag checking its contents, lipstick, cell phone, ID and some folded Lira. One more glance in the mirror. Unbelievable.... perfecto! Cara smiled; she was getting the hang of this language. She walked out the door to what she knew would be the most unforgettable evening of her life!

The bar was softly lit and she looked anxiously around to see if Bryan had already arrived. She didn't see anyone she knew. She started towards a booth and hesitated.

Hell, he'd spent a fortune on this dress he might as well get his money's worth.

She slid onto a stool at the bar. "Buon sera," Said the bartender, whose name tag identified him as Paolo, Cara took a chance that he had just said "Good Evening", so she replied, "Buon sera, Paolo."

He rattled off some more Italian and Cara apologetically admitted she was an American. "Americana, molto bene!

Molto bene!" Cara shrugged her shoulders again, "Mi scusi." He paused smiled and said in haunting English, "What will you have?" Cara repaid his kindness with a winning smile, "Your English is much better than my Italian. So far I know Bella, perfecto, scusi, bagagli and stupido. And let's not forget idioto."

"No Bella, those last two words should never cross your lips." He pouted out his lower lip and asked, "Please, Bella, do not tell me one of my countrymen used such unkind words in your presence."

She grinned at him, "Only because I knocked his wife to the ground at the airport." The bartender laughed, his eyes sparkling.

"Tell me Bella, do you wait for your lover?"

"You know I love the way you Italians talk to women! And yes I am waiting for my lover." She liked the way that sounded; her lover.

"That is a shame for all the men in Roma tonight. Would you like something to keep you warm or do you want to cool down?" He too had that way of speaking in double innuendos.

I'll bet all Italian men learn to flirt in the womb!

"I think I'll stay hot." Her smile telegraphed to him her plans for this evening.

He smiled and did the sign of the cross quickly with his hand and winked. She could definitely get use to this kind of attention. He returned with a clear liquid with a few coffee beans resting in the bottom of the glass. "Sambuca, it will warm you all night." He winked at her then turned and assisted others coming into the bar.

She sipped her Sambuca slowly, letting its licorice flavored liquid play over her tongue. She glanced around the bar and noticed several men staring at her with hunger in their eyes. One man almost fell out of his chair when she smiled at him which brought a sharp slap to his arm by his female companion.

This flirting can be powerful.

She glanced at her watch, it was 7:45. Bryan's flight must have been delayed but since he was on a private jet it couldn't be much longer. Her sambuca was nearly empty and she signaled for another. The bartender nodded his head in acknowledgement.

Unbeknownst to Cara, Vittore had slipped into the bar and was sitting in the back out of sight. He motioned for the bartender to prepare him a drink. Paulo knew him well and knew exactly what he would want. Vittore's eyes lingered on Cara as she sat at the bar. The dress she had on was perfect, his eyes slowly slid down her naked back until resting at the point where the blue satin finally covered her skin. She was totally oblivious to the fact that she was baiting every man in the room. Vittore chuckled, she was a temptress and did not even know it.

Cara's phone rang, she flipped it open and answered. It was Bryan, "Are you here?" her voice huskier than she ever thought possible. She was so hungry for him. There was a short silence.

"Bryan, are you there?"

"Hi, Cara. How are you?"

How am I? What was he nuts!?

"Bryan I am lonely, sitting at a bar with every man in

here about to attack me. You'd better get here quick to rescue me!"

"Ah that might be a problem Cara. I am back in the U.S."

"What!" her voice rang through the quiet bar, "What do mean you're back in the U.S.? You are joking right? You have to be joking!" Cara jumped off the barstool and began pacing like a caged animal.

"Cara, there was a problem with the paperwork concerning some assets for our client and we can't move forward until it is taken care of and I needed to get back to the States. I jumped the first flight out of Paris heading for the U.S."

"I don't give a damn if his damn company collapses to the ground Bryan. The deal was I come to Italy, we spend time together and you at least *act* like you love me. This is wrong Bryan!" Her voice quivered and she was on the brink of tears.

"I am sorry Cara I'll make it up to you. I promise." He sounded childish and unconvincing.

"Sorry! You have no idea how sorry you are! Do you know what you're doing Bryan? You don't ask your fiancé to travel half way across the world to stand her up! I hope you love this new client of yours, because he just got between us and I have had it!" Cara was having difficulty keeping her voice down and right now she didn't care.

"I'll be back in a few days, it's not like I am abandoning you. We'll just push back our sightseeing a few days. It's no big deal. You know how important this is to me. I thought you'd be more supportive." There it was, turning it back on her, trying to make her feel guilty.

Cara held the phone out arms length staring at it in disbelief. "Fuck you Bryan and go to hell." Cara threw her phone towards the floor and she heard it break apart and scatter across the dark stained wood. She sought the barstool for support shaking with rage as she lifted the sambuca to her lips. Her hand shook and her lips quivered.

She heard a soft voice, "Oh, Bella, do not cry. You are too beautiful tonight to cry." Vittore stood at her elbow holding various pieces of her cell phone. He held them out to her as a burnt offering.

She stared into his eyes and straightened her back. "Great! This is just a great bloody great day!" She quickly considered her options, go upstairs and cry her eyes out or get laid. "You know something Vittore? It's your lucky night! I just became unengaged." She gathered up her bag and started to get off the bar stool.

"No Cara," putting the pieces of her phone on top of the bar, Vittore placed his hand gently on her shoulder and sat beside her. He held her chin in the palm of his hand and softly stroked his thumb across her cheek. He lifted her head so her eyes met his. "I think that is what you Americans call revenge sex. No Cara, when I take you, you will be making love to me, not getting even with a man that has broken your heart. Come let's go out for a walk. You need air."

Vittore helped her off the stool and placed his hand at her waist, rubbing his thumb along the nakedness of her back. He leaned over and kissed the top of her head. "Cara, you are so beautiful. I am sorry your heart breaks." She leaned into his chest and they walked out of the bar.

Vittore let her wander, not directing her or talking to her. She had a lot to sort out in her head and he wanted to give her room to do so. It broke his heart to see the pain on her face, the tears welling in her eyes. How could a man be so callous of a woman's feelings? Vittore was quickly learning to hate Bryan.

Cara circled a fountain thinking of how Bryan had treated her this past year. She knew in her heart he didn't love her. Cara suspected he was seeing other women. The late nights, lack of communication and the total lack of sex spelled AFFAIR out loud and clear to everyone but Cara.

Jenna knew and tried to warn her how many times? Oh that would be every bloody time they got together. Katherine tried to tell her she deserved better, that if man does not respect a woman he dates, he will not respect her when they are married. Would she listen to either…noooo. Not the brilliant Cara!

Why the hell did he ask her to marry him? She stopped cold, *he didn't*! She did. What a fool! "I am so stupid!" She walked faster. Her engagement ring caught her eye. Suddenly it burned her finger; she tore at it removing it from her hand.

Staring at the diamond she knew, *she knew*; he didn't love her, may never have loved her. The revelation tore at her stomach and she felt sick, used, kicked to the curb like a piece of trash. She was on the verge of tears and decided he didn't deserve one more tear shed for him.

Cara stopped circling the fountain, squeezing the ring tight in her hand , she stared into the fountain trying to focus, to calm down; she allowed herself to be mesmerized by the rhythm of the water as it sprung out of different orifices. The water would spout and recede, only to spout again from some other hidden place. The wind carried the mist of spray towards the East. Cara began making her way to the eastern side of the fountain.

"Satin and water don't mix, do they?"

"No, Bella!" Vittore laughed running after her wrapping his arm around her waist, his hand slipping inside her dress as he pulled her into his chest. The warmth of his hand on her bare waist sent shivers down her back.

"I want to destroy everything he has given me." Cara whispered. Vittore pulled her closer, rubbing his chin across the top of her head. "I can't believe he just dumped me in a foreign country without a friend to turn to!"

"Tonight I am a friend." With his other hand he tilted her head back and smiled devilishly at her, "Tomorrow, I hope I am more."

CHAPTER FIVE

Cara brought her head down and leaned her cheek onto his chest. She heard his heart beating loudly and felt his warm breath on her neck. He pulled her closer rubbing his thumb along her bare waist. Cara began to cry, softly like that of a woman with a broken heart.

He caressed her neck and murmured softly, "Don't cry, Cara Bella, it breaks my heart. Shhh, Cara it will all work out." He kissed the top of her head holding his lips at the crown breathing warmth onto her body.

Vittore rocked her gently in his arms until she quieted. Cara lifted her chin, "I looked so beautiful tonight." Tears reappeared in her eyes and Vittore bent to kiss them away.

"Cara, you are beautiful. Just because your fiancé made the wrong decision do not think there isn't a man in all of Roma that would not desire to be with you tonight."

She lifted her head again and looked into his face, "Thank you for not letting me ruin my dress. I would have been really mad at myself in the morning. Did you see these shoes?" She kicked her foot out, "Real sapphires! Why would he spend a fortune, tell me how beautiful he thinks I am and then just dump me! I don't get it. I am so confused."

"It would have hurt me more knowing I would never see this perfect dress on you again. So maybe I was being a little selfish." Cara smiled at him and walked back to look at the fountain again.

Vittore came up behind her and kissing the back of her neck, he laid his hand on the front of her dress placing his palm wide on her belly, pulling her in tight to his body. Cara moaned and leaned her head back into his chest. She knew she was opening Pandora's Box with this guy; but Jenna's words kept playing in her head. "Find a guy that knows how to use what he's got!" Cara knew that this guy knew! And it wouldn't be revenge it was pure 100% lust.

With the sound of the fountain playing its watery tune, the scent of flowers heady in the night air and the warmth of Vittore's hand on her as he softly kissed the curve of her neck, every sense in her body was heightened. Suddenly she didn't give a damn about Bryan.

Cara turned in his arms and lifted her head and touched those beautiful full soft lips with her own. She held her breath, his mouth was so perfect. He moved closer pressing his body softly into hers, his hands roaming slowly, sensually across her back, stroking, caressing; inching his way lower until his fingertips brushed the gentle curve at the base of her spine. Cara's heart raced, Vittore's lips devoured hers, softly thrusting his tongue into her warm sweet mouth, separating only long enough for each of them to catch their breath.

He could not stop, he plunged his tongue deeper and firmer letting his kiss say what his body was aching to reveal, his desire, and his lust for her was almost beyond his control. Vittore was drawn to Cara the first time he laid eyes on her and had hoped he would be holding her in his arms. What he had not expected was her passion; her responsiveness to his caresses his desires, her wanton lust. It stole his breath.

He pressed his body hard against hers looking for some relief to the tension ravaging his loins. "Cara," he whispered her name he had never heard such a beautiful name. He could say it a thousand times and never tire of how it played across his lips.

He pulled her head into his chest and held her tight. Cara could feel his hard pulsing muscle against her, Vittore moved slightly to relieve the pressure mounting inside him. She matched his movements and he let out a soft moan and squeezed the round firm cheeks below her waist. "Oh Bella, do not do that, I might not live though the night." His voice was husky and breathy, his eyes cloudy with lust as he looked into her deep green pools.

Reaching up she held his neck, easing him towards her mouth, "I don't plan for you too, Vittore." She placed her lips softly on his and slowly inched her tongue over his full soft lips. She sank into his body, wanting him, cradling him between her legs.

Vittore pulled softly away, "Oh Cara Bella, we have to go now!" He quickly scanned the area looking for a taxi. Opposite the fountain was a scooter and sitting on the curb beside it, a boy eating gelato. Vittore kissed Cara's cheek and pointed a finger at her, "Do not move."

He ran to the boy and shoved some lira and his card into the boys' hand. Vittore jumped on the scooter, kicked the stand up and started the motor. Tearing across the piazza to where Cara stood laughing. Vittore reached across the few inches separating them and pulled her into his lap. Cara wrapped her fingers around the handles, "Is this safe?" positioning herself between his legs.

"Safer than staying here, Bella." He tore off in the direction of the hotel. Cara could feel his thickness building against her back as he swerved in and out of side streets begging more speed out of the little scooter. Finally they pulled under the portico of the hotel, Vittore lifted Cara to the ground; he stepped out, kicking the stand down hard and flung the keys to a valet as he flew past.

His large hand encircled Cara's wrist pulling her behind him as he hurried towards the elevators. Drawing out a card and swiping it over a card reader the doors opened immediately.

Vittore entered the elevator taking her with him spinning her around pressing her body into the mahogany wood paneling pinning her between it and his body. His breath ragged, his eyes burning, Vittore placed his hands on the wall caging her in. He lowered his lips and slid them over her mouth, parting her lips, moving slowly, softly asking her permission.

His hips pressed into her body, his leg inching hers open as he laid his thigh into her, pressing hard. Cara's body jerked slightly as a rush of excitement slammed into her. She sank her hands into the thick mane of his hair as his mouth devoured her.

He raised his head and looked into her eyes, he saw only desire. Removing his hands from the wall he pulled her in tight to his body. He fought the urge to pull the dress from Cara's shoulders and let it fall. No he had to move slowly, he wanted the delicious heat of desire to build.

Cara lifted her face to him; she wanted him to keep kissing her. His mouth was exquisite, soft and passionate. Her fantasies of their naked bodies touching sent a course of charges up her thighs leaving her weak. She wrapped her hands around this neck and guided him back to her lips.

Vittore read the desire in her; he could feel her passion

mounting with each thrust of his tongue. He could feel the tension of excitement in her grasp. He moved a hand to the back of her dress, easing the zipper down as his mouth claimed her, leaving no doubt that he intended to make love to her that night.

Cara gasped as his hands moved low over her bare back pulling her tighter into him, rocking his hips so she could feel how they were past the point of tender kisses. Making sure she understood that tonight she was his and he intended to take her. He felt no resistance from her. His impatience building, he had no restraint. He began easing her dress off her shoulder, just as the elevator doors opened.

Vittore took a deep breath and eased the dress back onto her shoulder. Laying his forehead against the top of her head, he smiled and shook his head, "This hotel does not have enough floors! It seems you have been saved, Bella."

Cara filled her lungs with air and nuzzled her nose into his neck, "More like interrupted."

Cara stepped out cautiously hoping they would not encounter any other hotel guest. She looked around quickly. The doors did not open to a hallway but to an opulent apartment. She looked across the living room to a wall of windows that revealed a breathtaking view of Roma. Vittore slipped his hand behind her back to the inside of her dress, down her waist and lower still until it rested on the bone of her hip. He splayed his fingers wide so that the tips feathered across her belly. She leaned back and looked up at Vittore, "I'm going to guess; you're not a guest?"

Vittore buried his face in her hair, "No, I am not, Bella." he whispered, "But try not to think too much of it."

"A little hard to ignore. So this is why you always stay here, it is your home."

"Si, Bella, living here is a convenience, nothing more." He pulled her hip in closer to his. "Would you like a drink, Cara?" He released her from his warm grasp and she immediately felt naked. She wanted his hand back on her skin.

As Vittore prepared their drinks, Cara wandered about the room. It was filled with antiques. Not the antiques you see commonly in the U.S., which are mostly from the Queen Anne or Chippendale period. These were Italian Romanesque pieces made of black walnut, carved with medallions and scrolls that were entirely masculine. The feet of several pieces had huge carved lion paws as feet. The massiveness and feral suggestions of the pieces seemed to compliment the strong sensuality of the man whose home they occupied.

Cara roamed around the room finally easing her way towards him. "Maybe you should zip me up?"

"I am playing a little game, Cara," He poured liqueur into a snifter, then leaned against the cabinet that served as a bar, crossing his arms in front of him holding her drink, raking his eyes over her body with brazen lust, "since I have seen you in that dress, I have been fantasizing of it falling from your shoulders. I had thought it would have happened by now, so I cheated a little and gave it even less to hold on to. So, no, Bella, I will not help you with the zipper." He smiled broadly and held out a glass of a warm lush amber colored liqueur. "Amaretto, sip it slowly."

She sipped her Amaretto, tuning her back to him revealing what little of the dress was actually in contact with her body. She looked out at the lights of Roma. The city knew how to romanticize its treasures. Everywhere under the night sky were lights illuminating and drawing attention to fountains or ruins. The view was amazing. She couldn't imagine having the privilege of feasting your eyes on this sight nightly.

Vittore studied her as she drank in the lights of Roma. "It is a beautiful view, no?"

"An amazing view. Do you realize how fortunate you are to see this every night?"

"Si, I am aware daily of how blessed I am. I am glad you too enjoy it"

Cara turned and looked at him across the room. His body language was so confident, so assured. *Who was this man?* He was handsome, wealthy and humble! He excited her in a way she had not felt in years. Just his gaze sent shivers down her back. And this giving out of her knees was something that has never happened to her before.

He was dangerous and she wanted to be reckless. Just imagining him making love to her was almost more than she could bear. Now here she was in his home, half undressed about to let him make love to her. Was she going to be ok with what she was about to do? It had been so incredibly long since she had made love and even then Bryan was disinterested. She studied Vittore's face, his desire was so blatant.

You are in Roma there is an Adonis that wants to ravage your body, why are you even hesitating?

"In this game of yours Vittore, is there a winner and a loser?"

Vittore moaned, "Cara, if that dress falls off you, I do not think either of us would lose." His eyes were hot with passion and his voice deep with desire.

Cara placed her drink on the credenza near her and with

the slightest wiggle of her shoulders the dress tumbled down her body pooling at her feet. She looked up smiling, "Oops."

Vittore's arousal shot through him like white hot heat, taking his breath. He took four strides and in seconds, was within inches of her. Wrapping his hands around her hips he pulled her into him so she could feel his hardened desire against her hips. His lips tugged at hers moistening and teasing them with his gentle kisses. Cara's body relaxed into his.

He smiled as he ran his hands behind her cupping her bottom, lifting her and placing her legs around his waist. He nuzzled her breast licking, playing with her hardened nipple. She stretched her torso and leaned back giving herself over to him.

He carried her to the credenza sitting her down on its polished surface. His hips pushing her legs further apart, he pulled her in tight to him. The height of the credenza placed her face level with his. He lowered his head and began stroking her nipple with his velvet soft tongue. Reaching up he took her breast in his hand and squeezed it so the nipple stood hard and erect as he began sucking and nibbling.

The pressure of his grasp and the strength of his suckling made Cara's body respond with a warm rush of heat. She wrapped her legs around his thighs and moved into him as close as possible. She wanted to feel him between her legs, feel his passion grow and harden. Then she felt his thumb between her legs flicking her soft wet entrance until she moaned with joy "I want you Cara, I want to make love to you until you cannot think."

Cara draped her head on his shoulder and she begged, "Take off your clothes, Vittore, let me look at your body, feel you." Warm moist honey flowed from her, as she moved with the rhythm of his hips, begging for him; she unbuttoned his shirt and let it drop to the floor, she ran her hands down his chest tracing the hard muscles beneath his skin. The feel of his body beneath her fingertips quickened her longing for him to be naked so she could look at him.

He stroked her back as he kissed her neck, her shoulder and upper arm. His breath was hot and sweet, his tongue swept lightly over her skin leaving a trail of fire.

She eased her hands to the front of his jeans, tugging on his belt. He lifted her chin so their eyes met and slowly shook his head, he was driving her insane. Cara removed her hand and thrust her hips forward in defiance and felt the cold metal of steel touch the hot swollen folds scraping ever so gently.

Moving her hips to the edge of the credenza, he lifted her to the ground.

She shivered and looked at him with hooded eyes. "What? Why? Are you trying to kill me? What's with all this "no" stuff?" She leaned her head on his chest, placing her palms on his chest. "What time is it?" The words came out ragged and breathy.

Vittore laughed," Why do you care about the time, Cara?"

Taking her hand he walked her to the sofa where he sat and pulled her hips towards his mouth, he began playing with her belly button, licking, prodding gently with the tip of his tongue.

"Just tell me." She whispered. Her hips rocked into him with each thrust of his tongue.

"It is past midnight, Cara. Do you need to be someplace?" he returned to licking and exploring her belly and the edges of her thong, his tongue sliding low hovering just above her heat.

Cara smiled as he tickled her belly with his attention. "Last night you were my friend." She held his head as he played, moving her body into his every movement. "I wanted to make sure we were in tomorrow because I think this is definitely something more."

"Oh, Si, Cara Bella, it is." He chewed the thin triangle of fabric that covered what he wanted so desperately to possess. Placing his hands on her hips he pushed her back a few feet, and then sank back into the cushions, his eyes drinking in her naked body. Vittore ran his foot up between Cara's legs, separating them until the tip of his boot reached the little triangle of fabric he had been playing with earlier. "I have never liked making love with my boots on."

Cara looked down at the toe of his boot resting on her and he wiggled it just a little. Cara smiled and looked at him, "You want me to take them off?"

"Si, Bella. One of many things I will want you to do tonight."

"Is that so?" Cara got one boot off and turned to remove the other. Cara's heart raced, *what was she doing she didn't even know this man?* "Should I be afraid?"

"Afraid, Bella? No, you do not need to be afraid of me."

Once his boots were removed he stood and allowed Cara to undo his belt and release him from the confines of his jeans. She knelt in front of him pulling the jeans from his hips, he wore nothing else. Her breath caught as she viewed him, thick, pulsing, ready to please her. He kicked the jeans with his foot as her mouth poised inches from his throbbing muscle. It was hot and as hard as a steel shaft; she glanced up at him and slipped her mouth over the velvet soft tip feeling the moisture of honey forming on its smooth soft surface. Vittore released a moan clutched tightly onto her hair as he thrust his hips forward sending his shaft deep into her mouth.

Her tongue worked over the entire surface of him feeling every ridge, every vein, and every pulse. She took him deep into her throat until her lips feathered against the base of his shaft. Cara played with him in her mouth, keeping him slick and hot; moving him faster and harder until she knew he was on the edge.

Vittore lifted her to her feet, his eyes filled with heat, "This game Cara, what is your fantasy?" He feathered kisses down her neck, his hand moved down her body and without warning he plunged two fingers deep within her moist hot sheath. Raising his head to watch the pleasure wash over her face and feel the withering of her body as he withdrew and plunged deeper a second time.

Cara cried out a loud visceral moan her hips bucking against his hand, her hands on his chest, eyes wide and mouth parted, silently pleading for him to take her. To take her to a place where rapture and joy overtook her senses, she desired to feel the ecstasy of him taking her here, taking her now, taking her with passion and desire that had no boundaries.

"What is it you want Cara, tell me. I will do whatever you want." She couldn't think or utter a word. She moved into his hand as it continued its assault and stared into his eyes and flicked his lips with the tip of her tongue, studying him and enjoying her need for him.

She slowly slid down his body and knelt before him. Teasing her tongue quickly over the hard surface of his desire she began licking and nibbling along its' shaft, feeling the rocking of his hips as she tormented him. Then she slowly turned, still on her knees and placed her hands on the seat cushions of the sofa. She turned her head looking back into Vittore's eyes.

Vittore roared as he flung the coffee table that sat in front of the sofa over onto its side, spilling drinks, books and a vase of flowers. He knelt behind her separating her legs with his knees as he placed his hand between her thighs rubbing the knuckle of his thumb into her wet folds. He ran his tongue from the crevice of her round plump bottom to midway up her spine.

He pulled her hips back into him and hovered for a heartbeat and thrust his hot hard shaft into her.

Cara's heart stopped for a second and when she felt him slide into her, felt his cock stretch her as she became a network of sensations, excited and uncontrolled. She moaned giving him complete control, "Ohmigod, Vittore."

He drove deeper with each thrust wanting to reach deeper than she ever had a man before to claim her as his. His eyes smoldered as he withdrew slowly and drove into her again.

Cara ran her hands up the back of the sofa, stretching like a cat to position her hips higher. She was trying to stay with the rhythm of his thrashing but was too enraptured to think and just let her body meld with his allowing him to control every movement. She gave herself over to him, letting him have complete control over her body, pulling and pushing her in his frenzied rhythm. Her body was his to do with what he wanted.

Vittore watched as he plunged into Cara and saw her accepting him by moving into his thrusts. He leaned his head back and closed his eyes, just focusing on feeling her surround him. Her soft slick hot folds played gently with his cock. When he totally withdrew only to plunge again, he felt the muscles in her tighten making his entry feel as if a strong hand was surrounding him, pulling him.

The sensation was so delicious he repeated it until he felt he would no longer be able to maintain control but he was not yet done with making love to Cara. He did not want to stop. He took a deep breath and withdrew.

He stood, "Cara you drive me mad!" looking down on her up turned ass, his feet on either side of her bent legs. "I want to see your face. I want to see you want me, Cara."

Cara turned so she was sitting, her back leaning against the sofa, her head tilted back onto the cushions. She ran her hands up his strong muscular thighs.

Reaching out to a lynx fur throw that lay across the back of the sofa he flung it to the floor and laid down on it resting on one forearm and with his finger beckoning her towards him all the while smiling devilishly, challengingly.

Cara smiled as she crawled to his side ready and willing to take on whatever he had in mind. Her eyes fixed on his accepting his challenge.

"How much do you want me, Cara?

He pushed her back into the soft fur of the lynx and looked at her with a desire that took her breath as he lowered his mouth to her breast and began teasing the hard bud of her nipple between his teeth. Cara moaned pulling his head tighter to her breast. A flood of excitement overtook her body as Vittore eased her legs apart and moved on top of her as he continued to lick and pull on her breasts. He felt her hips moving beneath him begging for him to enter her.

He rose; arms on either side of her and looked down, her face held such lust it heightened his desire. She wanted him so much her body shook. Staring into her eyes he slowly entered her. He felt her body jerk and then melt.

Vittore rose to his knees bringing her legs to rest on his shoulders, reaching over he took her hands as he plunged deep and hard moving with long deliberate stokes as he carried on the sweet assault. Cara heard her voice but her senses were so blurred she was only conscience of the sound of her heart, the blood rushing through her body. The sensation was visceral, primal, she screamed with pleasure. "Ohmigod!"

Vittore drove harder. A roar escaped his throat as Cara released a torrent of heat that bathed him in warmth and he released his warmth into her. He let go her hands and caressed her leg, kissing her ankles, "My god Cara!" His hips softly pushed against her as he moved his lips lower onto her leg.

He looked into her face and smiled, "And you were afraid of me, Cara. It is I that should fear you. You are a little wild cat!"

Lowering her legs to either side of his hips and although he was shaking and exhausted laid on top of her moving slowly inside her, allowing her to relax.

"You're an amazing lover. I don't want to ask how you got to be this good." Her body shivered again.

"I could wonder the same of you, Bella. You too are no innocent."

"I have a great imagination. And I have been imagining

making love like that for years!" her head hit his shoulder, "But wow, that was better than I could ever have imagined!"

Vittore laughed as he rolled off of her. He kissed her, tracing her nipples with his fingers. "I am glad you have such a creative imagination, Bella."

He stood, then lifted her into his arms and carried her to his bedroom. "I kind of liked making love on the fur, it felt amazing."

He kissed her temple, "I have another on my bed."

"Of course you do." She laid her head into his shoulder. This guy was nothing if not sensual!

CHAPTER SIX

Cara lay in bed with her eyes closed; motionless between the soft sheets that tickled her sensitized skin not certain if her over active imagination had played a cruel trick on her. She did a quick inventory of her body, accessing its delicious soreness confirming it was real and not imagined. She slowly placed her fingers between her thighs and felt the molten heat between her swollen lips. A smile formed on her face and she slowly opened her eyes to see the curve of an arm draped across a broad muscular chest.

She reached her hand out to stroke the ridges of those muscles, allowing her fingertips to move over the front of the body and softly down a hard muscular thigh. She felt a tickle on the inside of her forearm, she lingered and the tickle became a nudge, the beast was waking up, the nudge became a poke.

"What are you doing, Bella?" Vittore's voice was sprinkled with laughter. Cara tilted her head back and looked into his eyes; his hair was swept off his face revealing his profile. Her eyes explored his features, the curve of his jaw, his cheek and chin. Chiseled and perfect, truly an Adonis, she had made love all night long to a god.

Cara gave him a devilish grin, "Just checking."

Vittore propped himself up on one elbow and rolled to place the thigh she had been touching between her legs, bending his knee and sliding it along her inside thigh, gently spreading her legs wider, "Checking on what, Bella?" He sank his mouth into her hair; Cara kissed the base of his throat where it met the "V" of his clavicle licking his flesh leisurely with the tip of her tongue.

"You, making sure you are real and not a dream." She nuzzled her chin into his neck inhaling his scent.

Vittore played with a few locks of her hair, twisting them into little spirals then releasing them, watching them uncoil and spill down her cheek. His fingertips danced their way down the side of her face, along her neck, onto her chest finding the path between her breasts that led to her belly. He opened his hand wide just below her belly button, allowing his fingers to tease the wiry hair. "Um," she sighed softly easing her body into his touch. He moved his hand lower laying his finger into the folds of her swollen lips, pulsing gently.

Cara lapped his skin lazily, working her way across his chest and over his nipple, nuzzling and cooing with soft sounds of pleasure and contentment, "Um this is nice."

Vittore lazily explored her slick warm cavern. "Si, Bella, it is nice."

Cara looked up at his chin and began licking at the rough morning stubble. It created a strange sensation on her tongue, like a cats lick but in reverse, she licked again swirling her tongue down his neck, all the while tracking the roughness until ending at the pulse point of his neck.

"Do you want me to shave, Bella?"

"No, I'm exploring, leave me alone I'm having fun."

Vittore, smiled as he continued to explore her molten recesses, playing gently, dipping and rubbing, "I am as well."

Laying the bridge of her nose into his neck she rubbed her hand down his chest, past his belly, going lower still. Cara held him tenderly in her hand, exploring every ridge gently with her fingertips. Vittore thrust forward emitting a soft groan.

Vittore' eyes went dark and hooded. He brought his fingers to her lips. "Are you hungry, Cara?" She sucked on his middle finger, running it over her tongue and nipping it between her teeth.

He ran his fingertip over her lips, trailing down her chin. "Are you sure you got enough to eat?"

Cara's body shivered as his hand feathered over her body. "For now; you?" she whispered.

Vittore shook his head. "Never, Cara Bella, never, but unlike you I am not on holiday and as much as I would like to dine on you," He ran his fingers over her body, "I have a meeting I must attend."

"Tell them you need to postpone." Cara arched her back towards him never wanting this morning to end. She turned her head and licked his chest.

"I already have. Postponing twice in one day is not good business, Bella"

"What time is your meeting?"

"Noon," he trailed his hand up her thigh and placed it beneath her hips, drawing her closer.

"Then you have time for breakfast." She brushed his hair back from his face and smiled at him.

"We slept through breakfast, Cara and we have played through brunch. I am afraid I cannot delay these men any longer." He leaned forward and kissed her eyelids. "You sleep some more my piccolo, I will come back and we can discuss dinner. I think I will be very hungry by dinner." He nipped at her breast as he climbed out of bed.

Cara stretched like a cat and cuddled Vittore's pillow, inhaling his scent. Thoughts of last night played through her mind and for once, it wasn't a fantasy.

Vittore came into the room, wet with a towel wrapped at his waist. It was barely large enough to cover his hips causing one leg to peek out of the wrap. He walked to the desk and punching a button, spoke quietly so he would not disturb Cara's reveries. The wet towel stretched across his butt defining the muscular glutens.

Everything was perfect about him, Cara thought as she gazed at his broad muscular back. Still feeling him touching her, stroking her, teasing her, her eyes clouded with desire.

As he spoke he removed the towel and rubbed his hair, sending small beads of water dancing around him. Flipping the towel over his broad shoulders he placed the phone on the cradle and turned.

Cara had seen men naked, but Vittore's body was designed to be naked. Like the statue of David, putting clothes on it would destroy its beauty. Vittore walked towards her and put one knee on the bed and leaned forward to kiss her forehead.

"I have ordered you some breakfast and a masseuse. But no one will disturb you for an hour, so you can rest." As he got off the bed he smiled, "I asked the masseuse to pay particular attention to your inner thighs, Bella. You will be stiff today." He ran his knuckle down her nose and returned to the dressing room.

She pulled the pillow closer opening her mouth she screamed into its soft feathers. As good as she was at fantasizing she could never have imagined the last 48 hours; everything about them was "perfecto".

Vittore emerged from the dressing room in beautifully tailored dark tan trousers that flowed easily from his hips and a cream silk tee with a very subtle "V" at the neck.

Ok, Cara thought, *maybe you can put clothes on him and he would still be beautiful.*

He walked over to the desk and strapped his watch in place and slipped an amber ring onto his left forefinger. Cara had never seen a man wear such a large stone but it looked incredibly sexy on him.

He smoothed his hair behind his ears as he began filling his pockets with wallet, cell phone, and keys. He stood for a moment patting his pockets.

"Did you forget something?" Cara watched every motion Vittore made thinking how beautifully he moved.

"It feels as if I have." He lifted his hand to his forehead and touched it lightly. "Stupido, I know now what it is I have forgotten." He strolled over to the bed where Cara lay naked wrapped around his pillow. He ran his hand up her thigh and she quivered at his gentle touch. He bent lower and kissed her hip. "I was still a little hungry." He walked out of the room with a Cheshire grin on his face. "Ciao, Bella. Be good."

If Cara had been standing her knees would have given out. She buried her head into the pillow screaming and kicking her legs. *So this is what making love is like. Who knew?*

The masseuse, Carlo, arrived and set up his table. After having soaked in a hot tub for about an hour, Cara's muscles were pliable and Carlo found them easy to manipulate. But when he began massaging her inner thighs Cara knew that her muscles would be sore for days. Carlo had indicated he would be there for one hour but stayed until he was sure her muscles were relaxed. As Carlo, packed up his table Cara returned to the bath and donned a thick white robe.

He was gone when she returned to the bedroom. But on the bed sat a breakfast tray filled with fresh fruit, pastries, juice and coffee. Cara stretched out beside the tray and nibbled at the pastries. She heard the elevator doors open to the suite and stole a glance at the clock, Vittore had come home.

He came into the room and smiled at her stretched across the bed in his big robe, she looked like she was having the best day of her life. He lay down behind her and wrapped his arm around her waist and kissed the nape of her neck.

"Good meeting?" She popped a huge strawberry into her mouth, turned and smiled at Vittore, her cheeks full and the juice slipping onto her chin.

He brushed the juice away with the pad of his thumb, and licked it. "Very good, it is good that Italians understand amore, the American attending was not pleased that I was delayed because my priorities were not in line with his." He kissed her earlobe. "But I am the buyer he the seller, he can wait for me." He nestled his mouth into the curve of her neck blowing soft kisses.

A thought had just occurred to her, "What is it that you do?" She glanced back at him as she popped another but much smaller strawberry into her mouth. "These are really good!"

"I watch." He gently shrugged his shoulders and moved her hair from the nape of her neck. "I watch, then I acquire."

"Like this hotel?" She handed a huge strawberry back to him with a questioning look.

"Like this hotel. I watched it first and then I acquired it." He shook his head at the strawberry, "I like honey on my strawberries."

As Cara was about to pop it in her mouth he grabbed her wrist and took the strawberry from her fingers. He rolled her onto her back and leaned over her, holding the strawberry above her mouth, she reached for it with her teeth, he shook his head and gave her a devilish smile as his thigh spread hers legs apart and he lowered the strawberry.

It was cold and made Cara smile, but he kept swirling it until it warmed. Then he brought it to his mouth and bit into it letting the juice fall from his chin onto her breast. Then so very softly he whispered, "And you Cara, I watch you." He lowered his head and lapped up the spilled juice. "I told you I would be hungry." He licked his way lower knowing where the honey flowed hot and he drank.

CHAPTER SEVEN

"Do you think maybe we could get some real food? I understand you Italians like to eat but all I've had are strawberries." She and Vittore lay on top of the bedspread underneath a comforter made of mink. Vittore had pulled it over their bodies after making love and placed it so the fur of the pelt touched their naked skin. She had never felt anything as sensuous as the fur touching her, stroking her with little fingers every time she moved.

Vittore pushed the fur down his chest and patted his belly with his hand, "I am full, Bella! I do not need any more to eat." He turned his head towards her with a scowl trying to convince her of his distress by intentionally enlarging his belly under his hand as he patted it.

Cara pulled the pillow from beneath his head and began beating him about the chest as she protested "I am starving! What would your mother think knowing that she raised a sex fiend?" Vittore laughed as he fended off her ineffective blows to his body. They both knew they were like magnets, if they got within a certain distance of each other, they were just drawn together defying all efforts to stay apart.

"My mother, Bella? You think you can threaten me with my mothers' opinion? Oh, Cara Bella, have you forgotten you are in Italy? My mother would pat my cheek and tell me I was a good boy!" Vittore threw her back on the bed pinning her wrists with his hands. Laughing, he bit her lip then flipped her over on her stomach and gave her butt a sharp slap.

"Ouch!"

"That is for empty threats. Now get dressed, I am hungry." He jumped off the bed and was in the bath before Cara could launch her pillow. Cara ran in after him knowing they would make love again in the shower.

God she would never get anything to eat!

It was very late when they got to the restaurant and the tables were full. "Does everyone eat this late? Even in New York they begin closing their kitchens by now."

"Ah, Bella, the real question is does everyone come home from work and make love? And the answer to that is, "Si," Bella, they do. You see I am not the sex fiend you believe I am, it is, as you Americans say, in my genes." He knew she wouldn't be able to resist.

"It certainly is!" She held her hand as if she had a cigar and wiggled her eyebrows.

Vittore tucked her beneath his arm laughing. "You are so predictable, Bella!" He kissed the top of her head as he caught a waiter's eye motioning to a table asking if it was available. He got a "Si!" and guided Cara in its direction.

"Food!" Cara's eyes looked hungrily at the other patrons' meals as they walked by the tables. There was a dish whose aroma made her salivate, she pointed. "I want that!" It was a steaming bowl of broth filled with clams, shrimp, mussels and other fish.

She turned to look at Vittore with all the joy in her face as that of a child picking out her first puppy at the pet store. Vittore shook his head, she was a handful and he loved it!

What Cara did not know was that he had fallen in love with her over a year ago when he first saw her in Bryan's office at the law firm of Reed, Thompson and Fulbright. And he didn't know how he was going to tell her.

He had been in a meeting with his American lawyers that day and they had introduced Bryan to him as he would be working as the Junior Partner on some of the more mundane aspects of opening more of his boutique hotels in the States. Cara had shown up outside the conference room dressed like a snow monster. At least two or three layers of pants, a down coat that was so thick she could hardly hold her arms to her side.

She smiled and waved at Bryan through the glass and he shot out of his seat like a fire had been lit. Vittore watched as Bryan grabbed her forearm roughly and pulled her away and down the hall. He watched as Bryan yelled at her and as she made motions indicating they were to have gone sledding. Bryan shook his head no and gestured towards the conference room. He watched as Bryan turned and Cara stuck her tongue out at his back.

He was drawn to this woman, her playful feisty spirit. He was amused by her unabashed confidence and honesty. No woman in New York City walked into prestigious law offices dressed as she, unless that person was very comfortable in her own skin. He liked that, he had seen too many false images, she was refreshing.

When Bryan came back into the room Vittore was explaining to the Senior Partners the necessity of rescheduling the meeting for later in the week. He walked out without as much as a glance at Bryan. Vittore had watched enough and knew he did not like this man and he need not give him any consideration.

Vittore got to the lobby just as Cara was crossing the street. She was not difficult to miss. She walked along Fifth Ave. to the entrance of the Park. Vittore hung back far enough to be unnoticed. She wound her way along the paths to the sledding area where a group of people were gathered drinking steaming cups of hot chocolate to keep warm.

"Cara," one of them shouted and waived motioning her towards them. He played her name over in his head. Not liking the American pronunciation with its hard "r" the Italian way of saying her name by rolling the "r" was much more beautiful. "Cara, Bella, I am going to keep my eyes on you."

Over the next year Vittore had watched her work two jobs and he watched Bryan be unfaithful to her. He watched her eyes glisten as she fought back the tears when Bryan had left her waiting for a date that never arrived. Vittore watched and did not like what he saw. He had arranged for Bryan to stay in Italy doing insignificant inventories hoping Cara would come to realize she was worth more than Bryan was giving her. He watched until it was time to act. But how was he going to tell her all this?

Vittore ordered her meal assuring her he got her the dish she requested. "I have ordered you Caciucco Alla Livornese, Cara. It is a stew that this restaurant is famous for, you will enjoy it."

Vittore ordered antipasta of Crostini Alle Olive and Stracciatella, which he informed her was a Roman Egg Soup and a team of waiters brought the never ending stream of food. The restaurant was in no hurry for them to leave and they ate slowly. Laughing, enjoying each others' company, enjoying the night.

They sat sipping Frangelico after dinner and nibbling on Salmae Di Cioccolato, a rich dessert that looked remarkably like slices of salami but this was dense dark rich chocolate filled with almonds, orange peel and crushed sweet biscuits. It was heaven.

Cara looked at Vittore's left hand, studying the large amber cabochon. Reaching out she took his hand and rubbed the amber ring with the pad of her thumb.

"You wear this ring every day. It must have a special meaning." Cara looked at the unusual stone and its' even more unusual setting. The amber was called blood amber and one of the rarest of the ambers. She herself had never seen a stone of this type, this large or this perfect.

Vittore enjoyed feeling Cara's hand hold his as she inspected the stone. He could see her mind whirling as she tried to imagine where the stone was found and who the craftsman was. Vittore smiled softly, knowing neither himself, only how it came to be in his possession.

"Amber is actually organic, not mineral." She leaned closer, "It is made from tree sap that has hardened. Normally there are imperfections created by debris collected in the sap while it was still semi liquid. This stone has none, no imperfections or bubbles."

Cara glanced up from the stone and looked at Vittore, "Where did you get this? It is very rare amber; even the setting is unique, not modern. Is it an antique?"

"Si." Vittore retrieved his hand and twirled the ring thinking about its history. "I did not know the stone was rare amber, I just knew it had unusual properties. It is talisman for the men in my family. Once one finds true love it is passed to the next eldest male." Vittore looked into Cara's eyes and saw her amusement.

"I see, it is your lucky charm, does it bring you fame and fortune, too?" Cara loved the lore that surrounded stones and it was said that amber was made from the tears of a woman and provides its owner with sexual prowess and good fortune. She laughed, "On second thought it seems to have actually worked for you! Did you know Nero scoured the entire Roman Empire during his reign and collected every amber stone that could be found and brought it here to Roma? This could be a stone collected by Nero himself. Your little ring could be famous!"

"The ring was not found here in Italy but Russia." Vittore entwined his fingers in hers and brought her hand to his lips.

"Russia!" Cara had a sharp intake of breath, her eyes danced with excitement, "It could be from the Amber Room!" Chills went down her arms, "Do you know about the Amber Room?"

"No, Cara, but I think you are bursting to tell me!" He laughed at her enthusiasm.

"The Amber Room is one of the greatest mysteries of our time! It was constructed in Germany in 1710 then given as a gift to Peter the Great in1716. This is exciting Vittore! What if that stone is from the Amber Room?" Cara grabbed his hand and stared at the stone as if to see if it would speak to her.

"I would think someone would notice a chunk of stone had been removed." Vittore was amused with her excitement.

"No, Vittore, you don't understand!" Cara's voice mellowed, "The Amber Room was disassembled and stolen by the Nazi's during WWII. It has never been found. It is like the Arch of the Covenant, people are still searching for it!"

Vittore studied his ring for a few minutes then lifted his eyes to Cara's and grinned, "Cara, you may have discovered a piece of this Amber Room you talk about."

A chill went down Cara's back. "Ohmigod! Wouldn't that be amazing!"

"First I will need to tell you how it came into my Great Great Grandfather's possession. But it is not a story to be told in one sitting, Cara, so you will need to be patient over the next two weeks as I tell you about the amber ring." He opened her hand and kissed her palm and licking its center with the tip of his tongue, "And you, Bella, are not what I would call a patient woman. Can you behave yourself as the story is laid out to you?"

"I'm patient!" Cara paused realizing he just said something pretty significant. "Two weeks you said, so you want to spend my entire holiday with me? Wow and I thought I was tired now! I'll be a saint and show you how patient I can be."

She took a sip of her Frangelico. His commitment of spending two weeks with her was a little disconcerting. It's not that she wouldn't enjoy being with him, hell who wouldn't! But she didn't want him to feel obligated.

Vittore arched his eyebrows, "A saint you are not, Mia Bella, you are a little devil!" He drew her hand to his mouth and scraped her knuckles with his teeth.

"Come, let us enjoy this beautiful night." He stood

and drew Cara close as he turned to stroll along the Via Conditti.

These were the hours Vittore loved the most when in his beloved Roma; the hours when all others rested. The quiet allowed one to hear the birds' soft morning songs, fountains bubbling and in the distance he could hear dogs barking and cars speeding along a main artery. But everything was soft and hushed, relaxing and calm.

This was an experience most tourists did not have an opportunity to enjoy; for as beautiful and romantic as Roma is, the crime rate was staggering. But Vittore's size was enough to intimidate any thief that might be lurking.

He guided Cara to the Piazza di Spagna or Spanish Steps where, during the day it was so filled with tourists it was difficult to enjoy its beauty. Vittore had accepted that Roma belonged to the tourists during the day, but at night it belonged to the Romans.

At the foot of the Piazza di Spagna was the famous Fontana di Barcaccia, which trickled water from tier to tier rather than venting water in spouts. It fit the relaxed lazy mood of Vittore. Along the Piazza were the couture shops of Gucci, Giorgio Armani and Versace and baskets of roses and honeysuckle lined the walks filling the night air with their heady fragrance. Vittore picked several honeysuckle flowers for them to suck on and wrapped his arm around Cara's neck, pulling her to him so he could kiss her temple.

He loved her, but how could he tell her? To Cara they had only known each other for a little over 48 hours. He would need to be patient, when every fiber of his being wanted to tell her how much he loved her.

"Vittore?" Cara had a concern and felt now was the right

time to address it, especially since she was slightly drunk and knew she could not bear to do this when she was sober.

She drew away from his touch. "Vittore, you have been wonderful." She bent to remove her shoes hesitating not knowing how to phrase this. "You were there last night and witnessed one of my worst nights, and you were great in helping me to rebuild my self-esteem," she looked at him slyly, "Actually you were really, really great at that by the way."

She smiled thinking of last night and this morning, as she waded into the fountain crafted by Bernini himself, "But you do not need to keep me entertained for two weeks, just because I have a jerk for a fiancé. I'm sure you have plenty of gorgeous women more your type, lusting after you, to spend the next two weeks with."

"And what do you think is my type Cara?" He kicked his shoes off as well, rolled his trousers up to mid-calf and waded in after her to coax her out before they were arrested, wondering why she did not see herself as he did, as the most beautiful woman he had ever known. That first day he watched how she played in the snow with her nieces and nephews; he saw a woman that loved unashamedly and shared the joy of life with all those around her.

"Someone sophisticated, wealthy and well breed; the entire European elitist stuff," she flipped her hands in the air, "One in your own social class."

She looked at him and saw confusion in his face.

Man this guy's never been dumped! Go easy Cara!

"Don't get me wrong, I'm not complaining! In fact spending two weeks doing nothing but making love to you would be the vacation of a lifetime, but you have things to do and since I am in Italy, I should see it, so I have decided to catch a tour tomorrow and see Italy the old fashion way, from the back of a bus."

She kicked at the water sending a spray as she carried on with her litany unaware that Vittore had stopped chasing after her.

She realized she had been rambling but more than that she didn't want to say what she was saying. She didn't want to leave for a damn tour tomorrow but she knew eventually he would go on with his life and she with hers, so she wanted to be the one to suggest they bring their tryst to an end.

"Vittore, you have been very kind, but we both know spending two weeks with me is a commitment that is just unrealistic." She laughed a little, "Have you noticed I ramble when I get nervous and don't know what to say? So I just say everything that is in my head."

Cara tried to be cavalier but her insides shook, "Vittore, you don't need to babysit me, I know you have better things to do and there will be no hurt feelings. A beautiful romance believe me, I am *not* going to forget!" She shrugged her shoulders in resignation, walking in circles around the central water source; keeping her eyes diverted not wanting to see the relief in his face.

He stood there looking at her not knowing how to respond, completely confused. This was not what he wanted!

He had watched her for a year knowing he had fallen in love with her, doubting that his love could ever be expressed. Then two nights ago the opportunity presented itself. Cara was free, there was no obstacle standing in his way. No fiancé for her to betray. But it never occurred to him, she would think he didn't want her.

He wanted to scream in frustration because he couldn't tell her how much he loved her and have it make any sense to her. He had been too deceptive. He should have been honest and introduced himself on the plane and now he waited too long to tell her and was paying the price. She was convincing herself she was a passing amusement for him.

She stood there looking at him, waiting for a response. He had none; he was dumb struck.

He walked away from her pacing back and forth in the shallow water of the fountain, rubbing his face and glancing at her muttering in Italian. Cursing himself, Bryan, her, this night, his parents, life, if it came into his head he cursed it. He had never been at a loss for words.

What did she think? That she was doing him a favor by going away? He never wanted to be with a woman more in his life.

"Cara," it was all he could say. He stood only a few feet from her and looked into her eyes, "Cara Bella, do you not know how much I want you?"

His heart was breaking he despised himself for being no more considerate of her than Bryan had been. In one long stride he was inches from her mouth, pulling her into his body, possessing her mouth, his breath caught in his throat, he couldn't let her go or he would lose her forever.

He lifted her, wrapping her around his body and walked further into the fountain sitting her on a flat outcropping letting the water spill around their legs, reaching under her skirt he tore at her panties until they fell from her body. He freed himself from his jeans and lifted her onto him.

Cara laid her back against the fountains' curved wall and

through the thin cloth of her blouse Vittore captured her nipple with his mouth. Cara shivered as his teeth nipped at her swollen breasts as Vittore found his way past the cloth of her blouse to draw her in, suckling with an animalistic feral wildness. It was wild and unbridled passion, terrifying yet exciting.

She was a network of sensations building and exploding. She screamed and he drove harder and held her tighter. He took her until his back arched sending his final release into her as a primal roar escaped from his throat.

He collapsed his forehead onto her chest. His body shook. Cara cradled him to her chest, whispering, "I love making love to you."

"I was selfish, forgive me." He kissed her neck as he withdrew and placed her feet in the water.

She could barely support her weight, "Carry me to the edge and let me sit for a moment." She kissed the underside of his chin, her lips trembling, her breath rattled. He lifted her gently into his arms and carried her to a low wall surrounding the fountain and keeled in front of her and brought her hands together then leaned his head onto them.

"Cara, please forgive me." The fear of losing her drove him mad. His dishonesty made him feel ashamed. He felt like an animal that had to stake his claim. He was angry with himself. He wanted to hide, but he had to get her back to the hotel where he could hold her and soothe her.

"Vittore, I am fine, you didn't hurt me." She tried to reassure him, he looked so sad. She lifted his chin to make him look at her, "See, I'm in one piece, no arms and legs flew off and lying about. Although I don't know where my underwear ended up." She looked around hunting.

He stood nuzzled his mouth into her hair. "I will find them." As he stepped away he pulled out his cell to request a limo from the hotel to pick them up. As he was ending the call he found the remains of her pink lace panties. She shook her head and pointed to a trash can off to the side of the Piazza.

When he returned to the fountain, he sat next to her holding her across his chest waiting for the car to arrive. He didn't know what to say, to do, or how to make up for what he had done to her. Mia Bella, I am so sorry. Again his heart broke.

When they arrived at the hotel, he carried her from the limo to the elevator and held her in his arms until the doors opened into his suite. Without pausing he carried her to the bath and through a door she had not been through. It opened into a room that had a small Roman bathing pool. Vittore walked into the water and set her gently on her feet and undressed her.

He was slow and gentle as he removed her blouse and skirt. He held her very close as he let the clothes fall. When he had removed her bra he looked down on her body and felt ashamed. "Cara I am so sorry, please forgive me." He lifted her into his arms and carried her to a seat carved out of marble into the side wall.

He stood in front of her and removed his clothes and tossed them out of the pool. Without a word he gently lifted her onto his lap and began rinsing her body. Her nipples were still red and hard from his attention and he crooned his apologies.

He reached over to a shelf near the seat and removed a ceramic vial, pouring its contents onto her. The warm scented oil bathed her shoulders running down her back, between and over her breasts. He gently rubbed the oil onto her upper torso, tenderly licking her nipples trying to erase the redness, the mark of his frustration. How could he have done this to her?

He then sat her gently on the edge of the bath and spread her legs wide, as he poured the oil over her pelvis and between her thighs. Never would he again let his frustration control his emotions. He felt such guilt, about his selfishness and his deception, "Cara, I was too rough with you.' He said. "You are more delicate than you play at, I could have hurt you. Please do not let me get that rough with you again. You must tell me when to stop." His eyes pooled. "Please, Bella, you must learn to say no to me." His words whispered over her skin.

CHAPTER EIGHT

Cara stirred under the covers and reached over to Vittore, but he wasn't there. She opened her eyes and surveyed the room and saw him sitting out on the balcony hunched over a laptop and muttering "*miseria*" and "*maledizione*" as he jabbed at the keys. He heard her giggle and turned his head and looked into the room, "Mia Bella, bourn giorno, how are you feeling this morning?" He lifted a carafe and asked, "Cappuccino?" She nodded. He prepared a huge cup of the coffee, stirred it with a stick of cinnamon and brought it into her.

"Molte grazie!" she said as he sat it down on the nightstand.

"Scuzi? Parla Italiano?" He put his fists on his hips and his robe opened to reveal his chiseled chest softly draped by the black silk and smiled, "Molto Bene, Cara! I will now need to be careful what I say in your presence."

"Do you always have to look so damn sexy!? You drive me nuts every time I look at you, I want you so bad, but I can't move!" Cara groaned and slid down further under the covers. "Go put something on that would make you less sexy. Only I have no idea what the hell that could be. Shoo go away!"

"You do not like the way I look Cara?" he slid onto the bed and lifted her chin, "I always like the way you look, you do not hear me complain. Do I say Cara, put on clothes I no longer want to look at your body! But if you insist I can put on a pair of shorts and a tee shirt, trust me, you will not find me sexy in those."

Cara thought about him in a pair of shorts and her eyes narrowed and she shook her head, "Your right or a baseball cap, why is that?"

"Good Cara, we have established that I will not wear shorts, since it seems to repel you. But I thought that was the purpose?"

Horror crossed her face, "Please don't tell me you wear a Speedo to the beach." Cara held her hand over her opened mouth, her eyes spread wide. "Oh god, please don't tell me you wear a Speedo!" She rolled on the bed laughing at the image!

"Most women want their men to look good and you imagine ways for me to look ridicules. And no Cara, I do not wear a Speedo, I swim naked." He gently tweaked her nose, "Drink your Cappuccino, we travel to Umbria in a few hours and I still need to feed you."

"Umbria! Sounds like I'm not catching a tour bus? Have I changed my mind?"

"Si Bella. Your mind changed and you will enjoy having me as your tour guide." He kissed her lips, relishing the taste of the Cappuccino lingering I her mouth.

"What's in Umbria?"

"I have a villa there and partner in a winery. It has been over a month since I have been there, plus it is where my *gaio piccolo* lives and I want her to meet you. So get up and shower, I will order breakfast then we will leave."

"You've called me *piccolo* before what does that mean?"

Cara was determined to learn as many words of Italian as possible.

"Piccolo is little." He climbed off the bed and began packing up his laptop.

"And "gaio"?"

"I will let you discover that on your own. Now hurry, I want to leave the city this afternoon, it is several hours to Umbria."

Cara climbed out from underneath the sheets and snuggled her naked body against his bare chest, "Do you want to join me?"

He held her at arm's length, "Cara, I am staying away from you, you are dangerous! And I will not allow myself to be tempted. I decided last night no more fountains and no fruit!" He shook his finger in front of her face. "I am not going near you today, Cara, go shower!"

"The strawberry was your idea" she protested as she flipped around and headed to the bath, wiggling her butt at him.

He sent a prayer heaven ward.

Vittore had breakfast brought up and was sitting on the balcony sipping espresso. Below him were the sounds of morning traffic as Roma awakened from its sleep. Horns blared as drivers vied for the right of way and shop keepers swept the dust from the front of their stores. He gazed over the roof tops seeking out the dome of St. Peters Basilica.

The St. George sat on the east side of the Tiber River directly across from Vatican City on a street popular to Romans, Via Giulia. The street was filled with antiques dealers, churches and held an ancient palazzo that locals enjoyed gathering at. The side streets that surround it, such as via Del Pellegrino and via Dei Cappellari, still bore the ancient Sampietrini paving stones. It was an ancient street in this ancient city.

Cara emerged from the bath, flush from the steaming hot water, hair wet and smelling of the hotels signature scent, sweet figs. "That shower is amazing! I didn't want to get out."

She towel dried her hair as she too gazed out over the balcony capturing the morning activities. "How do men get ready so fast?" She turned and leaned against the balcony balustrade looking at Vittore dressed in black jeans, an Armani white on white shadow striped shirt and a black lambskin leather ¾ length coat. *Did he know how handsome he was?*

A gentle breeze teased the hair out from behind his ear and sent a dark strand dancing along his cheek. She stepped forward and eased it back into place.

Vittore kissed her wrist and smiled, "Magic. Sit Cara and eat. My mother would be proud of my sexual prowess but starving a woman is unforgiveable."

"Your mother; *gaio*, that's who you're taking me to meet, right? Your little mother?"

"No, my mother is not yet ready for you, I will need to prepare her for that encounter. No, *gaio* is not mother, that is *l'madre*." He was going to enjoy this game with her; he knew it would continue the entire trip to Umbria.

"I knew that! Sister?"

"Cara, *manjiare, manjiare*; eat, eat.

Vittore avoided the multilane Autoban that led out of Roma to the north, and opted for the Autostrada instead that wormed its way north then meandered northeast to Narnia.

"Cara, you are following alongside one of the worlds' most ancient roads." Vittore pointed to his left, "We are following the Roman road Via Flaminia built by Gaius Flaminius in the 3rd century. It is good to be your tour guide. When wonders are at your doorstep, one takes them for granted when seen every day. I am glad you allowed me to share this with you."

Vittore revved the engine of his Bugatti and slid it into a higher gear. The Autostrada allowed Vittore the pleasure of not only the speed but the maneuvering that his Bugatti did so well. He took turns at speeds that left Cara speechless and whenever they approached a turn on the mountain roads leading further north into the heart of Umbria, towards his home in Montefalco, she covered her eyes and squealed.

The drive home was perfect! Vittore became the consummate tour guide and shared with Cara the history of his beloved Montefalco, the home of his ancestors. "You will fall in love with Montefalco, Cara, it is a very ancient town that peeks over other surrounding villages and is referred to as "The Balcony of Umbria'. The views north towards Assisi or west towards Bastardo are magnificent. It is the picture of Italy all tourists come to see, but fortunately they look for it in Tuscany and Lombardy, leaving our village a secret."

Vittore was enjoying talking about Montefalco with Cara, it made it alive once again in his heart. "Not only is Montefalco the best wine producing region for the Sagrantino grape, it is the birthplace of eight Saints. We believe there is a connection and must be divine intervention. To have all in one town so many Saints and our fine Sagrantino, God must truly have blessed our village. No?"

Cara had to admit the views were spectacular and with every turn they took she was rewarded a view of heaven.

"What makes Montefalco such a good area for growing wine? The views are beautiful, but it's all mountains and hillsides. It doesn't look much like farmland." Vittore turned towards her as he took another curve, without looking. "Vittore, watch the road! You are scaring me to death!"

"I see I have much to teach you about wine, Cara Bella! Vines like it difficult. The more they struggle to survive the more robust they become. A vineyard is like a woman, Cara Bella. You must let it struggle if you want the sweetest fruit."

Cara punched him in the arm. "That's an awful analogy, where do men come up with this stuff?" But she must admit he was a 'piccolo' right. She smiled to herself she really was enjoying this vacation.

Considering how the vacation began it had all the earmarks of a disaster. It amazed her that the break with Bryan had not bothered her once since the night she finally realized he was exactly what Jenna had warned her about, a spoiled egotist. And here she was doing exactly what she would have wanted to do; but would not have done with Bryan, get away from the city and go into the hill towns to get know the Italian people.

Even when she traveled for business she found most cities were filled with people more concerned with their jobs then their families. So when she had time she would rent a car and drive out of whatever city she was in, go to a small town and go shopping in the family owned businesses. Have lunch in a locally owned restaurant and stop by any roadside stand or farm selling fresh produce. She found this brush with her roots kept her from becoming too self-impressed.

She loved living in New York City, but she saw over the

ten years of living there, it could take a small town girl or boy and hoist them up on their own petard and destroy them. She saw many tumble and never regained their confidence but remained rather than admit defeat to their families back home. One thing New York City was not lax in was ego.

Cara rested her head as Vittore tore up the mountains that led to Montefalco. "Are you going to tell me about your "gaio piccolo"? Or do I have to guess?"

"It should not be too hard to guess, Bella. Say the word slowly, you will find it sounds much like it does in English."

Cara sat saying the word out loud, slowly, "Jawya, jaw..ya, jaw....ya. Jawya...joy! It is joy! Your little joy!"

Vittore laughed, "Si, her name is Antinella and I am her godfather. She is the daughter of my boyhood friend, Rocco Conti and his wife Gabriella, they died two years ago when Antinella was four and she unfortunately witnessed their deaths and has not spoken in two years."

Vittore saw the sadness pass over Cara's face, "Oh, Vittore no. How can a four year old make sense of a tragedy like that? Who takes care of her when you are in Roma?"

"Rocco's parents had died years earlier, so I became her legal guardian and as Rocco's will requested, also the manager of Conti vineyards until such time Antinella can manage it on her own. I have had many things to complete and have asked Antinella's aunt to help with her care until I can give her all my attention."

Vittore would never forget the day of Antinella's christening when he gave his oath to Rocco that his friend would not regret his decision of placing two of the things he and Gabriella loved most in this world in his care, his beautiful baby daughter Antinella and the vineyard. However, no one could have imagined that responsibility would come to Vittore so quickly.

"Montefalco is a small village and the proper medical care is not available there, so I bring Antinella to Roma with me for a few days when I am home, but being in Roma scares her, so I am not sure that it is such a good thing. So I prefer to spend time with her at the villa. I only tell you this Cara, because you need to know you are not the only woman in my life. Antinella is my first love and you will need to learn to share." He smiled warmly. "Antinella will enjoy you Cara, you will be good for her."

"Tell me what happened to Rocco and Gabriella."

"It is a very distressing story Cara. Are you sure you want to hear?" Cara studied his face and had no doubt that he meant what he said, it distressed him just thinking of it.

"Only if you think it needs to be told." Cara did not want Vittore to remember something that would darken his day.

"It will be better for you to know before you arrive at the Villa." Vittore unconsciously slowed the Bugatti as he began talking.

"Rocco took over Conti Vineyards from his father when he was very young. His father enjoyed the winery but Rocco had the passion. It had been in their family for hundreds of years."

"Today small family wineries are being bought up by large commercial wineries because it is so hard to make a profit. The cost of labor, casts, bottles and equipment makes it nearly impossible for boutique wineries such as the Conti Vineyard to survive in the world of mass markets." Vittore slowed as the Bugatti took a sharp turn along the mountain road.

"Rocco was a good man but proud and stubborn. Conti Vineyard has some of the oldest vines in all of Italy. When the corporate winery began buying up vineyards, Rocco refused to sell."

Vittore paused and the thought flashed through his mind for the millionth time, what they all would be doing now if Rocco had sold. He and Gabriella would be alive, Antinella would have her parents, and she would have her voice. He jerked his head violently to erase the image of this idyllic life that cannot be.

"The corporation was not interested in the vines that have been the source of the Conti wines for ten generations. They wanted the land for road access to move the trucks more quickly. By cutting a road through Conti Vineyards it would save time and petrol and therefore make the cost of the wines more competitive in the market. But it would have meant removing vines that were hundreds of years old."

Cara listened in silence, she could tell by Vittore's cadence it was a story, though he may not have verbalize, he had certain played over and over in his mind. She heard the pain in his voice.

"The vineyards in this area are generations old and like so many business' of the father, the sons want nothing to do with them. Especially if it is agriculture, the sons want high tech and sterile rooms, getting dirt under the nails has little appeal even here in Italy's wine country."

"The vineyard to the west of Conti's is Del'oro and without Conti's selling, the large commercial winery did not want

Del'oro Vineyards because there was no easy access to the Autobahn from their vineyard."

Cara gasped, "Vittore, this isn't going where I think it is? Please tell me, No."

"As romantic as Italian wineries may sound there are some vineyards that have made paupers of their owners. The Del'oro's are one such family. The son saw the selling of his family vineyard as his way of making his mark." The Bugatti sped up; the curves taken a bit more recklessly, his hands gripped the steering wheel tightly.

"He was mixed up with the Mafia, drugs and alcohol." Vittore slammed the car into a higher gear, "He broke into Rocco's home after too much of both and murdered them. He shot Rocco then raped and strangled Gabriella. Antinella was sleeping in her parent's room that night, the best we can determine, Rocco woke before he was attacked and hid Antinella in the closet to keep her safe."

"No! Vittore, that poor child!' Cara gasped and began to shake. "Stop the car, you need to pull off right now, please." Vittore found a lay-by and Cara got out wrapping her arms around herself and paced. She felt Vittore's rage, which was terrifying enough, but the thought of a child watching and listening to her parents being murdered, violated every belief she had about the right of a child to grow up innocent.

Vittore came up behind her and held her. He too had walked off his anger.

"Life is cruel everywhere in the world Cara. Even in the beautiful hills of Umbria. Do not let Antinella's story distress you to the point you cannot enjoy her, Cara. She is a loving and beautiful child, surrounded by many people who love her. We will get her through this. Soon I will be leaving Roma and staying with Antinella in Umbria. I cannot bear to be gone from her for so long and I could never ask her to spend her life with me in Roma."

Cara smiled, "You're going to adopt her aren't you?"

"Si. I have been consolidating my companies, and will manage them all under one large corporation. The vineyard will be Antinella's legacy. When she is old enough she can determine its fate. But for now, I will keep it safe for her." Vittore drew her close and kissed her head.

"I have a lot to learn about you, Vittore. This has thrown me for a loop."

"You thought I was a rich playboy. What did you say, A European elitist?" Vittore smiled at her behind her back.

"Cara I grew up with the soil of Umbria in my hands. You have not known all of me in Roma, just a part of me. Do not judge me by my silk shirts and limousines, they are a means to an end and the end is a few miles away, jumping rope and playing dress-up. Come it is time to meet, *mio gaio piccolo*. You will fall in love with her, Cara. She loves as deeply as you. You two will be great friends."

CHAPTER NINE

The Bugatti sped up the central section of the Apennine Mountains heading towards the village of Montefalco. Cara felt like an eagle as they swooped out of the mountains and hovered above the little village. From this distance she could see the valley and everywhere you looked it was a deep lush green, filled with neat rows of vines. In the center of it all was the town itself, its' buildings awash with the oranges and purples of the setting sun.

"Vittore, this is beautiful!" She turned to him in awe.

"It is home." His smile broadened and his speed increased. Cara had to laugh; she had never seen anyone so happy to be going home.

Vittore blew his horn and waved to people on the street, as he tore through the little village. Once through the village he took a road that ascended a small hill and once on the precipice a vista opened before them that could only be described as picturesque.

A villa sat on a hill opposite them that caught the warmth of the golden hues of the late afternoon sun. The approach to the villa was lined with cypress trees and mulberry trees and on either side of that were hundreds of rows of vines and groves of olive trees.

When they were within a hundred yards of the villa, Vittore

began to hit his horn in short rapid bursts. First Cara saw a man appear from a barn, waving his hands vigorously shouting a welcome. They tore by him and headed straight to a courtyard beside a square two story villa with a red tile roof and huge sweeping verandas; some covered with arbors of wisteria.

Vittore skidded to a stop in front of the villa and jumped out by catapulting himself over the door. He took long strides to the steps of the villa holding his arms wide shouting for Antinella.

Bursting through the door there was a blur of pink, as Antinella flew through the air and landed in Vittore's arms, covering his face with kisses. She was giggling and squirming as he attempted to hold on to her and finally had to place her on the ground. He knelt in front of her talking and pointed repeatedly towards the car.

Cara got out of the car resting against the side, waiting for him to finish his greeting. She didn't know who was more excited, Antinella or Vittore. It was obvious the love they had for each other and Cara was amazed at the affection he showed towards this little girl.

Vittore was right she had made a huge assumption that he was a shallow playboy but there was nothing shallow about the man in front of her.

Vittore rose and held Antinella's' hand and walked towards the car. Cara was amazed at how tall Antinella was for a six year old and as they got closer she saw her sweet face full of expression and joy. *Moa gaio piccolo*, Vittore had given her an endearing name that fit her.

When Vittore reached the car, he swung Antinella up into his arms resting her on his hip. He began the introductions by telling Antinella that Cara was an American and then did the formal introductions which during the entire process Antinella giggled and buried her head into Vittore's neck. She smiled broadly and reached out and touched Cara's face lightly and turned her head towards Vittore and lifted her eyebrows in rapid succession and let her wrist shake in approval.

Vittore laughed saying to Cara, "Antinella seems to approve of my choice of a girlfriend."

Cara stepped forward and gave Vittore a quick look, "Girlfriend huh?" Smiling she held out her hand to Antinella, "Buon giorno, Antinella."

Antinella placed her little hand in Cara's and smiled. Antinella had dark brown curly hair that had been braided to keep it under control. Her eyes however were a brilliant blue and the two together were unexpected therefore breathtaking!

"Oh Vittore, you are right she is a joy! I can see how she would twist your heart, she is precious."

Approaching Vittore from behind was a woman flapping her arms and shouting endearments. He spun around and gathered the older women into his free arm laughing. He said something that made the woman blush and brought forth a gentle pat on his cheek. Cara watched Vittore. He was definitely much more than silk shirts and Limo's.

Vittore placed Antinella on the ground and gave her a gentle pat on her butt directing her towards the villa then turned and escorted the woman to Cara. "Cara, this in Maria Conti, Antinella's la zia."

He hugged Maria around the shoulder presenting her proudly. "Maria is my second mother and she knows much about me." He turned to her and said something in Italian shaking his finger and giving her a stern look before turning back to Cara, "I have warned her to not share too much about me that is bad. I have hopes that this visit will allow you to like me more, not less."

Maria hooked her arm through Cara's and started towards the villa. Cara caught a few words that she understood and gathered that Maria was going to prepare a light dinner for her and Vittore. She looked behind her as Maria led her into the villa and Vittore had taken off towards the barn greeting several men.

Cara was dizzy from the heat of passion in Roma to the contentment she was now feeling here in this little village tucked into the mountains of Umbria. She had always known she was a complex woman, but Vittore' complexities were staggering! No one was a gorgeous, sexy, wealthy, international playboy on one side of the coin and a loving, warm, compassionate man on the other. Or was one of these Vittore's not Vittore? He said her impression of him was wrong. But how does a simple farm boy from the vineyards of Umbria become so incredibly wealthy? There was a lot to learn about this man.

Maria pulled fresh vegetables from a basket sitting on the sideboard and motioned towards Cara to join her in rinsing and preparing them for a meal. Cara began cleaning and trimming mushrooms into thin strips while Maria prepared thick slices of what looked like mush and began sautéing them in a skillet filled with rich nutty butter.

Cara was a bit skeptical; mush was not something she had ever eaten and she was not looking forward to trying it, but how did you say "yuk!" in Italian without offending? Cara wisely kept her opinion to herself and allowed Maria to carry on with her meal preparations.

She was enjoying the silent camaraderie in the kitchen with

Maria when Antinella entered and slipped her little hand into Cara's tugging her towards another room. Maria nodded her head giving Cara leave to go with Antinella.

Antinella led Cara through a beautiful home filled with antiques and comfortable upholstery begging for those who passed from room to room to linger and rest. But the call of each room's tranquility did not dissuade Antinella from her goal.

They entered an office that had bookshelves lining three walls of the room floor to ceiling with a ladder attached to a brass track going around the room in order to gain access to the upper shelves. The room was masculine, warm and comfortable.

Antinella went to a large book she had opened on a table near the paned windows and motioned Cara to it. Lying open on the table was a huge atlas and Antinella pointed to the pages that were opened revealing a map of the US. She swept her hand over the pages and gave Cara a questioning look.

"You want to know where I live?" Cara asked. Antinella gave her another questioning look and Cara realized that although Antinella could hear, she did not understand English, so they had a challenge to overcome. Cara thought for a few minutes and thought of dear toothless Romano and his universal language.

"OK Antinella, we are going to figure out how to communicate. You game?" Cara smiled and thought hard back to the days she played charades with her family. She had always been very good, now she going to test the international applications.

Cara picked Antinella up and sat her on the table. Gave her a look letting her know something was about to happen.

Antinella's eyes were wide with expectation. Cara turned and walked a few paces away; then when she turned back to Antinella she pointed to her mouth and made talking motions with her hands as she bobbed her head back and forth.

Antinella caught on quickly realizing Cara was going to talk with her hands. Antinella clapped her hands and giggled waiting for the next clue from Cara.

Cara pointed to herself and made a question mark in the air then laid her head on her hands, hoping Antinella would get it. And she did. Antinella pointed to the map again and Cara pointed to New York City. "This is where I live."

Antinella pointed to the map, put her hand to her ear and then to her mouth and made her hands talk. She wanted to hear the name of the city Cara lived in. "New York City, Antinella, I live in New York City."

Antinella riffled through some pages of the atlas until she got to Italy and pointed to Roma. She looked at Cara and spread her arms wide then went back to New York City and spread her arms wide again with a questioning look.

"Si, New York City is a big city," Cara spread her arms wide, "like Roma. But," Cara held her forefinger out and shook it and her head, and pointed to New York and said, "Bella" then flipped to Roma and closed her eyes and said, "molto Bella!"

Antinella jumped off the desk giggling and wrapped her arms around Cara's waist resting her head on her belly. Cara stroked Antinella's hair whispering, "Si, Molto Bella," as she lowered her lips and kissed Antinella on the top of her head.

There was a rustle at the doorway and they both looked over to see Vittore standing there arms crossed, watching and smiling. "Cara you are in my home for less than a few hours and you have already stolen my most precious possession." He walked into the room looking at the atlas, "Are you two planning a trip without me?!" He turned to Antinella and asked the same question fining heartbreak.

"We're just talking." Cara winked at Antinella and moved her fingers alongside her mouth. "Antinella wanted to know where in the U.S. I lived. So she pulled the atlas out, she is a very clever little girl."

Cara looked around the room, "Is this your Umbria office? I have to say I like it!" Cara wandered over to a glass case located behind the huge antique desk that was filled with guns. "Now this I did not expect!! You collect firearms? I am not sure I will ever actually know you, Vittore. You are a bit confusing. Do they work?"

"Si, but do not be too confused; life in Roma and Montefalco are decidedly different. The animals in Roma are after your money, in Montefalco they are after your birthright. I can always make more money, Cara."

Maria called from the kitchen apparently dinner was ready and Vittore' eyes lit up, "Maria's dinner is ready! You are in for a treat! I owe my size to her and her good cooking!" Antinella giggled and joined Vittore's and Cara's hands together and led them both from the office.

"Ah, Vittore?" Cara made a little face, "I don't like mush, and I don't know how to politely beg out of dinner, could you extend my apologies and tell Maria I was tired and just went to bed?"

"Mush! Mush! Where did you get such an idea? Maria has made Polenta with wild mushrooms and truffles in a cream sauce. It is a delicacy Cara, you will love it, I promise! If you do not you can punish me for telling you a lie." His eyes twinkled. "Either way you win, No?!"

"I guess that would depend on the punishment." She cast him a wary glance.

"Um, I almost hope you do not like this meal, Cara." He was wicked!

Vittore and Cara sat outside after dinner sipping Amaretto. "It disappoints me Cara that you liked your meal so much! Not one serving, but two! What can we do tonight now, other than groan from contentment now that our bellies are full? You were supposed to turn your nose up at the meal than make me pay for lying to you. Now what are we to do Cara?"

"I thought you weren't going to touch me today. Just think of it as my helping you to keep a promise you made to yourself." Cara sipped some more amaretto thinking she had sufficiently held him at bay.

"Ah Bella, but it is past midnight, that promise is no more." He began to rise from the chair and Cara jumped to her bare feet with a squeal, running down the steps towards a row in grape vines, laughing as she turned to see Vittore give chase.

Cara was several feet into the vineyard when Vittore caught her around the waist and drew her to the ground using his body to cushion hers. Vittore rolled her on to her back covering her softly with his body, elbows either side her head, he lowered his mouth over hers catching her laughter with his kiss.

"We should be safe here Cara, no water." His smile was as wicked as a smile could get.

Cara swept her eyes across the field and looked into his with terrified eyes, "But aren't grapes fruit?"

He looked along the row of vines, "Si Cara they are, round

lush juicy grapes." He bent his head and pulled on her lower lip with his teeth. "I wonder where we could save them so I could have a snack later." His look was lustfully sexy and Cara gave a squeak, knowing exactly what Vittore had in mind. He ran his hand up the inside of her leg as the irrigation sprinklers turned on and they both began laughing.

"Water and fruit? I think you planned this Vittore." Cara laughed and wiggled under him trying to get off the ground to avoid getting any muddier then she already was.

Vittore pinned her to the ground with his hips watching her body get drenched. Her clothing became transparent as it got wetter and revealed the perfect curve of her breasts and their darkened circles and hardened peaks. Vittore moaned as he lowered his mouth to the inviting sight. He tore at the buttons on her blouse until they popped and he hungrily took her into his mouth. He wanted her every moment he was near her.

Vittore rose to his feet straddling her hips. As he gazed down on her lying between his legs, wet and dirty, his lust was overwhelming. He tore his wet shirt from his chest, "Mia Bella, you bewitch me. I want you Bella, here, now! I want you." His voice was trembling, his eyes hot as they raked over her wet clothes.

Reaching down he took Cara's hands and helped her to her feet. He ran his hands up Cara's arms and across her shoulders removing the blouse and throwing it to the ground. Cara smiled looking at the discarded piece of fabric. "It's a good thing you're rich, I've never destroyed so many clothes in my life!"

She felt his fingertips lightly touch her body, they trembled with desire. His hunger was so uninhibited it scared and excited Cara. She wanted him to possess her; to make love to her like no man had before, his strength and passion were electrifying.

Vittore pushed Cara back against the fence that supported the vines and undid the waistband of her skirt allowing it to fall at her feet. He knelt before her cupping her cheeks and drawing her hips towards his mouth. The spray of water ceased as he shredded the delicate lace, removing all obstacles and tilted her hips forward to devour her. Spreading her thighs apart with his rough chin he plunged his tongue into her liquid recesses, playing with Cara until she thought she would not survive the attack. Then he withdrew and began suckling, licking, teasing her trigger.

She screamed, lifting a leg over his shoulder leaning her back against the fence digging her fists into his hair, pushing her hips forward. Vittore balanced her as he nipped and suckled pulling the swollen slick button of ecstasy into his mouth. She wasn't going to survive. She thrust herself into him again wanting him to stop because she had lost control of breathing. The rush of heat hit her in waves that should have destroyed her but she would die if he stopped, die if he continued.

She couldn't see, the heat had destroyed her ability to focus, she begged for more; begged for him to stop. The rush was so intense it could not be controlled. Vittore licked her trying to calm her heat to help her stop trembling. But he couldn't calm her because he couldn't calm himself. He had to bring her to a climax again. She excited him like no other woman ever had.

He sucked on her button and flicked it with the hard tip of his tongue. Cara brought her fists down on his shoulders, "God Vittore, ohmigod!" She was spinning into a different universe. He licked, nipped and plunged his tongue deep, scraping his rough chin along her slick folds, Cara wanted more and she drew him in closer. "Don't stop, oh god please don't stop!" she couldn't breathe, she couldn't stand, she couldn't stop moving into him, she couldn't stop the surge of her excitement; she was going to die.

Vittore stroked her swollen folds with his warm tongue, pulling on her lips with his perfect mouth, coaxing her. He never knew a woman who could give herself so completely, it took his breath away. Her craving was so intense he could not imagine an end to her desire. He plunged deeper and pulled harder on her hot slick button until she nearly collapsed.

Vittore rose holding her with one arm supporting her weight, she was like a rag doll, he buried his mouth into her wet hair as he kicked off his shoes then with his free hand removed his jeans. She felt the warmth of him pressing into her belly, hard like a steel rod, her knees went weak. Vittore felt her hand gently touch the velvet tip of his arousal.

"Cara, I want you now!" He desperately scanned the area. ""Oh, Cara you are driving me mad. Why do I want you so?"

His eyes landed on the fence behind her, he spun her around, putting her hands on the fence and covering them with his, bending over her, his weighted muscle falling between her thighs. Cara gasped; she was so weak she wasn't sure she could do this.

He slid his hands up her arms, across her breasts, lingering long enough to gather the full soft mounds into his hands and feel the weight, squeezing gently. He held one breast while positioning himself into her rich, moist well. He slipped into her slowly and placed his arm around her waist, pulling her into him hard.

Cara grasped the fence and dropped her head between her forearms. He withdrew and entered her again, watching her bottom quiver with each thrust. The sight excited him, he drove harder, deeper, faster.

Cara screamed with pleasure, "Vittore, I can't, I can't..! No! Don't stop."

Her mind was a confusion of desire and exhaustion as he found a rhythm that drew him out of her warmth then plunged back in with reckless desire. His hands forcing her hips into his frantic thrusts, he moaned and threw his head back as he spilled his seed into her, bathing her with his molten heat.

He kissed her lower back and she shivered releasing another flow of warm rich honey. Softly trailing kisses along her spine he said, "Mia Bella, so you still have more to give? Cara you will kill us both."

He withdrew leaving her wanting. She whimpered and moved her hips back towards his, she couldn't take any more but she did not want him to stop. "Please no, please don't stop," she whispered.

Vittore turned her to face him and he took her face into his hands and kissed her lovingly, tenderly. "Please don't stop," she whispered again. Looking into his eyes searching for his consent his agreement to not stop making love to her. "Please."

He stepped back a few inches and smiled as he played with the Amber ring on his left forefinger. He looked into Cara's eyes and her heart skipped a beat. Vittore removed the ring from his hand and moved it to his right forefinger. "This ring was given to my Great Great Grandfather by the Czar of Russia to thank him for saving the life of his beloved Czarina."

Cara stared at the stone, even in the faded light of evening it glowed a beautiful dark honey color bordering on red. She watched Vittore play with it. He held it out and placed the stone inches from beneath her chin. "Did you ever place dandelions beneath your chin as a child to see who your sweetheart was?"

Cara nodded her head slightly. "Yes, we all want a test to make sure the one we love is our true love for all time."

He bent his head peeking under her chin, "What if I told you this ring will identify my true love?" He looked into her eyes, "Shall we test it?"

Cara could only nod her head. She couldn't hear, she couldn't think she just wanted more of him. She wanted to die making love to him.

He placed his foot on the bottom rail of the fence and lifted Cara, straddling her legs on his thigh. She held tight to his neck for balance, he kept his left hand securely at her waist. He looked at her soft folds as they opened to him, then he very gently allow the warm surface of the stone to glide against her.

Cara had closed her eyes and was relishing the intense pleasure of this gentle act. She concentrated on the touch of the ring. She shivered sending another wave of honey spilling from her body. Vittore continued to move the ring slowly. "Does that feel good, Cara?"

She nodded slightly, trying not to let anything distract her from this pleasure, "Delicious." She shivered again.

"Good Cara, because we will have a lifetime to enjoy, for it seems you are my true love."

Cara gave a little laugh and opened her eyes and saw Vittore continuing to watch his hand. She kissed his temple, feeling the heat of the amber stone increase.

She moaned and thought if it could only be true. "You are such an incredible lover, Vittore. I could actually enjoy this for a lifetime and never tire of you making love to me. It is a beautiful dream."

"It is no dream Cara." He smiled as he raised the ring to her eyes. "it appears that you are my true love."

Cara gasped, "How did you do that?" The stone had turned from deep reddish amber to a scarlet red.

"I did not Cara, you did. Only a true love can change the stone's color. I knew it would be you Cara."

"No really how did you do that?"

Vittore laughed, "You do not believe me Cara? You turned the stone red. As have all the women in my family for many generations."

"You're telling me Great Great Grandpa Falco used this little trick on your Great Great Grandmother and she fell for it?

"As did my mother and my fathers' mother before that; did I not tell you this ring had properties you would not be able imagine?"

Vittore held her against his chest as he lowered his leg, placing Cara on the ground. Her hands rested just above his abdomen and she kissed the hard muscles that stretched between her palms. "Why can't I stop wanting you? It is not natural."

She tilted her head back and smiled, "You do realize that at one point we will have to start acting like adults and not a pair of sex starved teenagers?"

He brushed a few strands of hair from her face. "And why is that Cara?"

"Because if we don't I will die with an embarrassing grin on my face!"

"And what is wrong with that?" He laughed at her expression.

"You're being difficult!"

"No Cara, I am being selfish. I want you, every inch of you when I have you alone like this. We do not need to be in control when it is just you and I. What we do is between us." He kissed her temple as he lifted her into his arms and began walking towards the villa.

"Ah, we left our clothes back there, shouldn't we attempt to cover up before we go in?"

"I will get them later, right now I want to shower and lay with you in my bed and make love. Slowly, very slowly Cara Bella," he bent and tugged on her hardened nipple with his mouth. She was going to die. She knew she was going to die.

CHAPTER TEN

Cara woke the next morning to shouts, dogs barking and what sounded like a raging bull. She leapt from the bed grabbing a robe and as she ran to the balcony.

Vittore was standing over a man holding him by the shirt and driving his fist into the man's face repeatedly. She screamed running from the room and out the front doors into the yard. She got to Vittores' side just as a man was pulling Vittore off the man who lay prone on the ground.

A lot of things were being said she could not understand, she hated not knowing what was going on! She looked at Vittore and her breath caught in her throat. She saw such raw hatred, such rage it was like looking into the eyes of a stranger. This couldn't be the same man that held her so gently last night attending to her every desire. No this man was the face of evil, what happened? She stepped back away from him afraid whatever demon possessed him would unleash its rage on her.

His eyes met hers and they were cold and dead. No apologies for her having witnessed such brutality, no care that she stood before him terrified. Hatred and rage coursed through his body leaving in its wake barren emotions. He almost hissed at Cara as he pushed past her and went into the winery.

She looked around the yard. Everyone was quite and

staring at her. The only person she knew who spoke English was in a state of fury and unapproachable. "What the hell is going on?" She directed her question to no one in particular.

Two men hoisted the man who lie on the ground to his feet and shoved him unceremoniously towards his truck, depositing him in the drivers' seat. Again words were spoken and without knowing what was said it was unmistakable to misunderstand the intent, it was a threat.

As the truck drove away, the larger of the two men approached Cara, his head slightly lowered. "Scusi, Signoria, I am Vittore's brother, Davide. I am sorry that you had to wake to all this." He motioned towards the truck spewing dirt as it tore down the drive.

"What happened?"She held her arms tight to her chest trying to keep from trembling. Vittore's face scared her, she had never seen such hatred, such rage! If Davide had not pulled Vittore off that man Vittore would have killed him with his bare hands. She shook with fear and the fear was evident in her eyes.

"Come, you need to sit." He led her to the side porch covered with an arbor supporting the heavy, branches of wisteria. He pulled out a chair for her and poured her an espresso placing it gently in front of her. "Drink this it will warm you."

Davide sat opposite her slouching in the chair, rubbing his eyes wearily, elbows on his thighs, head in his hand. He lifted his eyes to meet Cara's. "Hell of a way to meet, huh?" A very small smile crossed his lips.

She sat in stunned silence, confused and afraid. Davide continued, "That was a Del'oro brother. Did Vittore tell you of Rocco and Gabriella?"

Cara nodded. Then panic rose in her chest. "Antinella, where is Antinella!" She began to rise to run to the child.

"Sit Cara, Antinella is in the village with Maria, she didn't witness this, nor see the brother of the man that killed her parents, she's safe."

Tears began to form in Cara's eyes. She was raw emotion; it was too much, going from joyful bliss a few hours ago to paralyzing fear. "Why was he here? Vittore could have killed him!'

"Vittore would have killed him." It was a simple fact. Davide knew that side of Vittore, a side Cara had no idea existed.

Her hand trembled as she removed the cup from the saucer. Davide watched her hand tremble, "Maybe I should have gotten you a whiskey?"

Cara tried to ignore her emotions, "You sound very western?"

"I attended college in California at UC Davis. After I graduated I stayed in San Francisco and worked in Sonoma. I came home to Italy only a few years ago, after Vittore decided to build Conti Vineyards into an inheritance for Antinella." A warm loving smile spread across his face. "Who was I to say no to my big brother? Vittore asked me to manage the winery and like Vittore, I have known the Conti's all my life and Vittore has a good plan. I'm glad to be a part of it."

Cara was calmer, "Why was that man here and why was Vittore so angry?"

"Niccolo? He is as stupid as his brother! Both brothers were mixed up with Mafia, but even they couldn't tolerate the stupidity of the two of them. When Roberto was tried for the murders of Rocco and Gabriella, no one from the brotherhood came to his aid. Niccolo still thinks he has the weight of the Mafia behind him. He's too stupid to realize he has been cut loose."

"You talk of the Mafia so casually. Aren't you afraid?"

Davide laughed, "Americans think of the Mafia as they were in the '20's. They have evolved here in Italy. Don't get me wrong, they still are not people you want to climb into bed with or cross. But the Mafia today is more of a crooked business than a bunch of murderous thugs. Now they intimidate with law suits and takeovers. Not that they still don't make it a point on occasion to let you know who is really in control, but it is more likely your crops will be destroyed with a pesticide than having a horses' head placed in your bed."

"Ah the Godfather," Cara smiled. This was relaxing her. "So you don't fear the Mafia?"

"I didn't say that, we just do not cross them. Roberto made a big mistake murdering Rocco and Gabriella, it put too much of a spot light on what the Mafia was doing here in Umbria. They have been flooding the area with drugs and were trying to keep a low profile. So the Mafia was happy to let Roberto swing."

"But why did Niccolo show up here and what did he do that made Vittore so angry?"

"Hell all Vittore needs to do is see a Del'oro and he comes unhinged. Several of the wineries that did not sell to the wine conglomerates banded together to buy the Del'oro vineyards. The Del'oro's have allowed their vineyard to decay and it really isn't worth that much, but we all want the family out of the region before someone gets hurt. They are not happy with the offer and think Vittore is behind keeping the offer low."

"Oh," Cara was now beginning to understand what had taken place in the yard earlier. "Do you think Vittore is OK? He scared me and I think he knew it. I want him to know I think I understand."

"He'll be fine Cara. I think he scares himself more than anyone when he loses his cool like that. It really pisses him off how they can push his buttons. He's out in the fields somewhere hacking away at some innocent vine that I'll have to nurture back to health later." He smiled and shook his head as he rose from his chair, "Cara, it was a pleasure, but I need to get back to work. Try not to worry. I don't think Vittore is a homicidal maniac."

Cara leaned back in the chair enjoying the fragrance of the wisteria, espresso and wet earth. Well things certainly were not dull around Vittore! And she thought she was the one always landing in it!

Despite Davide's assurances Cara was worried about Vittore all morning. Shortly after his disappearance Antinella and Maria returned from the village and Cara then spent the remainder of the morning helping Antinella create a stage for a ballet she wanted to perform for everyone after dinner. Cara helped her with costumes and music selections. They broke for a short lunch and joined Davide and several other vineyard employees under a large tree near the winery enjoying the cool of the shade.

Cara saw a few horses corralled by the side of the winery. "Horses! When I think Italian I don't think horses!" She turned to Davide with a surprised look. "They are beautiful!" Cara approached the fence and several huge pure black stallions moved closer inspecting her hand for treats. Their soft noses nuzzled her palms. She turned to Davide who was only steps behind her, "These aren't quarter horses or Arabian? What breed are they?"

"They are unique to Italy, they are called Murgese." Davide offered forth two palms each holding a piece of carrot. "They are an ancient breed from the Puglia region in what is called the heel of the boot. The Murgese is a national treasure."

"Are they work horses?"

"No! Nooo, not these babies; they are pure pleasure. This one is Fortuna and this big guy is Vincere. Vittore must have saddled Vento." Davide stroked the nose of each horse.

"They seem so docile. How do they handle strangers riding them?"

"The Murgese is bred to be accommodating; either would let you ride them. Do you want to go look for Vittore?"

Cara nodded her head, "I knew you were worried. Hey why don't I saddle Antinella's pony too and the two of you can go out. She knows where he goes to brood and her Piccolo Cavallo hasn't been ridden in about a week."

"Sounds like a plan. I'll get Antinella changed and we'll pack some food. I am sure once we find Vittore he will be starved. We should be ready in about 30 minutes." Cara paused, "And thank you Davide."

Davide just nodded. He knew she wanted to get out and start looking for his brother. Although Davide knew Vittore was safe, it was Cara's first sight of his rage. It seldom happened and only lately when it concerned the Del'oro's, but Cara wouldn't be comfortable until she saw Vittore him with her own eyes.

Cara ran to the villa and informed Maria, in her now well developed pantomime language, that she and Antinella were going to locate Vittore. She asked Maria to pack some food and then turned to track down Antinella. Cara found Antinella in her bedroom playing. She entered and sat on the bed facing Antinella and asked in very broken Italian if Antinella would join her to find Vittore. She jumped at the offer and began tearing through her closet for a sturdy pair of jeans.

Cara left her to get ready while she herself changed and grabbed a backpack to fill with food and water. The two met in the kitchen where Maria had made several sandwiches and had a vast array of fruits, vegetables, cheeses and bottled water. The three of them began packing Cara's backpack stuffing every inch with food. Maria mentioned several times that Vittore would be very hungry.

Cara and Antinella walked to the barn where Davide had both horses saddled and ready. Cara paused and looked at the saddle, it was not a western but she hadn't expected one, but she did think it would be an English saddle, she'd ridden an English saddle before, but this was different. "What kind of saddle is that!?" it could best be described as a padded leather blanket over the back of Fortuna.

"It's a French Saddle, designed for riding not jumping or herding as your western. You'll do fine, it looks strange but the same principle as any saddle. Do you need help?"

"You know I think I might! There is nothing to grab onto!"

Davide walked Fortuna to the side of a platform; which Cara climbed putting her level with Fortuna's back. She slipped her leg over the back of the horse and set herself into the saddle. Antinella got special treatment. Davide lifted her into the air and swung her on top the saddle sitting on her pony. He shook his finger at Antinella and said something that made her laugh.

Cara smiled, "Something I should know?" She began leading her horse out of the barn.

"I warned her not to show off to you. Antinella is a champion rider here in Umbria and we don't yet know your abilities. She will need to pay attention to where she takes you. Some areas are dangerous."

Cara winked at Antinella and said to Davide, "Oh I think I can keep up." She flicked Fortuna's reins and crouched low in the saddle and Fortuna shot off like a bullet. Cara turned her head to steal a glance at Davide who stood there shaking his head and threw his hands in the air.

Cara slowed to allow Antinella time to catch-up. When they were side by side Cara said, "I guess I am the show off, huh?" They rode in companionable silence for several miles when Antinella caught sight of something up ahead and set her little pony riding hard. Vittore was asleep under a tree and heard the thunder of hooves. The morning had been tense and his adrenaline was still high so the sound sent him into alert mode and he rose quickly, ready to encounter a fight. But rather than an adversary approaching it was his gio piccolo! Antinella drew her pony to a stop and slid off the saddle running to him, knowing her would lift her and twirl her in circles, making her belly tickle like she was on an amusement park ride. After several turns, he held her out, hands under her arms, feet dangling, "Antinella, you should not be this far from home on your own. We have spoken of this." He scolded her, but she giggled and pointed behind him.

Vittore turned and saw Cara seated on Fontuna. She looked dazzling seated high on such a magnificent beast.

Her hair wild about her head, face flushed, the mid afternoon sun intensifying the red in her hair. She sat easily in the saddle obviously accustomed to riding. She took his heart. He wanted to declare his love, but it was too soon. He had not played this right, nor had he intended to fall in love, he had just intended to rescue her.

Vittore set Antinella on her feet and walked over to Cara, never taking his eyes from hers. When he reached her side he held Fortuna's reign and stroked the horses quivering flanks. He was ashamed that she had seen him so out of control. Twice in her presence she left him speechless, both due to unforgiveable actions he had taken.

"Hey stranger, are you going to help me down?" She was smiling with joy at having located him and seeing him safe. "Although once I am down I have no idea how I am going get back up. At the barn I slid on from a platform, great horsewoman, huh?" She reached out her arms to grab his shoulders while she dismounted.

Vittore held her waist as she slid from the saddle and onto the ground. "Cara, I am sorry you saw that." His voice held such shame. He laid his chin on top of her head. Cara could smell he grass he had been laying in, it smelled good, earthy and warm.

She leaned into his chest, "Davide explained a little of what was going on." She stole a glance at Antinella who was gathering field flowers, "You should have called me, I would have held the bastard down for you!"

Laughter ripped from Vittore's throat so loud it scared the horses. His heart soared. He had a tigress, it is what he wanted, a tigress that would do anything to protect what she loved. He drew her into his chest, "Cara Bella, you will make me love you if you keep attempting to protect my piccolo!" unbeknownst to Cara, Vittore' eyes welled with tears as he held her tight. He kissed the top of her head as he guided her to the shade of the tree.

"Oh wait I forgot," Cara ran back to Fortuna who grazed lazily on the deep green grass. She freed her backpack from the horse and held it triumphantly. "Food! We thought you would be hungry!"

"Cara Bella, you are a Saint!" He spread his arms wide to show his appreciation of her thoughtfulness. Taking the pack from her, he headed to his spot under the tree. "I am starving! I took off without breakfast and missed lunch and wasn't sure I'd be welcomed for dinner! Grazia!"

Vittore opened the pack and dumped its contents onto the grass. He sorted through the cheese, sandwiches, fruits and vegetables before settling on an apple and a hunk of cheese. He leaned against the trunk of the tree and pulled Cara to his side as he watched Antinella pick flowers.

She dipped and swirled in delight as she compiled a bouquet in her little hands squeezing the stems tight so as to not lose one precious flower. She looked over and smiled at Vittore and Cara, waiving excitedly. Vittore held up some food indicating her to come and sit with them.

Antinella presented her bouquet to Cara. "Grazie, they are molto bella!" She looked to Vittore, "Did I get that even close to right?"

"Close enough, Antinella knows what you meant." He took a Swiss Army knife from his pocket and placed his half drunk bottle of water on the ground while he produced a blade. "Here let us give them some water." He cut into the plastic about an inch above the water line and took the flowers from Cara and arranged them in his makeshift vase. Antinella gave him a long hug about his neck.

They spent the rest of the afternoon chasing each other around the field and playing blind-man's bluff. Cara laughed watching Vittore, this huge, perfect specimen of a man blind folded stumbling about the field, his arms outstretched seeking to capture one of them. When his hands landed on Vento, his horse, Antinella squealed with laughter. "This does not count as a capture mia Bella?"

"Nope!" Cara piped up, he turned immediately to the sound of her voice and sought her out like "the mummy" from a late night horror show. She was laughing so hard she didn't pay attention to the terrain and fell over a tree branch, giving Vittore the time needed to claim her as his captive.

As soon as he ran into her body on the ground he fell upon her and ripped off the blindfold and threw it aside. "I caught you!" He yelled triumphantly. "Antinella, venire rapidamente! Io raggiungre, Cara! Presto, Presto!" Vittore crept up Cara's body smiling, laughing. "Got you!"

She smiled, "You certainly do."

Antinella flew on top of Vittore's back slamming him into Cara and the three of them lay in a tangled heap, laughing and rolling in the sweet grass. When the rolling stopped Vittore found that he lay with Cara in the crook of one arm and Antinella in the other. He beamed up to the heavens and sent a prayer of thanks. He turned and kissed each of his girls on the temple. "Perfecto!"

Cara and Antinella peaked at each other over his chest and in that brief moment each saw the plan hatch. They leaped on top of Vittore tickling him and pinching him until they all were exhausted.

After a brief rest Vittore began gathering the remnants of lunch and the flowers. "Do we have to go?" Cara pleaded with him. She knelt before Vittore with her hands folded, Antinella mimicked her giving him her most pitiful look. He stood above them both and shook his head.

"You two are the same! I am in trouble. Double trouble!" he reached out and gently toppled Cara and gave Antinella a firm shake of his finger. "Maria will have dinner ready and it is not good to miss a meal by Maria."

Antinella grabbed Cara's face to get her full attention and twirled like a ballerina. "Oh that's right, we need to get going! Hurry up!" She began shoving things into the backpack with no regard to the preservation of the remaining food. "Come on Vittore, get a move on."

He stood there stunned a few seconds ago they both wanted to stay now he wasn't moving fast enough. He thought this was one of the most perfect days he had ever had.

Antinella vaulted herself on to her pony and Vittore managed to swing himself up effortlessly on Vento. Cara stood at the side of Fortuna staring at the side of the horse like it was Mount Everest, she really had no idea how to mount this saddle. She looked helplessly over at Vittore, "Ah, a little help here please?"

Vittore walked Vento over so he was parallel with Foutuna with Cara between the two animals, he reached down lifted Cara up from under her arms high enough so she could slip a leg over her saddle. "Grazie." She said as she turned her horse and coxed it into a gallop. She might not know how to get onto the damn thing, but she sure knew what to do once she got there! "Presto, Presto!" She shouted to the two of them as she sped away.

They all arrived within site if the villa galloping at full speed, somewhere along the way it became a race. Vittore and Cara allowed Antinella's pony a sizable head start before the two of them unleashed the speed of their horses. As Vittore and Cara speed along side by side they would glance at each other challenging the other to take the lead. Finally Cara couldn't stand it any longer, she whipped the reigns and took Fortuna into a full gallop. Vento followed right behind with Vittore laughing at her impatience.

At the barn several of the men came out to cheer on the horses, whipping hats from their heads and slapping them alongside their thighs. It was clear the favorite was Antinella for when she was the first to arrive into the corral there was a universal shout of joy! Cara followed and finally Vittore. They all dismounted breathing heavily and looking at each other with knowledge that they had all just spent one of the best afternoons of their lives. Vittore lifted Antinella onto his hip and laid his other arm around Cara's shoulders.

He caught Davide out of the corner of his eye and called him over. He removed his arm from Cara, but she continued walking towards the villa.

Davide stood alongside his brother while Vittore reached around Antinella and removed the Amber Ring from his left hand and placed it in Davide's palm. Davide cocked his head, "Are you sure?"

"Definitely, Davide, Definitely!" He couldn't be more sure of anything in his life. He made his way towards the Villa thinking of ways to make Cara be as sure as he. He hugged his piccolo unto to his neck. He was happier than he had ever been in his life.

That evening after dinner Cara and Antinella set up the

outdoor stage for the ballet. Cara had transformed one of Antinella's black bathing suits into a costume a prima ballerina would be envious of, she used a skirt she had brought that was a leopard print and cut it into petals and adorned the edges of each petal with glitter they found in an art supply box. And then onto one of Antinella's headbands she fashioned fuzzy ears and attached them securely and then adding makeup transformed Antinella in to a lioness from the Lion King.

Antinella slunk onto the stage as the music from the Broadway musical began with it distinctive primal cries. Cara was the stage assistant and raised a cardboard sun above the painted mountains of the set; morning dawned on darkest Africa. Then the music began a low melodious rhythm and Antinella mimicked its mood as the lioness woke and prowled.

She captured the audience in her interpretation and graceful moves that led up to the high point of the ballet. She had made certain the audience knew she was a lioness to fear and very protective of her cubs. She growled and paced as imaginary hunters got too near her den. During one turbulent element of the musical score, Antinella fiercely feigned an attack scaring the hunters off. After protecting her cubs she curled beside them and began licking their faces and ears. She had kept her family safe, the lights dimmed and thunderous applause erupted!

She stood beaming as everyone cheered. Vittore was the only one in the audience that had tears, the ballet expressed so much it broke his heart. He silently made the promise to Rocco for the millionth time that he would never let anything ever hurt her again. She was his to protect. Antinella bowed and bowed, loving the attention, then swept her arm towards

Cara indicating her appreciation of her help. Cara bowed, she too was crying.

Cara ran to Antinella after the performance and hugged her and squeezed her, "I am so proud of you! That was brilliant, better than anything on Broadway!" Cara was bouncing up and down with excitement.

Vittore stood aside watching the two of them. He was so flooded with emotions he couldn't differentiate between them, pride, sorrow, joy, bliss, dread, contentment..it was endless. Cara caught sight of him, she knew he would want to congratulate Antinella and turned her head towards him and let nature take its course. Antinella ran to him with her arms outstretched. He crouched and let the little lioness bury herself into his chest. He murmured his congratulations and expressed his pride in her performance. He caught Cara watching them, knowing she had fallen in love with his piccolo gaio.

After packing the stage away and clearing dishes, Cara flopped into an overstuffed chair in the living room. Vittore had been reading while the villa quietly began to make preparations to end the day. He lowered his book and smiled. "It was a beautiful ballet Cara, thank you."

"It was all her idea, I was just the muscle." She smiled and flexed hers.

"Oh, frightening," Vittore gave a fake shiver of fear.

She leapt to her feet and stood before him fists clenched. "Oh Yeah! Think you can beat me huh?" She started bouncing on the balls of her feet in front of where he sat, swinging punches and flipping her nose with her thumb. "Want to fight big boy? Think you scare me?'

Vittore sat there watching her for several minutes then made a lurch towards her that made her squeal and start running. She ran through the villa laughing ending up in his bedroom trying to hide under the covers. He fell upon her wrestling the covers from her trying to get close enough to pinch her. She squirmed and giggled, flopping around on the bed like a fish out of water. "Si Cara, I think you are afraid of me!" He finally found a piece of flesh and pinched hard.

"Ow," she screamed laughing peeking out from the covers, flopping onto her back. "No fair!"

"What is not fair, Cara?" He loved that she played. Life was so hard, someone in it should still have a joyful heart and that someone was his Cara. He was within inches of her lips. He brought his fingertips to her mouth and began tracing the edges watching his hand move about her lips. "You are the one who does not play fair, Cara. How am I supposed to fight you when you are so irresistible?"

Cara gave it a few seconds enjoying his touch, "Irresistible? Like in cannot resist? Out of control? No turning back? You mean that kind of irresistible?"

"Si, exactly that kind of irresistible, Cara Bella."

"Well what's holding you back?" Her voice came out very husky and breathless. The anticipation of making love to him rocked her to her core.

CHAPTER ELEVEN

There was a soft commotion coming from the kitchen as early morning meal preparation began; coffee being made, bacon frying, gentle morning laughter. Cara was beginning to feel lazy always being the last to rise, but then she remembered this was her vacation. She stretched as she walked into the kitchen anxious to get some espresso. She stopped mid yawn as she detected unfamiliar faces in the room.

Her hair rumpled, creases on her face from the pillows and wrapped in a robe two sizes too big, she suddenly felt embarrassed. "Opps, sorry." She turned to go, thinking she should come back dressed and a little more presentable.

"Cara Bella, no come back." Vittore lunged after her returning her to the kitchen. "Do not leave, I must introduce you to my gentitori."

She had no idea what "gentitori" was but she wasn't so sure she wanted to be "introduced" right then and stood wide eyed in amazement that Vittore thought it was the appropriate time and place. What the hell was he thinking? He nudged a reluctant Cara before two people seated at the table, "Mamma, Papa this is Cara; Cara my parents, gentitori, Bianca and Giovanni Falco."

She sighed thankful to get that misunderstanding cleared up, but still self-conscious of her appearance. She tried to smooth her tussled hair and straighten her robe to have some semblance of dignity. This was not how she had imagined meeting "the parents".

Signora and Signore Falco, Bianca and Giovanni, greeted her with smiles and warm hugs. "It is good to meet the mysterious Cara at last. We have heard of you from everyone in the village! Everyone has been running up to us asking if we have met Vittore's woman. We are sorry we could not get here sooner." Bianca spoke perfect English.

"It is a pleasure meeting you," and under her breath and directed right at Vittore, "but it would have been nice to have been warned!" She flipped her knuckles at Vittore' chest and gave him an evil eye.

He held his hands up in defense. "Mamma, this woman hits me all the time. Please ask her to stop!" He laughed as he pleaded with his mother for protection.

"Oh give me a break!" Cara laughed as she poured an espresso. "You deserve more beatings than I'll ever be able to dole out!"

Giovanni looked at his son, "She is a handful Vittore! Will you be able to keep her under control?"

"No Papa, and I think that is what I love about her!" He came up behind Cara and pressed his body into hers kissing her neck.

Davide came into the kitchen from the back door, "I'm hungry! When are we going to eat!" He stole a look at Vittore who stood behind Cara with his arms wrapped protectively around her. Vittore's smile was so wide it about cracked his face in half. Davide shook his head as he played with the Amber ring on his left forefinger.

"Hey, wait a minute!" Cara reached down and lifted

Vittore's hand looking for his Amber ring, he didn't have it on this morning. She flicked him on the arm, "You are such a liar!"

"Mamma, she how she beats me!" Nuzzling her hair with his mouth, "What is it you think I lied about Cara?"

She pointed to the Amber ring on Davide's hand, "You both have one! Heirloom, my foot! And to think I almost believed you, boy am I a sap!"

"Papa, she does not believe me about the Amber Ring. You will have to tell her the whole story, please. I cannot convince her it is true!" He rocked her in his arms.

"Vittore, it's an exact duplicate! You are so full of it!" She sipped her espresso confident that she had uncovered a fraud.

Davide twisted the ring on his finger, "It is the same ring, Cara. Vittore gave it to me yesterday when you returned from your ride." He smiled broadly wondering if she knew the significance of his older brother passing the ring on to him.

All eyes were on Cara, everyone in the room waiting to see if it connected. She glanced around wondering if she dribbled coffee down the front of her, she lowered her eyes to check, *nope no dribbles. What the heck is everyone looking at!*

She tried to nonchalantly continue drinking her espresso, then it hit her! Vittore had said the ring was passed on to the next eldest son when one had found his true love. The removal of it meant he had stopped searching. She turned very slowly in his arms, "But you don't even know me!" It was slightly above a whisper.

"Ah, but I do Bella, I know all I need to know about you." And he drew her into his arms and kissed her with such tenderness, tracing her cheek with his thumb, she melted into him.

She nuzzled his chest, "I'm going to miss the ring."

Coffee flew out of Giovanni's mouth and everyone in the kitchen began laughing. Cara buried her head into Vittore's chest. *Damn! Damn! Damn!* She looked up at Vittore and mouthed, "Sorry" and retreated back into the safety of his chest shaking her head. How the hell was she going to get herself out of this embarrassment!

Cara finally turned and faced "the family", "Opps."She smiled and sipped her coffee. What else could she say?

After the second most embarrassing moment of her life they all sat down for breakfast. The table was a riotous jumble of laughter and talking. Vittore's family had no problem carrying on multiple conversations at one time, but she was totally lost all she could do was laugh at their joy. She liked this. Vittore's family was warm and familiar.

"Cara," Vittore turned to her, "I have forgotten to tell you, we have some very busy days ahead of us. In two days Davide is presenting the Conti Winery's finest vintage in a competition here in Montefalco during wine festival. Davide developed a Sagrantino wine that has some unique properties. He located some very old vines in an area completely neglected and Davide pruned and pampered them, bringing them back to life. The grapes they have produced are excellent. If the wine does as well as we expect, it will be the base for the winery in the years to come. It is the most important day for the winery."

There was so much excitement on Vittore's face it was difficult to believe this was the same man she met a few days ago. He was still not only confident and bold but he was joyous, happy; genuinely happy. It tickled her belly to see him grin so broadly. She raised her hand involuntarily and touched his face. He turned her hand and kissed her palm. "Mia Bella." His eyes twinkled.

"Well that doesn't sound too busy." One festival, true an important festival, still only one. "No problem, just tell me what I can do to help." She directed that statement to Davide and Vittore took exception.

He puffed up his chest and gave her a stern look, "Hey Bella, I'm the boss of this operation." He tried his best to look offended!

She smiled sarcastically at him, "Ya, but Davide is the brains!"

Vittore's eyes popped wide and he landed on her tickling every possible spot on her body. Cara was literally on the floor, back against the cupboards trying to fight him off laughing so hard she couldn't catch her breath. "Stop, Help! Someone help me!"

"No Cara, you will have to deal with him on your own. I have to put up with him in the winery!"

Vittore turned like a cat after more interesting prey. His eyes lit on Davide. "Put up with me, il fratello piccolo." The bull roared and Davide sprung for the back door with Vittore right behind. Vittore flew off the veranda landing on top of Davide and wrestled him to the ground. They tossed around on the ground like two puppies letting off steam, each trying to show the other who was the stronger.

Antinella couldn't stand not being part of the fun and dove into the fray, doing her best to beat them both. Maria, Bianca, Giovanni and Cara stood on the veranda laughing watching the three of them unleash some energy. Davide and Vittore ever mindful that a il piccolo had joined them.

Davide was the first to give in to her superior strength, Vittore fought on a little longer finally ending in begging for her pity. Antinella strutted around the yard like a cock! Cara laughed, what a little actress! She was very funny!

Everyone dispersed after a few minutes of congratulations but Vittore remained lying in the grass. Cara went over to him and poked his side with her foot, "Hey big fella, you still alive?"

He opened his eyes and looked up at her. Hair a mess, no makeup and wrapped in a robe that could only be described as ugly. She was a complete mess. "I love you, Cara."

This time she couldn't pretend she didn't hear him say the words. She was looking as his mouth as he spoke. She stood looking down at him until she fell on her butt. He rose on his elbow almost eye level with her now.

"Knees give out again, Bella?" He leaned over and kissed her toe then her ankle. Stealing glimpses to her face waiting for her to say something. Afraid he was too impatient, he should have waited. He was kicking himself inside, willing her to say something, anything!

Cara finally got some composure and snapped back to the moment. She wasn't sure where she went; her mind was a rush of emotions, questions, fears, apprehension. He said he loved her. What did that mean to him? Love meant different things to different people maybe it was just an expression and she was taking it too literally. Yeah, that was it, he just meant he enjoyed her company. She stared at him tongue tied. Not meaning for the words to actually be said she whispered, "What does that mean?" She stared at the toe he just kissed.

Vittore laughed, "Cara Bella, I think you are in shock." He lifted her chin so her eyes met his. "It means that I love you, I do not want to be apart from you, that you are my joy, Cara." He ran his finger down her nose. "Cara?"

She looked at him. "I don't know what to say. You're insane, maybe?"

"Si, Cara Bella, I am." He rose and helped her up, putting an arm around her, he walked to the villa.

As Cara took a long shower to clear her head, Vittore went in search of Davide. He found him sitting behind the winery tasting some of the latest productions. Vittore sat in the chair next to him. "Davide I think I am not handling this right. I do not think Cara can love me." His forearms rested on his thighs and head bowed low.

"What have you told her?"

"Nothing." He admitted

"Vittore that is a big thing between you, it needs to be dealt with, the sooner the better."

"I am afraid, Davide. Nothing has scared me so as her knowing."

"Well if I read her right, nothing is going to piss her off more than finding out. When does she fly back to New York?"

Vittore groaned and held his head in his hands, "Seven days! Oh, Davide how did I get in this mess?"

"The question is how are you going to get out of it?" Davide took a sip of wine.

Vittore groaned louder and dropped his head lower.

He knew when she arrived at the hotel that Bryan had

already decided to fly back to New York. He spoke to Bryan seconds before he turned and saw Cara standing in line to check-in. His heart broke. She deserved so much more. This was a woman alive with passion. He knew he could not let Bryan ruin her trip. He would find a way to soften the blow.

He placed her in a suite, sent her two dozen roses and he bought her the most beautiful dress Roma had to offer. Having the sapphires added to the shoes and purse was an extravagant impulse but he really didn't care. He just wanted her to be happy when she learned that Bryan had abandoned her, again.

It was silly, dresses and shoes cannot mend a broken heart but it was all he could think to offer. Because he knew that Bryan was going to destroy her dreams. He had to be there to hold her when it happened. He just was not aware that it would not be until her heart broke that his would be born. He was not prepared to fall so hard so fast! But he had no doubts this is the woman he will love until he takes his last breath.

Cara stood under the shower head wishing it was more brutal. She wanted to feel needles assaulting her body, any pain to distract her from her confusion.

How could he love me! How does he expect me to respond to that? Damn Him! Damn! Damn! Damn! She hit her forehead against the tile wall of the shower. "Ow!" She reached up and rubbed her forehead. *Brilliant, Cara, you are such a bloody idiot. Idioto! Stupido!*

How was she going to handle this? He was confused, on an adrenaline high; thoughts of launching the new wine, adopting Antinella, all the incredible sex, being back in Umbria. It was going to his head. He'd get back to normal after she left. She just needed to be cool.

That works for her, she is going to pretend he didn't really say the words. He is probably kicking himself right now and she shouldn't add to his embarrassment. Just carry on as if nothing happened. When in doubt do nothing! Isn't that a survival skill? If not maybe it should be.

She felt much better! She climbed out of the shower and decided to go into this village where her name seemed to be bandied about. She wasn't sure how she had become the celebrity of Montefalco, but she was going to find out! Hum, what to wear into an Italian village? Shocking or Subdued?

Cara walked into the yard dressed in a grass green halter sun dress with tiny white buttons down the front. Her hair was swept up into a ponytail tied off with a ribbon that dangled four-leaf clovers on its ends, courtesy of Antinella. She wore a delicate strand of small pearls interspaced on a thin white gold chain.

She popped into the winery looking for Vittore and drew a few whistles from the crew. She swooped a curtsy to the gentleman and rewarded them with a grin and a twirl that drew applause; she really did love Italian men!

The whistles and applause brought Vittore and Davide in from the back of the winery. They entered just as Cara was taking her last bow. Davide looked at his older brother and in his best California surfer impersonation said, "You're screwed Dude!"

Vittore just smiled and chuckled, yes he was!

He didn't give a damn about what happened an hour ago, it would work itself out. He just wanted to enjoy every moment with her, whether for a life time or seven days. Like Davide said, he was screwed. He walked up to her standing among the wine vats and grabbed her waist and twirled her some more. Placing her feet on the ground held her at arms' length, "Mia Bella, Cara!"

She beamed, "I'm going into town. Your mother said people were asking about me, so I thought I'd see what all the interest was. Want to join me?"

Vittore looked up at Davide, he waived his hand, "You think we can't run this place without you, go, enjoy! Hey while you're in town talk up the wine, maybe we can influence the judges."

Vittore held the door of the Bugatti open while she slid in; he vaulted over the driver's side door and slide down. "Show off." Cara laughed as he turned the key and the engine purred. He eased it into drive and took off down the drive.

They entered a modern city that was busy with preparations for the upcoming festival. Tents were being erected, kiosks being placed about and shop windows being adorned with enticing treats. Cara loved the feel of this little village. So different from Roma where it seemed everyone was a tourist. Here everyone was a neighbor.

As they parked, an older man with a walking stick stopped and looked at the car, gave a harrumph to express his disdain but was caught by the beautiful woman sitting in the passengers seat. As soon as his eyes landed on Cara, he removed his hat and gave a polite bow. Then leaned over and graciously opened the door for her. Leering at her leg as it exited the Bugatti then smiling as her skirts swished in place around her once she stood.

Vittore exploded into Italian nearly scaring the old man to death, apparently accusing him of something. The man raised his walking stick to begin a fight when he finally focused his attention on the driver of the car. "Vittore Falco! Vittore!" The man hobbled his way closer to Vittore who made the approach easier by taking long strides towards the man cutting the older man's efforts by half.

The man gave Vittore a big hug and held his face saying something that made Vittore laugh! They chatted awhile then Vittore finally turned his attention to Cara and introduced them. Cara caught the names Martin and Cara and then heard Americana. Vittore no doubt informing him that she was clueless of what he was saying.

Martin stood back and looked at Cara then over to Vittore, his head bobbed up and down and a sinister smile formed on his lips. He chuckled and slapped Vittore on the upper arm and went on his way.

"Ah, do I want to know what that was all about?"

Vittore laughed, "Probably not Cara, probably not!" It felt so good to be home, Vittore drank in the air. He wrapped his arm around her neck and guided her towards a pastry shop.

When they entered the women squealed like teenagers, but these women were way past their teens. They flocked around Vittore like hens to a chick, smothering him with kisses and questions. They kept glancing at Cara, raising their eyebrows and pinching his cheeks. Cara began to laugh because Vittore obviously loved the attention!

He finally was able to grab Cara's wrist and make some introductions, again, Americana! They all nodded understandingly, like she was mentally challenged, not language challenged.

One of the woman reached out her hand and began pinching Cara on the arms and midriff, shaking her head looking at Vittore like he did something wrong. "Troppo magro, mangia, mangia!" She kept pinching!

Cara cast a pleading look to Vittore. *What!? Why is she pinching me!?*

Cara stood there taking the assault and all Vittore could do is laugh. He kept trying to reach in and rescue Cara, but then another set of fingers would start pinching her and making this margo/mangia remark. She was starting to get sore.

What was with Italians, all this pinching and nipping?

Finally Vittore put his body between Cara and the flock of hens but every once in a while one of them got their fingers in and got in a hard pinch.

"Ouch! Vittore!" She really couldn't keep quiet any longer it was starting to hurt. "What is this, an Italian torture test?" She actually slapped one wrinkled hand as in came near her. Vittore was trying his best to keep the ladies in control but he was laughing too hard at Cara's predicament.

He finally steered her towards the door as a large bag of pastries was thrust into his hand followed by yells of "mangia". Outside the door he doubled over in laughter as Cara rubbed her body all over like she was knocking off fire ants. He laughed so hard tears came to his eyes. Whenever he lifted his head to look at her he doubled over again.

Cara was indignant, "What the hell just happened in there!" She kept rubbing her arms and midriff. "Vittore stop laughing that hurt!" She was getting angry but was also finding it hard not to laugh.

Vittore held out the bag to her laughing, "Mangia, mangia

Cara! My aunts and grandmothers think you are too skinny, they want you to eat, mangia!"

Cara stood there with her mouth opened, "They were family!" She turned on her heel shaking her hands above her head, "No, No No!" She spun around to face him, "Aunts and Grandmothers! They almost skinned me alive in there!" Vittore tried hard to stop laughing.

Cara grabbed the bag and dug out a pastry, "Hell! Give it to me! I'd gladly put on some weight then to go through that again!" She stuffed a cannoli in her mouth. Her eyes got wide, "Wo, dis gwod!"

He looked as whipped cream spilled out of her lips, "Oh Cara!" He used the pad of his thumb to scrape off the cream and licked it. "Um! That is good!" He dove into the bag himself. The two of them strolled down the street stuffing their faces with cannoli.

CHAPTER TWELVE

After several more introductions to the misfortunate "Americana" Vittore took her towards the old city of Montefalco sitting high on the mountain side, home of his ancestors.

Cars were not allowed in the old city. The streets were too narrow and the turns too sharp. But at the entrance to the city, there was a small lot where Vespas were parked in a jumble. Cara mused that this must be Montefalco's answer to a parking garage.

Further along the street a few tourists were milling about the buildings complete with cameras and fanny packs. There was one tour guide collecting his charges and encouraging them to follow him to the view that spawned the phrase "The Balcony of Umbria." Almost in a trance, people followed the guide, unquestioningly.

Vittore steered Cara in a different direction, Cara protested. "I'd like to see that view. Why aren't we following them?"

"Cara, I have lived in Montefalco my entire life, who do you think knows where the most beautiful view of Umbria is, a tour guide or me? Come, I will show you."

They traveled along cobbled streets that rose gradually in never ending turns left and right. Cara was amazed at the excellent condition of the village's buildings. Most of the houses appeared to be lived- in, having curtains and flowers in the windows. All the buildings were of stone, but rather than mortar holding the stones in place, it appeared as if the stones were cut to fit perfectly together as if a jeweler had set them in a pave design. She reached out her hand to touch one of the buildings.

Vittore understood her amazement. Archeologists had come to Montefalco for years to study the building construction of this little village. "The stones are held together with mortar developed during the Roman Empire years. Come we are almost there."

Vittore entered a building and began making his way through its darkened interior until finding a door that revealed stairs that led upward. The stair case was made of stone and spiraled in tight turns making the steps very narrow at the end closer to the interior wall and broader towards the exterior, making the climb not only treacherous, but also causing Cara to become dizzy.

Cara stopped to regain her equilibrium. Since the stairs turned so sharply she could not calculate how much further they needed to climb. She really wanted to sit. Fainting on these steps would not be such a good idea, but since the treads were so narrow she opted to lean her back against the cold stone of the exterior wall. The cold against her bare back helped shake the cobwebs from her brain.

"Vittore, how much further? I am getting dizzy!"

"Come, Cara a few more steps and you will have fresh air. It will clear your head. Come and see what no American tourist will ever be shown."

Pushing off the stone she trudged up about 15 more steps to find a low doorway leading out to a turret with crenellated stones surrounding a small walkway. She had to bend low to get through the opening and when she emerged and stood, she unconsciously held her breath.

Vittore stood, his hands resting on the ancient stones of the battlement and turned to catch Cara's reaction. "It is beautiful? No?"

Cara had to look down to assure herself she was standing on firm ground. They were so high it seemed as if they were floating in the air on a magic carpet. The vista was more beautiful than anything she had ever seen. The tower wall followed the line of a sheer cliff that seemed to drop hundreds of feet into a valley of lush green foliage. There were hills that softly undulated like waves spreading towards flat lands before more hills extended further towards the horizon.

What was disconcerting is they were above it all as if suspended on a cloud in space. Cara walked around the battlement and saw off into the distance a small outcropping of stone, surrounded by a guardrail and within the rail the tour group. They were at least a hundred yards below where she and Vittore stood. Cara knew their view could not compare to what she had the privilege to see.

"Vittore," she whispered and turned to him eyes wide in awe.

"Si, I told you I would be a good tour guide." His face held such pride as if he had created the view he was now sharing with her. "In reaching the building we were ascending at a slow incline so you did not notice how elevated we were, but the climb of the stairs will shorten your breath at this altitude."

"No wonder I thought I was going to faint! I feel as if we are in the clouds!"

"I have been up here when there were clouds below me. It was raining in the village, and I was dry. It was amazing!" He stood staring out over the ledge drinking in the scenery.

"How did this get built? It had to be dangerous building this tower."

"It was built in 1425. Si, many hundreds of lives were lost not only in the building of the tower, but in several being thrown from it!"

"Ug! That sounds gruesome! Who was the maniac that used that method of justice?"

Vittore gave her a sly glance from the corner of his eye and smiled softly, "The Lord of the Manor, Vittore Falco."

"What!" Fear tore through Cara's stomach as she cowered towards the door leading to the steps.

"Bella!" Vittore's voice tore out of his throat with a laugh, "Mia, Bella. You are not thinking that the maniac is me! Bella, you do have an overactive imagination!" Vittore continued to laugh as he looked at the terror in Cara's face. "Cara, I was named after my ancestor that built this castle and founded this village. Oh, Bella! I know now something of you I did not know. You have a very suspicious mind!"

"Well it is scary enough up here without being told the name of the person who threw bodies over the ledge is the name of the person I am standing up here talking to!" Cara was still ashen and tense and getting angrier by the minute as Vittore continued to laugh at her. "You could have put it a little differently." She studied Vittore as he stood there and laughed. "You did that on purpose didn't you? You are awful!"

"Will you beat me again, piccolo?" He smiled broadly.

"To a pulp!"

"Then we should go, it sounds as if you have a busy day of teaching me a lesson." Vittore ducked low through the doorway, turned and offered his hand to Cara as she stepped through. "I will go first, so if you lose your balance I will stop your fall."

Cara and Vittore returned to the villa as the bustle of meal preparation was underway. Bianca was conducting the mayhem and their arrival did not slow her; "Vittore, Cara! The evening is beautiful, so we are eating in the garden. Davide is getting boards from the winery to create a table. Vittore, go help him! Cara, Maria needs help in the kitchen, Antinella, mi puoi aiutare la candela trovare, velocemente!"

Cara looked at Vittore, "Well all-righty then, let's get moving!" and started towards the back door. As Cara made her way across the yard, Bianca reached out and lightly took Cara's wrist.

"Cara, thank you. You have brought joy to Vittore's heart. It is good to see." Bianca's eye shifted to the side as she saw Giovanni sneaking away towards the winery. Without looking at him she called, "Giovanni where are you? I need your help with the candles." She then lowered her voice conspiratorially and said, "Cara, come back to the garden in twenty minutes."

Cara saw the mischief in her eyes, "Are we going to get into trouble, Bianca?"

"No, Cara, our men are! Now, go help Maria." Bianca winked.

After helping Maria wash lettuce and chop vegetables for a salad, she went back into the garden and noted two pails filled to about half with water and Bianca standing over them.

"Cara, you are going to learn something very bad about the Falco men. As we work hard preparing a lovely meal for them, they sit in the back of the winey 'tasting' wine, not drinking, no, tasting, very businesslike! Here you take a pail and hide it behind your back, I will do the same."

She was a devil! And Vittore said he had to prepare his mother to meet her, what about preparing Cara for Bianca? "Mamma, are we going to break up a business meeting?"

Bianca gave that a little consideration. "I like the way you put things, Cara! Si! We are going to break up a business meeting! Our men are easy, just a little flirting should allow us close enough to break up the meeting, No?"

The two women walked quietly into the winery and from the far end of the building, beyond the back doors, they heard the sounds of male laugher. Cara felt childish, but excited, knowing that what she was about to do, would send Vittore chasing after her. She glanced over to Bianca and saw the same excitement on her face too and a thought flew into Cara's head, Bianca and Giovanni still make love! She is well into her 60's and Bianca has butterflies in her stomach too! Oh, to love someone so much to never stop making love!

As they stepped into the back of the winery, Bianca shot Cara a look of caution, they have one chance. The three Falcone men sat in a semi-circle enjoying the breeze coming down the hillside, filled with the heady scent of earth and grapes. Each had a tumbler of dark, cherry-colored wine and were in the middle of a conversation, when the women drew their attention.

Cara locked her eyes on Vittore and gave him the sultriest

look she had, accenting it by wetting her lips, then slowly dragging her forefinger along the bottom lip. Vittore's eyes went hot and he slowly inched forward in his chair, just waiting for her to ask him to follow her.

Cara couldn't see what trick Bianca played on Giovanni, but whatever it was worked, because his eyes were as large a saucers. When each woman was near enough to their prey, they glanced at one another and smiled as they swung the buckets out from behind their backs and drenched Vittore and Giovanni. Both men jumped with surprise, looking at their soaked clothes in disbelief.

Bianca shook her finger at Giovanni and Cara mimed her by shaking her finger at Vittore. Then father and son charged at their respective women. Bianca and Cara went flying in opposite directions, laughing as the men chased them.

Davide yelled, "Hey, what about me!"

"Find your own woman, I gave you the ring!" Vittore yelled over his shoulder on the run.

Vittore caught up with Cara near the big shade tree at the side of the winery. He reached out and caught a handful of fabric. The restraint was enough to make Cara stop. "This is my favorite dress! You are not going to tear it, Vittore!"

He stepped closer, let go of the fabric and grabbed her waist, slamming her into his body. His mouth fell upon hers as he pushed her back into the trunk of the tree and with his free hand, cupped her breast as he devoured her. He trailed hungry kisses down her neck, pressing, squeezing her breast. He bent low and kissed her chest, going just low enough for his tongue to slip into the cleavage that her lush mounds created. Her knees gave a bit and Vittore grinned. "Did your knees give out again, Cara Bella?" He finished his lick and raised a twinkling eye to her.

Cara hit him in the chest, "You're awful." She laughed. Then she suddenly looked quickly around her to make sure they were alone. "Vittore," she was just above a whisper, "your parents still make love!"

Vittore stood and looked at her quizzically shaking his head, "I would hope so Cara, but what has brought this to your attention?" He was laughing at her.

"Your mother! When we were scheming this little attack I saw the same excitement in her eyes as I had in mine. She knew your father would chase her and make love to her, she couldn't wait! She wanted your father to do to her what you are doing to me!" She looked around to make sure she was not being overheard.

"Cara, why does this seem so strange to you? Of course my father still makes love to my mother. Why would he not? She is a beautiful woman," he nuzzled her neck, "as are you, Cara."

"Vittore! Doesn't it seem strange that your parents are so, so…. lustful!?"

Vittore was laughing at her, "No Cara, what I find strange is that instead of us making love as my parents are, you have interrupted our love making to focus on theirs. Why does this knowledge puzzle you Cara?"

"My parents never conveyed to us that they have any," she lowered her voice to a whisper, "sexual feelings for each other!"

Vittore's head fell back and he let out a great roar of laughter. "Mia Bella, do you think you reach an age where the," he lowered his voice and looked around to mock her, "sexual feelings stop?"

"Stop it! You're making fun of me!" She pouted, not knowing where to take this conversation, because she really did want to get back to making love to him.

"Si, Cara Bella. But I think our moment has passed. Maria calls us to complete the garden dining room. Dinner will be ready soon." He kissed her neck and took her hand and led her to the veranda.

The western sky was streaked with gold and purple as the September sun began to set. The breeze was still coming down from the hillside softly disturbing the wisteria that was entwined in the arbor over head, the air filled with its sweet fragrance.

Cara watched as, one by one, family and vineyard employees gathered at the long table. There was such an air of contentment among them Cara had to remind herself she was a voyeur in this happy scene. As comfortable as this felt, it was not her world.

Cara thought of Rocco and Gabriella and the life they had built here. How could such a tragedy befall these wonderful people? How could that kind of evil be spawned in the beauty of these mountains? Her eyes drifted towards Antinella who had been lifted onto the lap on one of the employees and both were laughing wildly. He spoke to her with such animation and expression, Cara was mesmerized and delighted, even though she had no idea what story was being told.

Davide and Vittore were in deep discussion about preparations for the festival. The other vineyard employees were joking with each other and punctuating their merriment with wild arm movements. Maria and Bianca were still twittering about making sure every detail of this evenings' dinner was complete. Giovanni sat at the head of the table, enjoying his wine and, like Cara, enjoying his family. He caught her eye and held his glass in a salute to her. She replied, and a rush of serenity overtook her.

Couple that feeling with the intoxicating aromas wafting out of Maria's kitchen and Cara thought she would be the happiest woman on the planet if she could stay right here, in this moment in time.

Maria and Bianca had prepared an antipasta plate filled with salami, olives, fennel and endive which everyone nibbled on as they eagerly awaited the main course to arrive. Cara didn't know much about Italian cooking but she was quickly becoming intoxicated with the aromas that wafted out of Maria's kitchen. And she now agreed with Vittore. One should never miss a meal prepared by Maria!

Bianca and Maria laid bowls of Gnocchi Allo Zafferano, Ravioli Di Barbabietole, Peperronata, Fricassea Di Funghi, and Broccoletti All'Olio and everyone dug in and began passing the bowls across, to the right, to the left; total chaos. The aroma left in the wake by the passing of each bowl, made Cara want to grab it and get more. Everyone was making guttural noises, enjoying the food before it even hit their palettes.

After dinner the employees returned to their own homes in the village, while the family remained on the veranda enjoying the wine and pleasant evening. Vittore had pulled Cara onto a chaise with him and she lay between his legs, her head on his chest.

"Mamma, we went into town today and stopped by La Dolci."

"Vittore! You did not subject poor Cara to that! Did you warn her?" Bianca cast an apologetic look towards Cara.

"You knew!" she laid her head on his shoulder looking up at his face. "You Beast! You knew I'd be assaulted!" She gave him a hard pinch to the inside of his upper arm.

"Ouch, Cara, that hurt!" He gave her a pout and rubbed his arm.

"You bet it did, and those little hands grabbing at me earlier were experts and knew how to inflict pain. Do you have any idea how much that really hurt?"

"Honestly, Cara, I did not know it would be so bad! I had heard rumors, but," he looked over to his mother, "they were brutal, Mamma."

"The worst is your grandmother! She not only pinches she gives it a twist. Oh Cara, I am sorry!" She laughed. "When Giovanni and I began to date, his mother would pinch me so hard, I would bruise!"

"Me too!" she held up the underside of her arm and revealed bruises of different sizes and colors. "If they weren't your family, I would have filed assault charges!" She rubbed her bruises and said more to herself then anyone in particular. "Why do they do that?"

"It is a rite of passage for the women of the Falco family. If we can endure the women of the family, we can endure the passion of the men." Bianca glanced at Giovanni and smiled.

Cara hit Vittore in the arm and nudged her head towards his parents, "SEE!" she mouthed.

"Cara Bella, I can see you are not going to stop thinking of this!" Vittore shook his head laughing at her.

"Papa, Cara would like to know," Cara cast him a look of death if he breathed one word of their discussion earlier, "the story of the amber ring. She is a gemologist and knows about amber. She does not believe me that our ring can change colors," he glanced at Cara and raised his eyebrows and whispered, "under certain circumstances."

Cara was going to die! What Vittore did with the ring, what that ring has done in the history of the ring! *Please God, Cara pleaded, make his father tired! Send him to bed. I don't want to talk about this!*

"It is beautiful, no? My Great Grandfather, Darius, was given the ring when he was in Russia attending Saint Petersburg State University as a doctoral student of Alexander Kovalevsky." Giovanni settled back into his chair and studied the deep rich plum of his wine.

"Kovalevsky was doing remarkable research at the time in embryology and Great Grandfather was fortunate to have the opportunity to study under him. It was December 10, 1895 during the age of Czar Nicholas II."

"Being Italian, his love of opera was known, and he was invited to attend a performance of the opera, *Christmas Eve,* by Rimsky-Korsakov at the Imperial Mariinsky Theatre. It was opening night and Czar Nicholas II and Czarina Alexandra were also in attendance."

Cara was mesmerized as Giovanni wove his tale of how the ring came into the possession of the Falco family.

"Nicholas II had only been Czar for a year and had just married Alix, which was Alexandra's German name. Alix had not yet embraced the Russian Orthodox Church and remained a Lutheran, which was a concern among the people of Russia." Giovanni looked around at his family to assure the implications of that were clear.

"To have a Czarina that was not of their faith was an insult and although years later, she did become Russian Orthodox, and changed her name to Alexandra, the people of Russia never forgave poor Nicholas and never allowed Alexandra much latitude when she invited Rasputin into the Czars court. Although that is another story, tragic on its own, it helps to explain the events of that night."

Cara watched the intensity on Giovanni's face as he told the story. He was in his element. He had his audience spell bound, even though Cara was the only one who had never heard it. Knowing the revelation of how the ring came into Darius' possession was near, Cara leaned forward slightly, in eager anticipation. Vittore smiled behind her back, pleased that she found the history of his family so interesting. He reached out and lightly stroked her hair.

"December in Russia is very cold and very snowy." Giovanni continued, "After the performance as everyone stood to wait for their carriages, the Czar and Czarina were in polite conversation with friends."

"My Great Grandfather was fascinated to be so close to royalty, he never took his eyes off them, he watched. Out of the corner of his eye he saw a man who had hatred in his heart." Giovanni was an animated story teller and his eyes became sinister and his voice bolder. Cara now saw who had honed Antinella's talent.

"The man was looking directly at the Czarina as he walked towards them, and that is when Great Grandpa saw the glint of a blade reflected by the gaslight. He knew the man meant to harm the Czarina. He pushed through the crowd just as the man was poised to strike and when the blade was brought down," Giovanni had his hand raised and brought it down with incredible force, "it was my Great Grandfather who received the blow. The knife caught him in the left shoulder just below the clavicle." Giovanni pointed to his upper chest indicating where the blow struck.

"Many people rushed to the aide of the Czar and Czarina. The 'would be' assassin was wrestled to the ground and captured, but they seemed to have forgotten the young man who had saved the Czarina's life. As Great Grandpa sat bleeding and in shock, he felt a hand slip that ring into his hand," he nodded towards Davide's hand, "and a whisper of "Danke schön!"

Cara gasped, "The Czarina gave it to him?"

"Darius did not see who slipped it into his hand but since the Czarina was German…" Giovanni gave his shoulders a shrug and took a sip of wine

Everyone held their breath, Cara wanted to hear more. "Please don't stop!"

"But that is the end, Cara! It has been passed from one Falcone' male to the next until such time that the one possessing the ring has determined he has attained all the good fortune the ring has to give! It is then passed to the next oldest to pursue his dreams. When my father gave me the ring he said it had brought him a lifetime of joy and it was now time for me to find my passion and my love. He said that the ring had a way of clarifying the right path. It is the same I have told Vittore and will now tell Davide."

"But what about the ring changing color? And the purpose of the ring to identify your true love?" Cara insisted, looking up at Vittore to get support for the telling of this part of the rings, history.

"Ah yes, the color change, Vittore did say that interested you a great deal." Giovanni smiled having forgotten that he had not made that clear. "As I mentioned, my Great Grandfather was a doctor. In that time doctors did experiments and research in their private laboratories. My Great Grandfather had on the ring one day while working in his laboratory. The experiment he was performing needed heat and moisture and he noticed after some time that the ring had darkened its hue to a deeper red. It is an oddity nothing more."

"That's it! No great love detector?" Vittore could feel the coiling of Cara's muscles ready to attack at the first opportunity. He smiled behind her back and winked at his Papa as he pulled Cara closer to him. Feeling her squirm broadened his smile.

"Cara, that is the lie all the men of this family tell the woman they fall in love with!" Bianca added laughing. "Giovanni told me if I was meant for him the ring would deepen in color by my kiss." She reached over and tapped Giovanni on his cheek, "He is lucky I had already fallen in love with him, I must have spent over an hour kissing the ring waiting for it to change hue. When I found out it was a story, I felt like such a fool to be so easily led. But he already had my heart. So I forgave him!"

Bianca turned to look at Cara and saw her flushing red with anger. She darted her eyes to her son, "Vittore! What lie did you tell Cara! You did not play the same game with her as your father did with me?'"

Vittore held Cara tight, "Not quite the same, Mamma."

Vittore's voice deepened and was above a whisper. Cara had no idea if anyone heard, but her.

"Vittore let me go! Let me go! YOU are no gentleman!" Cara squirmed in his grasp and the longer she struggled the more she began laughing. How had she fallen for that line! She couldn't believe she was that gullible! "Vittore, I swear if you don't let me up, I'll,"

Vittore nuzzled the nape of her neck and whispered, "You will do what, Cara Bella? Tell my Mamma?" He kissed her softly. "You know what happens when you threaten to change my mamma's opinion of me, Cara."

"You are going to pay for this!"

Vittore roared, "I do not doubt that Cara Bella, I do not doubt that!"

Giovanni rose and held Bianca's hand, "I think we have told enough stories tonight. We have a long day tomorrow preparing for festival, and I think our son has a doghouse to build." He led her and Antinella off the veranda and into the villa.

Davide watched them enter the house, then turned to Vittore, who was trying to control an increasingly angry Cara, "You are going to have to explain more about this ring, brother! I think there is something I have not been told!" He too said his goodnights and left Vittore and Cara alone.

"You are awful Vittore! I don't know whether to be angry with you or me! Here I was all freaked out that every woman in your family had been "tested" the same way. And you let me think it! You are rotten!" She thought for a moment, "If everyone but you and your creative imagination had their lovers kiss the ring, why did your father almost choke this morning on his coffee?"

"Because Cara, you said you would miss the ring, and my father is also very creative."

A glimmer of hope rose in Cara, "So no one really knows then? And your father just suspects?" Cara seemed to calm. "I swear if you tell Davide, I will kill you!" She looked up at him again. "You really do need to learn manners!"

Feeling Cara shiver in the cold of the night air, Vittore rubbed her arms. "If I get you a sweater, will I regain my reputation as a gentleman?"

"Vittore, you cannot regain what you never had." Cara kissed his cheek. "Stay here I'll run in myself. Pour me another glass of wine."

When she returned, Vittore was standing at the edge of the veranda. Sipping his wine, he spoke to no one, "We have done it my friend. We will bring this winery back for your piccolo. Salute."

"Promises kept?" She spoke softly

Vittore turned and smiled, "Si, Bella, promises kept. It will take work but we will begin with the best Sagrantino wine ever produced in Montefalco." He raised his glass to his lips and took another sip.

"Why the winery Vittore? You could provide for Antinella without it. There are so many ways you could provide an inheritance."

Vittore closed his eyes and tilted his head slightly and let out a sigh. He turned and gazed at her, "Come sit with me Cara. It is a beautiful night, and the quiet relaxes me."

He straddled the chaise and placed his wine on the table next to it, motioning for Cara to sit. When she had tucked herself in between his legs, he wrapped his arms around her. "It is not I who am providing the inheritance, Bella, it is Rocco and Garbiella. When Antinella was born and they asked me to be her godfather, I swore that night, if anything ever happened to them, I would watch over her as if she were my daughter but raise her as they would wish. They loved this vineyard. They gave their lives for it. Antinella needs this vineyard to ground her. I need this vineyard to ground me here with her. I have been too busy and the only thing that is really important is here in this villa, in this winery. This is where I need to be. This is a legacy, not just an inheritance."

The past several days sped through her mind. How had all this happened? How did she come to be on this veranda, in this village, with this man? "I may be falling in love with you." She whispered and softly leaned against his body. She couldn't believe she said it out loud. It was insane, you don't fall in love in six days.

Vittore stroked her hair and kissed the back of her head "Be sure, Cara, for my heart aches to hear the words spoken with no doubt." He kissed her head again.

Cara lay curled in Vittore's arms thinking about the past several days. She was on her way to meet her fiancé, and less than six days later is in the arms of a complete stranger and saying that she may be falling in love!

The silence was comfortable, Cara nestled deeper into his chest thinking about Vittore. Not his wealth, or his perfect mouth, *Lord, she loved his mouth!*, or how incredible the sex had been. She thought about the man she had begun to know, the one who promised to protect a little girl out of love and honor. She thought of the man who was mischievous and funny, the man who was as comfortable in the powerhouses of Roma, as on the dirt floor of a winery in Montefalco. This man, who held her rubbing his chin on top of her head, she listened silently to the night, content and at peace.

Cara listened to the steady rhythm of his heart. Vittore felt the weight of her body go slack and he knew she had fallen asleep. He enjoyed just holding her in his arms. He was in no hurry to go in. He took another sip of wine, held its contents so it was reflected in the nearby candlelight. Tomorrow would be a busy day. It would be the beginning of a new life.

The quiet of the night, the warmth of Cara in his arms brought such joy to his heart. He prayed it would never end. Vittore gently lifted Cara into his arms and carried her into his bedroom. He smiled when he entered, Cara had filled the bedroom with candles and the glow was warm and relaxing. He kissed her forehead, "I think not tonight Cara. I think tonight my pleasure will come from just holding you."

He sat on the bed, holding her in his lap as he unfastened the button of the halter dress and slid the zipper down. Placing her on top of the bed he gently drew the dress down her body. The chill of the night air caused his sleeping Bella to curl against the cold. He laid the comforter over her before he undressed and slid in next to her.

Vittore pulled Cara's back into his chest and held her tight around the waist, softly kissing her neck. Cara moved at the touch but remained deeply asleep. Vittore had no intention of waking her, for tonight, he just wanted to hold her. Nuzzling into her neck, Vittore drifted off to sleep.

CHAPTER THIRTEEN

Cara woke to the weight of Vittore' arm around her, it felt good. Since arriving at the villa, she had not woken with him and forgot how comfortable it felt. The room still held the scent of the candles and she realized her plan of candlelight seduction had not developed. Vittore had to have seen the candle lit room and suspect her intent, but rather then wake her, he let her sleep. She snuggled deeper into his hold, resting silently until she knew he was awake.

Vittore felt Cara's gentle stirrings and woke enjoying the feel of her in his arm. He drew her close and kissed her hair. "Buon giorno, Mia Bella. Did you sleep well?"

Cara turned and snuggled into his warm chest. "Um, Buon giorno, it's nice waking up with you. I kind of missed it."

"I am being lazy. Papa and Davide have been up for hours getting things ready for festival tomorrow. I woke and heard them having breakfast, I knew I should get up, but I did not want to leave you this morning." He nuzzled her neck and gave her shoulder a kiss.

"We should get up. You know, you were less busy in Roma! Remember back when we could lie in bed and play until noon? Ah those were the days! How long ago was that? Four or five days?" she kissed his chest and made moves to get out of bed.

He a kept tight hold of her, "Cara, do not get up yet. I too have missed waking to the feel of you."

She kissed the underside of his chin as she snuggled in closer to his body, "Ok, but don't blame me when Davide gives you a hard time." The hardness of his chest muscles made her feel small and safe in his grasp.

Vittore kissed her neck and made a path to her breasts. Just lying there playing seemed the most natural thing on earth to do. Both were exploring each other's bodies, feathering fingers lightly over the skin. His attention was tender but firm leaving no doubt as to his desires and his eagerness to make love to her.

"I could do this forever." She whispered looking into his eyes she saw the same longing in him. He hung his head slightly just enough to watch himself slip into her. His movements were slow and relaxing, measured and controlled. Then his strokes lengthened, penetrated deeper and became more forceful. Cara gasped and held his forearms tight in her grip, he lifted his head and smiled knowing she was enjoying him, enjoying herself. They both released a warm flow of heat. Both satisfied but not spent.

He remained in her, liking the feeling of her surrounding him, "We should go and help, Bella , not only will Davide demand some answers, but Maria and Mamma will scold me for being lazy."

They showered and dressed and made their way into the kitchen, where Maria was busy preparing food for an army.

"Maria!" exclaimed Cara, "Who are you cooking for!?" Vittore repeated her question in Italian. There was a lot of hand waving, smiles and giggles, as Maria informed Vittore the reason for the busyness of the kitchen.

Vittore's eyes rose in surprise and approval. He picked Maria a few inches off the floor and gave her a quick turn and kiss.

"Hey, are you trying to make me jealous?" Cara playfully scowled and placed her hands on her hips.

"This is why I am in no doubt of my abilities, Mia Bella, the wonderful women in my life!" He kissed Maria full on the mouth, to which she pushed him a way and flicked her hand. "Maria and Momma have invited the village up after tomorrows' festival to celebrate the vineyards success at the competition. We had planned on friends coming over after the festival but Maria and Mamma decided to have everyone up for a celebration! I had better make calls to finds more tables and chairs. "

"Well, I think I know where I am going to be needed. You had better go see if you can get Davide to forgive you. And don't you dare blame me!" Cara sent Vittore off to the winery.

Cara, Maria and Bianca spent the remainder of the morning chopping, boiling, sautéing, basically if it was a food preparation method they did it, and there was still more to do! Cara put down a knife and looked at the two older women bustling about the kitchen effortlessly. "How do you do it? My back is killing me and my feet hurt and I am half your age and right now I feel twice it! I need the Italian energy secret."

Bianca smiled and placed her hand on Cara's cheek, "Take a rest, go out to the barn and check on Antinella and Papa." She turned and started to put together a tray of snacks and refreshments, "Take this, they will both be hungry. I have not seen them since they entered the stables early this morning."

Cara lifted the weighty tray and struggled across the yard

to the stables. She punched the door with her hip and turned into the arena area and gasped. "They are beautiful!" She placed the tray on a nearby bench. "Vento you are a very handsome man! And Fortuna you will be the envy of every filly at the parade!"

Antinella slid off Fortuna and ran to Cara, grabbing her hand she pulled her towards the two horses. The closer Cara got she saw the hard work that Antinella and Papa had placed making all the horses parade ready. The mares had their manes braided and decorated with ribbons and beads in the colors of the Conti vineyard, purple and green. The stallions' manes had been brushed smooth and oiled so when they shook their heads the hair fell about them softly. All the horses had polished hooves and their coats glistened.

Vento, Fortuna, Vennito and Piccolo Cavella stood side by side and bowed their heads and scraped the ground with their hooves as if to say thank you.

"So this is what has kept you two so busy!" Cara laughed at the horses, they knew they looked beautiful and they were prancing and rearing their front legs in an attempt of garner more complements. Antinella still holding Cara's hand, led her over to where several hooks on the wall held deep purple vests decorated in green and gold embroidery each depicting a scene of vineyard activity; the harvest, the pressing or the celebration of the season.

Antinella gave Cara a vest and indicated for her to try it on. Cara slipped it over her shoulders and turned asking, "Bella?" Antinella nodded yes! She went to remove the vest and Antinella stopped her. "You want me keep it?" She looked questioningly at Giovanni.

"You will need to talk to the boss, who was adamant that

you be recognized as part of the family." Papa grinned and winked at Antinella.

"Where is he, in the winery?" Cara started to leave when Papa spoke.

"No Cara, Vittore is the vineyard manager, Davide the winemaker. The owner of the winery is Antinella."

"Oh," Cara smiled brightly at Antinella, "I guess the boss has spoken! I would consider it an honor!" Cara nodded yes and leaned over and kissed her on the cheek. Then looked to Papa and asked if she could help with the tack.

Cara hardly saw Vittore all day, when she did he was on the phone organizing tomorrow's event. It appeared that the after festival celebration was turning into a rather large affair and Vittore was in a groove, but he still had time to joke with the workers and tease Davide.

Only once did she have a moment with him and that was shortly after a delivery was made and he sought her out. Cara was in the tack-room alone polishing saddles and reins. She has hot and perspiring, her auburn hair hung in her eyes and as she pushed it back from her face she saw Vittore standing in the doorway watching.

Her smile lit him from within. He pushed off the door frame and approached Cara with a package.

He gave a soft laugh as he took her chin into the palm of her hand, "You, Mia Bella, are all dirty from the saddle soap, here let me." Her brought her face closer to his and sensuously licked a spot on her cheek and then on her neck. She weakened.

"You do that on purpose don't you? You know that my knees will give out. How do you make everything so damn sexy?' She wrapped her arms around his neck and kissed him. "You are habit forming." She pulled on his lower lip and moved in closer to his body, wiggling her hips to get as close as possible. She immediately felt him respond. She pulled back and smiled. "Turn about is fair play, no?"

"I want you now, Cara!" he whispered softly in her ear.

"I know you do, that was my plan." She smiled devilishly at him, "And you, sir, will just have to wait!"

He swatted her butt hard. "Ouch, that hurt!" she pulled away and rubbed her butt. "Don't like the rules?"

"Si Cara, I dislike the rules very much!" he placed the package in her hand. "I ordered this from the U.S. five days ago. I hope it has everything you need in it."

She looked at him curiously, "What is it?" Cara began tearing the wrapping off the package. "My cell phone! What did you do? Order a new one for me? Why?"

"I was able to save the sim card and sent it back to the states to get a new phone programed. I thought you might want to call your friends. Most of your contact list should have been on your sim. Those that were not I did not bother to reprogram. I also added a few numbers I thought you would like to have."

She kissed his cheek, "Thank You! I had been thinking I should call Katherine and Jenna. By now they have seen Bryan walking around and are dying to know what's going on. What time is it in New York?" She counted back 6 hours, "around eleven, I'll finish this saddle and call them." She was flipping through her contact list and saw one name suspiciously absent.

"Hum, seems like you didn't think it necessary to put everyone's name in here." She gave him a sideways glance.

He smiled and leaned over to kiss her forehead and left. Thinking to himself, *Not at all necessary, Bella.*

When the day's chores were done, everyone was exhausted. After dinner Antinella fell asleep sitting on Vittore's lap. She really needed a bath, but he decided to let her sleep and Maria or Mamma could give her a good scrub in the morning before the parade.

He looked around the table and saw his family sharing in conversation and laughter. He pulled Antinella closer and buried his lips into her sweaty little head and smiled. He did not know he could be this happy. Cara shot him a brilliant smile and turned back to Davide whom she was having an animated conversation with about the words to a Beach Boys song. She insisted he had the words wrong.

Cara began singing, "East coast girls are hip I really dig the styles they wear; and the southern girls with the way they talk they knock me out when I'm down there. The mid west farmers daughter really makes you feel alright and the northern girls with the way they kiss keep their boyfriends warm at night. I wish they all could be California girls" That's how it goes. You don't need a "West Coast girl" Californian girls are the west coast girls."

Davide continued to insist a verse was missing so the debate continued. Bianca came to Vittore's side and put her hand on his shoulder, "I like your Cara, Vittore. She has character."

"Si Mamma, she has lots of character." He loved watching her, she was animated and alive! She used every part of her body when she spoke, her arms, hands, shoulders and her face was so expressive you couldn't help but watch her talk. "I will take piccolo to bed, can you help her with a bath in the morning? She is really in need of one, but I do not want to wake her for something we can do tomorrow."

"Give her to me Vittore, I too am tired and am going to bed." She looked at Giovanni and said, "Come Papa, we will put Antinella to bed and go to bed ourselves."

Davide, Vittore and Cara stayed up for a few more hours laughing and enjoying the evening. Davide admitted he was very nervous about tomorrow's competition and though doubted he would sleep, said his good nights and headed up to bed himself.

Cara and Vittore were on the sofa in the living room finishing their wine and Cara started to laugh. "What is so funny, Cara?" Vittore asked.

"I feel awkward!" She pulled away from him and gave a nervous little laugh, "I've been sitting here trying to figure out how to say, 'let's go to bed'. We've never gone to bed, we just always ended up there. So how do we do this?"

Vittore put his wine on the sofa table behind him and took her glass from her and placed it beside his, "I prefer ending up there, but knowing we are going there, it is fun too Bella." He gave her that smile, that damn smile that started it all. That perfect mouth, those lips, she weakened as he laid her back among the cushions.

He was right this was fun.

Vittore ran his hands up the inside of her shirt and found her soft, warm breasts. His hands encircled them, squeezing gently. Watching her face as her eyes closed in expectation.

He leaned low and kissed her belly and dipped his tongue in to her navel, licking tenderly.

Keeping one hand on her breast, he withdrew the other to unbutton her shirt, leaving her exposed for him to enjoy. He then undid the zipper of her jeans and pulled them from her body. She lay on the sofa before him naked, but for the shirt still on her shoulders. His eyes became pure heat.

"I will take you to bed, Cara, but Mi Bella, you have no idea the pleasure you will be enjoying tonight." Her breath caught.

Vittore took her hand and helped her up from the sofa. The hem of her shirt fell softly around her hips, the front covering her breasts, but exposing the white flesh from her neck to her lace. He stared for a few moments and slowly closed his eyes and took a deep breath.

"Bella, you will never survive this night." With his free hand he feathered his fingers down the path revealed, hesitating just above the lace of her panties, then raised his gaze to meet hers.

"Tonight Bella, tonight we do not make love like sex starved teen agers, tonight we make love like lovers." He put a fingertip into the waist of her panties and pulled her into him, "with maybe a little sex starved teen enthusiasm."

He smiled his wicked smile as he took the back of her neck into his large palm and drew her lips to his and whispered softly. "Tonight, Cara Bella, you are mine. To do with what I want."

Oh God! Cara's knees were weak.

He kissed her softly, slipping his tongue in between her lips gently entering her mouth caressing her tongue. He licked the roof of her mouth. She shivered and released a soft moan.

Vittore smiled, "Oh Bella, I am going to enjoy this." He took her hand and led her to his bedroom.

He walked her to his bed and smiled as he pushed her backwards with one finger until she was seated. He traced his finger over her shoulder to her neck and down the front of her opened shirt to her breast. Using just his finger he moved the cloth back and exposed her nipple. He drew ever decreasing circles around the surface of her breast until the tip of his finger gently teased her. He let his fingertip play over the hardened tip of her breast then traveled to her other breast and reenacted the same movements.

When both breasts were hard and firm, tight with desire he lowered his mouth to swirl his tongue over their surface always ending at the tender tip made hard with his attentions. Cara was so mesmerized she barely felt the shirt slip from her shoulders. He covered his teeth with his lips and rolled the buds hard until Cara moaned with sheer pleasure.

He whispered in her ear, "Lay on the bed, Cara." She moved back to the center of the bed and laid her head on the pillow, as she watched Vittore remove his clothing. His movements were so slow, so sensual she quivered in anticipation of what was to come. He said she wouldn't forget this night, what more could he possibly do? Her expectation heightened as she watched, waiting for him to keep his promise.

He stood before her naked, his body sculpted by hard muscles making it tight and feral, like an animal waiting to pounce. His hair hung loose but tucked behind his ears with a lock escaping on the side, touching his cheek like a whisper.

His thighs rock hard pillars and between them, Cara's heart stopped she held her breath, *oh god between them!*

Vittore lay down next to her, stroking her face, gently tracing her cheeks, jaw, lips. His touch was so whisper soft it seemed like a light breeze blowing over Cara, she closed her eyes to just focus on the touch, so soft caressing. His fingertips tickled their way down her neck and over her breast down her belly and feathered past her sweet hot mound to her thigh. There the fingertips lingered moving her legs apart gently. He leaned forward and whispered into her ear, "Open for me Cara, open for me now, Bella."

Cara felt as if in a trance. There was nothing he could ask of her she wouldn't do. She slowly opened her legs and he placed his palm over her thick mound of curls and gently letting the tip of his finger touch her moist hot trigger. He swirled his finger slowly softly, building pressure and speed the more aroused she became. He kept his movements controlled.

Vittore's ability to control his passion heightened Cara's. She bucked against his hand begging for him to take her. He moved a strand of her hair off her face as her eyes challenged him.

He smiled, leaning forward he tugged on her lower lip with his teeth, "Si, Bella you are not patient are you?" His eyes twinkled with delight as he shook his head slowly. "No Mia Bella, not patient at all. But you will be patient tonight, Cara." He bit her lip again, "Tonight Cara, you will do as I tell you, when I tell you. Do you understand, Cara?"

Her heart was pounding and she couldn't breathe, all she could do was to nod her head in acceptance. "Good Cara, now let us begin."

Vittore placed a knee between her thighs and spread her

legs wider, then knelt between her legs pulling her hips up onto him, draping her calves over is forearms, he slid into her. He then kept control of the pace; each movement causing a sweet delicious wave of desire to wash over her body.

When she became excited and demanded more. Vittore would softly stroke her and whisper, "Ssshh, Bella, enjoy. We have all night. I want you to feel every second of my making love to you, every touch, every caress." He moved ever so slowly into her rocking her hips with his hands, controlling their pace. "You will remember this night, Bella. Tonight I make you mine, you will never want for another."

Cara's muscles contracted on Vittore's hard shaft causing them both to release drops of honey. His eyes hooded as mellow warmth flooded his torso. "Ummm, Bella, you will need to be patient." He moved ever so slow making each stroke a delicious death.

For what seemed like hours he demanded her calm acceptance for his directive of controlled pleasure. Cara screamed out a cry of pent up desire that was rushing ahead of his rules. She was breaking into a million pieces, barely hanging on to control, then he thrust hard and deep into her, quickening the pace and depth with each thrust. Cara's body coiled and rose from the bed grabbing his forearms, demand in her eyes.

Vittore's eyes slowly blinked and a rush of warmth flooded him again, his teeth gnawed on his upper lip as he fought to get back in control, slowing the pace, eyes challenging Cara to lie back.

She thought she would faint, her breathing became labored, her head swam in a pool of confusion and desire. She wanted this to last forever, but she wanted to feel the rush of heat consume her body and make her quiver in exhaustion. Knowing she would lose one in order to gain the other. She looked into Vittore's face begging for help, "Lie down Cara. Tonight you will shatter. Ssshh Cara, lie back. Let me take you, relax, Mia Bella, relax." His words were a whisper, Cara eased her back onto the covers.

"I am a wreck, Vittore. I can't think. Please Vittore, oh god please." She whimpered as she lay looking at his body move into hers. "Omigod, Vittore, please." A stream of honey released from inside bathing Vittore in warmth.

"Si Bella, shattered." Again he held her hips high as he attended to her every desire.

Cara screamed her body having no other recourse but to play to the demands of his game. Tears came to her eyes, tears of lust, desire. She involuntarily drove into him again, he bent and kissed the thigh resting in his forearm as he held her hips in place. "Ssshh Cara we will get there."

Her senses were keen making the control unbearable. Her eyes wild, breath shallow, Vittore's upper teeth scraped his lower lip as he pushed in deeper, "We will get there Cara."

He leaned forward and with one hand, played with her nipple, she was going mad! She released another scream and moved her hips into his, slowly shuddering against the explosive nerve endings sending uncontrollable pulses through her body. She quivered, trembled and shook with excitement, "Vittore please, I can't."

"Yes you can, Bella,." He pulled hard on a nipple and thrust in deep causing a scream to spring forth from her throat. He removed himself and thrust forward again.

"Vittore," Her muscles within became uncontrollable and

took on a series of contractions she could never have imagined, she rose off the bed holding him around the neck, lifting her hips to a sitting position on to his, she screamed into his shoulder, "Vittore, I can't."

"You can." He drove in harder and felt one strong contraction against his shaft pressuring his muscle like a steel hand, he knew it was her final release and joined her in the ecstasy. Her head flung back and his hips pushed forward to seek the joy of her release. She shivered uncontrollably nestling into his chest seeking refuge. "I have never felt anything like that. What did you do? Ohmigod, I can't stop shaking. I want more but I can't. I am…what happened?"

He kissed her lips, softly and gave a little tug with his teeth on her lower lip. "Bella," Vittore softly laughed, "You have never felt that?" He released her lip and looked into her eyes and smiled. "I am glad it is I who delighted you so."

"I've been made love to before and nothing, nothing like that has ever happened. I am still shaking." She rested her head against his chest and was quiet for a few moments.

"Ohmigod," She took a deep breath and stared into his eyes smiling. "Ohmigod! All those years of making love and this is what I have been missing?" She laughed from pure joy!

Vittore was laughing at her she was so excited; "I do not know Bella." He kissed her neck, "If it is; then you have not been made love to."

She shivered again, "And here I thought I was wonder woman having multiple orgasms…" She just smiled and looked into his eyes. "Wow, maybe I won't let you go."

"That would make me very happy, Cara Bella."

CHAPTER FOURTEEN

Cara woke late and lay in bed, it was so quiet. Normally the household was busy in the morning. "Festival!" Cara flew out of bed grabbed a robe and started towards the stairs. She ran into Bianca and made her apologizes that she had slept in.

Bianca laughed at Cara's excitement and told her that everything was going fine and that she had time to have breakfast. Vittore and Davide were in Montefalco getting the tasting set up, Papa and Antinella had taken the horse trailer and are getting ready for the parade.

"You will not need to be in town until midafternoon. Breath Cara, we have been preparing for weeks." Bianca smiled lovingly, "Maria and I are going to leave for Montefalco in a few minutes. Salvatore and Antonio are remaining completing some duties in the winery. Vittore has asked that they bring you into Montefalco."

Cara checked a mantle clock, it was 10AM. She forgot to call Jenna and Katherine last night, it was too early in New York to call now, she decided to call just before leaving for town. She knew Jenna would answer no matter what time she called, but she wanted her semi conscience, there was a lot to talk about.

Cara went into the kitchen and fixed a small breakfast of fruit and bread. The villa was always so busy it was strange listening to the quiet. She sat on the veranda enjoying the wisteria and the sound of bees flying among the flowers. After an hour she went to shower and get ready.

As the hot water cascaded over her body, she gave thought to the last few days. It was a whirlwind of experiences and emotions. If she thought too much about it she would get dizzy. From the excitement of the trip itself, Romano!, Bryan!, and Vittore, *oh dear lord Vittore.*

They were in those frantic early days of a highly charged sexual relationship and as worldly as Vittore was it surprised her that he didn't see it. He was enfolding her into his world and she wasn't sure how she felt about that.

In a few days she would be going home and she would be a distant memory. She was having fun and was defiantly enjoying the sex, *dear god was she enjoying the sex*, but he wasn't really interested in her. She knew he felt sorry for her, he saw how upset she was that night when Bryan stood her up.

Stood Her Up In Italy, who the hell does that?

Vittore was a good man, her distress would affect him. She knew he had a lot on his plate. She knew all this; it was so easy to say in her head, so easy to explain, but she was falling in love with him.

Cara laid her head in the shower wall and the tears mixed with the water. She was such a dope! Thinking Bryan loved her, all those years he was using her, just like Jenna said. Now going weak over a gorgeous international hunk! She wanted to go home. She wanted Jenna to kick her in the butt, Katherine to hold her while she cried. She wanted to sit in her office at the Metropolitan Museum and catalog stones. She was exhausted with all the emotions.

She knew Vittore was trying to be kind, but the end result

was she was again single, alone. She was in her early 30's and Bryan had taken the best years of her life and used her!!! She cried, Vittore had no idea he was hurting her more acting like he really liked her.

I should just leave, go now. No one was here, I could leave a note. There was a train station in Montefalco.

She decided to call Jenna she needed her friend to tell her what's what.

Pull yourself together you dope, you are a grown woman! He is a flirt, it is his nature! Errr...call Jenna!

Cara got out and wrapped a huge fluffy towel around her body, she was going to miss this luxury! It was a little past noon, heck with it she was calling Jenna as soon as she was dressed!

Jenna answered on the second ring, "Where the hell you? And what the hell did that jerk do? Don't you ever do this to me again, I have been sick with worry!" Jenna was yelling and obviously angry.

Cara listened and the more Jenna scolded her, the harder she cried. Finally Jenna heard her soft sobs coming over the cell phone. "Oh, baby, I am sorry! I didn't mean to make you cry. Things must have gone horribly wrong. What happened?"

"He stood me up! In Italy, Jenna! Then Vittore has been so nice but I know I am going to get dumped again and I love him!" She choked the words out between sobs, barely coherent.

"Don't waste your love on that bastard, Cara!" Jenna was really mad.

"But the sex has been great! He is beautiful and he said he loved me! I don't know what to do, Jenna."

"Who the hell are you talking about?"

"Vittore!"

"Who the hell is Vittore?"

"He was there, he saw everything, he felt sorry for me, he has been really, really nice and I had a real orgasm, Jenna, I never knew! I never had one, I didn't know!"

"What the hell are you talking about? What have you been doing in Italy? Vittore, orgasms, never had one," Jenna pause for a few seconds, "What do you mean you never had an orgasm!"

"Jenna I want to come home. He's not here right now and I could leave. He'd never know, but I don't know how to get out of here, he brought me to his home in the mountains.."

"Stop!" Jenna yelled, "you are not making any sense Cara! Have you been kidnapped by this Vittore guy! I am going over to Bryan's right now and kill the little bastard. Cara, if you can get out run like hell, get to the nearest house and call the police. Cara, are you listening to me? Get out of there now!"

"But I don't really want to Jenna," she cried, "not really, I think I am falling in love, but I don't know him Jenna, what should I do?"

"Well first stop talking in circles! What is going on! Be calm, forget about Bryan, I'll deal with that weasel, but be CLEAR on everything else before I call Interpol and create an international incident. Breath, Cara, calm down."

Cara began relaying the past several days to Jenna, with gentle probing Jenna started to unravel the story. Her friend was not in danger, well at least from no one but herself. She got the jest of the trip. Bryan abandoned her, this rich Italian Adonis, Vittore, picked her up, has made her laugh and has screwed her in every tourist spot in Roma brought her to his vineyard and gave her the first orgasm she has ever had, and now she wants to come home because she afraid of getting hurt.

"Hell no girl, you stay right there and get that Vittore working on another orgasm! What do you mean you never had one, what did you and Bryan do when you screwed?"

"Jenna that's not the point! The point is I don't know what to do! I am falling for this guy and I just met him!"

"Cara I was right about Bryan so trust me; do not come home! You deserve this, even if it only lasts two weeks, honey you deserve this. Do you hear me?"

"But what if I really fall for him? I don't want to get hurt, Jenna."

"Cara, you have already fallen for this guy. No matter if you come home now or in five days you're going to be hurt. Stay and make some great memories to get you through."

Cara heard some shouting out in the yard and stood to look out the window. She saw the man Niccolo and someone else fighting with the two men from the vineyard. "Jenna, I have to go!" she pressed the end button and threw it in her pocket.

The man who drove in with Niccolo swung something out at one of Vittore's men and it slammed into his head and he dropped like lead! The other man from the vineyard ran into the barn.

Niccolo went to the back of the truck and pulled a small dead animal from the truck bed and began walking into the winery. Cara ran to Vittore' office and threw open the gun case and grabbed a Beretta.

Shit she hadn't used a gun in ten years, shit shit shit!

She found the ammunition for the Beretta and filled the clip and ran to the winery. Growing up in Arizona she learned to ride and shoot. But she'd been a New Yorker for ten years.

Please God don't let me really hurt someone.

As Cara entered the winery, Niccolo was climbing the wine-tasters staircase that lead to the top of the vats and the man who came with him stood over the collapsed body of the other worker. He was holding a make shift billy-club made of a sock with something heavy in the end.

"Stop," shouted Cara pointing the gun at Niccolo. They both laughed at the woman they saw before them pointing a gun. The man with the billy-club walked towards her.

"Damn it I said stop!" she turned the gun on him. He began swinging the sock around in circles to intimidate her. "I will shoot you, you bastard, stop!"

He kept moving forward, Cara aimed at the ground at his feet and pulled the trigger, her hand jerked up a little and hit the man in the kneecap. He went down writhing in pain.

She lifted the gun to Niccolo, he stared at her dumb founded. "Get down! Or I swear I will shoot and I don't give a shit where it lands! Get down, Di sotto!" Thank god for airport signage! "Di sotto! Presto!" She fired a shot into the air, "Di sotto".

Niccolo looked at his friend writhing in pain on the floor and back to Cara. His face should have revealed fear, but it turned smug, Cara swung around just as the man on the ground threw the weighted sock at her head, she ducked and it grazed her shoulder. She grabbed the weapon and turned to Niccolo, who was now running up the steps the dead animal swinging in his hand. Cara raised the barrel of the gun and took aim she prayed she really wouldn't hit him, and fired.

The bullet caught the animal's body and Niccolo dropped it turning horrified to Cara, "Damn it! Di sotto, you fucking bastard!" he started climbing down.

Cara looked quickly at the man on the floor of the winery, he was screaming in pain. "Shut up!" he screamed louder. "Shut Up!"

Without thinking Cara hit him in the head with the billy-club knocking him out. She turned to keep her gun pointed at Niccolo. As he got lower she started to worry about how to contain him.

"Stop!" she shouted again. She decided she was safer with him half way up this contraption then on the ground with her. "Sit!" she motioned the barrel of her gun for him to sit, "Sit!"

What the hell was she doing! Now what! She can't hold this guy at bay until someone comes home. Plus Vittore's men probably needed help. She pulled out her cell phone, what the hell do I dial!? She hit 911, nothing. She saw the European emergency code somewhere, what the hell was it? She stabbed 999. Someone spoke, she had no idea what they were saying and she prayed they would understand enough to get help right away.

"Sucai, I am an American. Conti Winery. Help!"

Please dear God, send help! What was she thinking!

"Conti Winery, Montefalco. Mafia." Hell why not she didn't know how to say trespassers, everyone knew mafia meant trouble.

The woman kept saying, "Ault, Ault." Finally someone who spoke some English got on line.

"We send someone now. Wait we come. Call Montefalco poliza now. We come Conti Winery."

Cara said. "Ambulance presto three di sotto," She was pretty sure ambulance was international.

"Si, police and ambulance."

Cara sought out a chair and placed it at the foot of the stairs holding Niccolo prisoner. She sat back and kept the barrel of the gun pointed straight at Niccolo.

What the hell was she doing!?

She pressed her phone icon and checked if Vittore had programmed his phone number in, and of course he had. She dialed.

"Mia Bella. Hurry you will miss the parade. Antinella rides for a prize and she wants you here, hurry, Bella!" He sounded so excited, she was ruining the most important day of the vineyard!

She whispered holding back a cry, "I am sorry Vittore."

"Sorry? Bella for what?"

"You need to come home."

"Cara what has happened? Are you hurt?"

"No, but I shot a man and the police are on their way, I think I may be in trouble. I need you Vittore, I am so sorry." Tears welled in her eyes.

"Cara, are you in danger?"

"No. I have Niccolo at gunpoint and I knocked the other one out, but both of your hands have been knocked unconscious." She lowered her voice not wanting Niccolo to hear, "I'm scared Vittore, please hurry." She disconnected the call.

Vittore tore through the crowds looking for the police captain, he had seen earlier. He spotted him just getting off his phone and turning to shout for some of his men. The captain caught Vittore's eye and motioned for him to come. The captain explained, he was just informed of an American woman at the Conti Winery that needed help. He told Vittore to come with him.

Running to the police vehicle, Vittore dialed Davide and hastily explained what was going on.

The police blared their sirens as they left the city. Vittore sent a prayer, "Cara, be safe, be safe!"

The cars raced up to Conti Vineyards leaving clouds of dust and reached the villa in less than ten minutes. Everyone piled out and approached the winery cautiously. One of the officers checked on the man lying on the ground outside the winery, felt his pulse and nodded an ok to his chief. The site of the man on the ground sent fear coursing through Vittore, "Cara!"

"Vittore!" They heard a cry come from the winery. Everyone rushed forward to find two more men lying motionless on the ground and Cara seated pointing a gun up the wine-tasters steps at Niccolo. The police chief cautioned Vittore to stay back as he approached Cara, speaking softly. He came slowly to her side and gently placed his hand on the barrel of the gun.

Cara sat motionless, in a daze. Her arms were locked and pointed straight at her prey. The police chief spoke again, trying to lower the barrel.

Vittore's voice snapped her out of her shock, "Cara, please we are here, lower the gun. You have no one to fear, Bella, I am here."

She looked at the policeman and let her hands drop away from the gun releasing it and Niccolo into his authority. She began to cry as she looked at this total stranger. She was so scared, she began to shake. Vittore was at her side in seconds pulling her into his arms, cradling her, letting her cry.

The police were asking him to allow them to question her, he wanted to protect her, but he knew he had to let them.

"Cara, we need to know what happened. Come let us go to the villa." He turned to the police chief and said something then walked Cara to the veranda.

The police were walking Niccolo off the stairs and taking him into the tack room to question him as the ambulance arrived. An EMT began to administer first aide to the bleeding mans leg and two others were attempting to revive Salvatore and Antonio.

When things had quieted the police came onto the veranda to begin asking Cara questions, Vittore acted as the interpreter. They drew the story out of her, between sobs.

Vittore held her tightly to his chest when she began to shake uncontrollably, she was in shock. He said something to the officer and led her into the house. Wrapping her in a blanket, he sat with her on the sofa and cradled her head on his chest, "Cara Bella, You frightened me." He kissed her hair and a little smile came to his mouth, "Where did you learn to shoot like that Cara. To hit a man in the kneecap is no small fete."

Cara pulled away from him abruptly and stood. "You don't know anything about me! How can you say you love me when you know nothing about me!" She shook like a leaf as her hand reached up to move hair from her eyes. She paced in front of Vittore gushing words. Not yelling but stabbing the words out, "I was raised in Arizona. I ride, shoot and hell even know how to rope cattle, but how the hell would you know any of that, you don't know me! What am I doing here, with you in this villa?

What am I doing shooting at people I don't know, protecting something that isn't mine!"

She stopped pacing and looked at Vittore. "I don't know you. We don't know each other. What am I doing?" Terror crossed her face and she fell on her butt to the floor and whispered, "Oh God, I am going to jail." Her lips trembled in fear as she raised her face to Vittore, who was already helping her up.

He held her tight into his chest. His heart broke. She was terrified, in shock and his feelings for her were making things worse. He was not handling any of this correctly and now this. He had to get her through this moment, and then he would address the rest. Get her through this Vittore he told himself. Get her through this experience.

"Cara, please, you need to sit. You will not go to jail. I will keep you safe. We need to know why Niccolo came here today. The police are questioning him, we will find out. Do not make stories in your head that do not exist. You are not going to jail." He tried calming her by stroking her hair and kissing her temple as he rocked her in his arms. He held her for what seemed hours, not talking just comforting her.

The Police Chief returned to relay information to Vittore who nodded and turned to speak to Cara. "Niccolo came to place a dead animal in our wine vat to ruin our production, you stopped that Cara, you did a brave thing for Antinella." He leaned her back to look into her eyes, "You did a good thing Bella." He drew her into his chest again.

"Niccolo being a stupid criminal left a bag of cocaine in his truck, so not only will he be charged with trespassing, assault and criminal intent, but drug possession as well."

He pulled her closer, "You may be charged with discharging a weapon." He felt her body tense and shake, she began crying again. "I will not let them arrest you, Bella. You are an American. They can do little since it was self-defense. My lawyers will clear it up Bella, do not worry. What is important is you are safe. Niccolo did not ruin Antinella's future and now maybe the battle between the Conti and Del'oro will end." He held her face, "You did a good thing, Cara Bella."

The officers came back in to the living room and kept motioning towards Cara, she shrunk into Vittore' arms. He held tightly on to her letting her know he would protect her. His voice exploded into some harsh words and he pulled his cell out and punched a dial. When the other party answered there was some discussion then Vittore handed the phone to the police chief.

The officer nodded and the only thing Cara understood was American Embassy.

Oh god they are deporting her!

He handed the phone back to Vittore; again all she heard was American Embassy, then "Presto". She started to cry. Vittore continued to talk while stroking her head, trying to comfort her. Vittore and the police chief seemed to come to some agreement because they shook hands, then Cara and Vittore were alone again.

"What? I am being deported, aren't I?" she shivered.

"I do not know Cara," He kissed the top of her head. "For now you are in my custody, so no running or I too will be in trouble!" He tried to get her to smile, she was so afraid. "We will stay here in Montefalco until tomorrow then go to the American Embassy with my lawyers to see what can be done. I do not think anything will come of it Bella. You were protecting my property. It will be seen as that."

Vittore's phone rang. He gave it a quick glance fully intending not to answer, but he saw it was Davide. "Yes, Davide."

"We won! Damn it Vittore, we won the competition. We did it, god damn, we did it!" Davide was so excited Vittore could feel the ground shake from Montefalco to the vineyard. His smile broadened, "Congratulations, my brother, you are the genius of this vineyard. Cara and I will be with you shortly to celebrate. He closed the phone, "A new age has begun, Cara."

He held her until she fell asleep and he continued to hold her until he heard the faint rustling of someone in the kitchen. They were returning from festival. He needed to wake her and encourage her to help in the celebration. He kissed her head, her cheek and finally her mouth. She opened her eyes, they were still puffy from crying and he kissed them as well.

"Cara, the celebration is now at our villa. Do not worry about tomorrow. Let us enjoy tonight, Cara. We have much to celebrate and the festivities will ease your mind. Come let me help you shower and get ready. I will wash your body and ease all your worries, Cara. Come." he rose and held her hand as he walked her towards the stairs that led to the bedrooms.

CHAPTER FIFTEEN

They got up early and drove to Roma. On the drive back Vittore was constantly on the phone. Cara wasn't sure what he was working on and really didn't care too much. Saying goodbye to everyone was hard for her. She had only known them for a few days but she would miss them terribly. And Antinella, tears streaked down her cheeks, she didn't want to say goodbye to her. She laid her head back on the headrest and let the wind hit her face.

She knew she would be going back to the States in a few days. The reality of what she had feared was coming to pass. She turned her head to looked at Vittore and smiled. *I knew it would end like this*, she returning to her world, him to his. It hurt, even though she had prepared herself.

There was a spot where Vittore was unable to receive a signal and he put his phone aside. "The attorneys do not think we will have a problem, Cara. You will not need to go to the Embassy tomorrow. They will call the police in Montefalco and see what they intend to do. So please relax and enjoy the drive. This is the scenery all Americans come to see."

He looked over at her; he knew she had been crying. "With the success of the wine yesterday I have sped up my consolidation of companies. I have made arrangements to make a formal announcement in three days, there will be a banquet. I would like for you to stay and enjoy this moment with me Cara. Would you do that?"

"I'd love to, if I don't get kicked out of Italy first!" She gave him a weak smile. "Are you sure you want to fraternize with a know felon?"

"I rather like dating Annie Oakley. You developed quite a reputation in my village." He wanted to cheer her up. "Did you notice that my grandmother and aunts did not assault you last night? I overheard that they are in fear of you. I do not think you will need to worry about any more assaults."

She did smile at that, "Hey it was almost worth it not to get pinched!" She went melancholy again, "Vittore, this has been fun, thank you. Sorry I ended it with a bang, pun intended!" She stole a glance at him. "But I have a feeling I am on my way back to the states."

"Cara, let us get though the next few days and not worry about what we do not know. And as for the banquet, we will be very busy while in Roma. You will need to help me buy a new evening suit and to buy you a new evening gown."

"Vittore, no, you don't have to get me a dress." She looked over at him, he really was very sweet. He must have more money than Cara imagined to be throwing it away on her. "I'd love to shop with you, or rather for you. But you have been too generous already. Even though these are your lawyers they are going to charge you and I will never be able to repay that debt. Please don't rack up any more guilt for me. I ruined your celebration, embarrassed you, caused you to leave Montefalco before you were intending.."

"Stop, Bella." He smiled at her, "Do you also think it was you also that caused the rain to fall last night? Cara, you did not embarrass me or Conti vineyards. Your American wild-west arrest of Del'oro was the most excitement Montefalco has had in years and the whole thing happening on the day Conti vineyards won the award for producing the best Sagrantino in all Umbria. It will only draw more attention which would have cost me a fortune otherwise." He looked at her to make sure she was listening.

"And I intended to return to Roma if we won, to hold this banquet and announce my resignation as head of a few of my companies. I will be introducing the new management at the banquet. And as far as the purchase of a little dress, consider it payment for the best marketing campaign we could ever get!" He looked at her and saw how sad she still was. "Cara, please, do not worry, it will all be fine." He reached out and placed his hand over hers and squeezed gently.

They arrived at the hotel around noon. Vittore had made arrangements to meet his attorneys in the suite at one that afternoon. Cara sat on the balcony, trying to relax waiting for their arrival while Vittore worked in his office. She called Jenna back, knowing the way she had cut off their conversation yesterday, Jenna would be worried. And she was worried and mad again but in spite of that, Jenna did calm her down.

Jenna's husband, Hank, was an attorney and he came on the line to discuss Cara's situation. Hank said since it was a clear trespassing issue he didn't think it put her into any jeopardy. "It's not like you have a criminal background Cara. Plus didn't you say this Del'ore family has a history with the Conti's and that drugs were found on this Niccolo? The man came to that house with intent to do harm, Cara." Hank tried his best to ease Cara's mind.

"Discharging a weapon is minor here in the United States, I do not think it is a big deal in Italy. This incident should be glossed over. If you need help you know I am here, but it sounds like this Vittore guy has good lawyers."

"I think he does, it just seems so weird to be in a foreign country and having the police looking at you. I have been really scared!"

"Don't be Cara. You'll be OK. Call if you need me, but I have to go." Hank hung up.

"So tell me about this orgasm?" Jenna could not believe she had never had one!

"God Jenna, can we get past the fact I never had a real orgasm? Jeez. I'll bet there are lots of women who haven't." Cara was reliving in her mind that feeling. "Jenna, are you sure you've had one?"

"Hell yes! If Hank couldn't give me one, he'd be gone!" Jenna's voice held total amazement that Cara could even consider such a thing. "How long were you and asshole together?"

"Six years. Before that it was pretty much inexperienced boys from home. So no, it wouldn't surprise me that I was clueless." Cara thought for a few moments, "Jenna this guy makes love like no man I've ever even heard of! I am just near him and I can't control myself. I have never been so excited about being with a man. Is it like that with you and Hank?"

"Depends on how pissed he made me earlier, but yeah when we first started dating we couldn't keep off each other, I thought I was in heat all the time, it wore me out!"

"See it was never like that with Bryan."

"Go figure!"

"Jenna I know you told me, I know. Look the attorneys

will be here soon, thank Hank for me he really calmed me down."

"Sure sweetie, enjoy your Adonis and come home with lots of stories! Hank and I have gotten a little complacent. Maybe you can share something new."

"I'll do my best." She had that twinkle back in her voice. She really was feeling better. Cara ran to the bath, put on fresh make-up *better not to look the part of a crazy pistol packing mama* and joined Vittore in his office.

"Good, no gun case here." She stood in the door way waiting until he was off the phone. He looked up and smiled.

"I guess we are all safe. It seems you are feeling more like yourself again." He was glad to see it. Seeing Cara sad broke his heart, it had since the first day he saw her.

"Sorry." She knew all the emotion of the last 24 hours was triggered by the incident at the winery but her fears were so much more then what the police might do, it was leaving. Leaving this man who was so kind, so loving. "Vittore, thank you," she looked at him sitting at his desk eager eyes, smiling at her, "for everything."

He stood and approached her, "Cara Bella, you have nothing to thank me for, it is I who should thank you." Cara watched him glide towards her. He always took her breath away. Just the simple motion of his body walking across the room was primal and sensual. Her knees gave, just a little, and then she was in his arms.

"Cara, these days we have spent, has not been about a playboy seducing a beautiful woman. I know you think that is all it has been, that you were a toy for me, a distraction." He tilted her chin back to look into her face. He held her in his gaze for moments, saying nothing, just studying her face, "You do not understand this and do not think it possible when I tell you, Cara, that I love you."

She opened her mouth to speak, but Vittore covered her mouth with his and pulled her tight, allowing his tongue to play with hers and explore its warmth. He slid a hand softly over her breast and kneaded it gently, each thrust of his tongue brought his fingers to hold her more firmly. He gently pulled away to look into her eyes and said with such conviction, "Do not doubt this, Cara Bella."

Just then an intercom sounded announcing the arrival of his attorneys. He kissed her again on the lips and then on the forehead. "Please, Cara, allow it to be a possibility in your mind and see how it feels, do not dismiss my statement of love so quickly. Please Cara." He leaned lower and kissed her neck, just behind her ear, shivers coursed through her body. "I must let our attorneys up." He released his hold and moved to the desk, picking up a phone giving permission for them to come up to his suite.

Cara was clueless as to what was being discussed, neither of Vittore's attorneys spoke English and although Vittore would explain periodically what was going on, it was a difficult way to determine your fate. The inability to keep up with what was happening was very nerve racking and Cara began to get impatient.

"Vittore, please," she interrupted a conversation, "this is hard not knowing what is being said, bottom line, will I be kicked out of Italy? And if so when?" She looked at him pleadingly.

He knew her distress and touched her face gently with just the tips of his fingers, smiling, "They do not think Cara that this will be cause for the Italian government to ask you to go home. You are here as my guest and it has a little weight in your defense." His eyes danced with affection.

"Tomorrow my attorneys will meet with an Italian magistrate and someone from your embassy to discuss the incident. From the preliminary conversations they had with them today this will go nowhere. Relax Cara," His fingertips traveled to her neck and gently caressed her, "you will not go to jail nor will you be asked to leave Italy. My attorneys tell me the local government of Umbria is grateful to you for getting Niccolo behind bars. I will explain to you later the extent of his involvement with drug trafficking in Umbria. You may become a hero, just like Anne Oakley." His eyes laughed and Cara did laugh!

"You and Anne Oakley, how long have you been fantasizing about her?" Cara joked with him.

"Never her, Cara, just you." He turned back to his attorneys discussed a few more things, and then everyone made motions that the meeting was over. Briefcases repacked, chairs moved back from the table, handshakes and a kiss to Cara's hand. Then they were gone. It seemed surreal to Cara and only the lingering warmth of a kiss to the back of her hand remained as evidence that the meeting even happened.

Vittore voice brought her back to reality, "Cara, it is too late to shop but I know what I would like to do." Cara looked at him and those devil eyes and smile were a staring back at her.

She laughed, "And what would that be, like I can't guess!"

He pulled her body into his, "Si Cara, but the how, Bella, how is it I will make love to you?"

"How?"

"Oh Cara, there are many ways of making love to you."

"Is that a fact?" Her stomach was filled with butterflies.

"Oh si, Cara, many ways, it may take a lifetime to show you them all." He captured her mouth with his full soft lips and made his desire known. He pulled her hips in tight to his and she felt his hardened muscle, throbbing against her. He lowered his mouth over hers and began stroking the top of her mouth with his tongue. "Tonight I will be the cat and you the little mouse and I will play with you all night."

Cara's knees gave a little. "I am going to die, aren't I?" She asked.

"Si, Bella but you will love every minute."

Vittore laughed at her as he guided her to his bedroom.

CHAPTER SIXTEEN

Cara couldn't believe she was still alive. Every inch of her body still shook with desire. She had never felt like this, not sore, spent. Tired but wanting more. Exhausted but re-energized.

How did he do all that?

Vittore had already risen and was in the dining room having breakfast when Cara entered. "You do not play fair!" She scolded.

He turned to look at her, she was still flush from a night of making love and her body was still shaking with desire. He rose from his chair and crossed the room to take her into his arms. "I told you that you had no idea how wicked I could be, Bella. But you had a good time, no?"

Cara hit him in the chest, "What now you're fishing for compliments? You turned me into your pet, you beast!"

He smiled broadly, "Umm, does that mean you are now mine forever Bella. No other man could make you as happy as I?"

"You have spoiled me for all other men! There can't be more of you out there, no one would ever leave their bedrooms, economies would collapse, you are dangerous! Very, very dangerous."

She worked out of his grasp and sat in a chair opposite

his. He loved watching her eat, her hands were sensual as she picked at toast and fruit and placed them in her mouth. Her lips full and wet from the juice of the berries, he wanted to lick them. He wanted her again. It was not he that made her his pet, but she who had made him hers.

"So what are we doing today?" Excitement filled her eyes. Every day with Vittore was an adventure.

"Today Bella we shop!" He grinned at her as her eyes went wide with anticipation.

"You know I actually had a little time to give some thought to that offer of buying me a dress. I decided after last night, you owe me a dress. I have never had a workout like that in my life and I wasn't allowed to do anything!" She smiled brightly at him, "Where do we go first?"

"I was thinking Versace."

"Really, just like that, 'I was thinking Versace'. Boy would I love to live in your world! Hell, why not drop into Cartier later and pick up a few baubles while we are out and about?" She tossed her head back and flicked her wrist sending him a brilliant smile!

"Si, Cara, Cartier is a very good idea! Go get ready we have a very busy day. And tomorrow Antinella comes to Roma with Davide and Mama and Papa. They will be coming to the banquet, so we need to buy Antinella a dress as well."

"Vittore, are they all coming?" Tears welled in her eyes. She thought she would never see any of them again. Her hand shook as she wiped her eyes. "Oh my god, look at me, I am such a dope!" She smiled at him, knowing she was being silly.

"Cara! You make my heart sing! Now go get ready. I will order a car."

Cara walked out of the room shaking her head and laughing, "Of course you will, another planet, I swear you live on another planet."

Shopping at Versace was an experience beyond her wildest dream. Vittore and she were led to a private dressing room filled with overstuffed chairs and a sofa. On a sofa table was a bucket of ice and inside was a bottle of champagne. Vittore explained in Italian to the sales lady what they were there to purchase, the event they would be attending and the way they sized her up from across the room; her dress size.

When the woman left, Vittore poured them each a flute of champagne, it was 10AM and she was drinking champagne. Different world! "She will return with some items that will be appropriate." He handed her a flute.

Cara looked around the room, it was a large room and one wall was all mirrors with pull out mirrors on piano hinges to allow the customer to see a 360 view. There was the door to the shop, but Cara did not see a dressing room door. She spun around in a circle, "Where do I change?"

Vittore was sitting on the arm of a large chair, his foot on the cushion and resting his forearm on his knee, champagne flute in his hand, watching her, "Here Cara." He took a sip looking at her.

"What do you mean, "here"? Right here, with you standing there, with her coming in, no really where is the other room."

"This is the only room, Bella. You remove your clothing

and she will return with a dress." He loved how uncomfortable it made her and it made him laugh quietly inside.

"With you, standing there, just watching?"

"It is what I do Bella, I watch."

"I am sure you're supposed to leave the dressing room and come back in when I am dressed." She was embarrassed, he has had his tongue on every inch of her flesh and the thought of stripping in front of him, in this dressing room, knowing that woman would come back to see her standing almost naked with Vittore standing there looking at her embarrassed her.

Vittore slowly shook his head, "No Bella, I am to stay, you are to undress and she will return to dress you. That is how it is done in Italy, Bella. Shopping is sensual and what good is a dress if I do not approve." He sipped more champagne.

She looked at him suspiciously, "If you're teasing me and putting me into a situation that will embarrass the hell out of me, I will never forgive you!"

"Bella? I would not intentionally embarrass you. Here you seem to not know how to get started." He put the flute down and walked to the center of the room where she stood and began unbuttoning her sweater, kissing her jaw line. "Let me help you."

He removed the sweater from her shoulder and one arm, he held her flute while the sweater slid off her other arm and onto the floor. Cara's eyes were half closed. She couldn't believe she was being made love to in a dressing room of Versace's, no one would believe it, not even Jenna.

He was standing very close as he began to undo the button of her skirt with his free hand pulling on her waistband inching her closer to him, he got her close and let the skirt drop to the floor and then squeezing her soft round bottom, pulling her into his hard stiff shaft. Cara's head fell back and she let out a loud moan, just as the door opened and in walked three women, all carrying dresses.

Cara dropped her head into Vittore's shoulder.

Why can't she control herself around him? Damn.

She peeked an eye over at one of the women hanging gowns on a hook, who smiled sweetly at Cara.

Damn! Damn! Damn!

"You've brought me nothing but trouble since I met you!" She pushed off his chest with her forearms. "Damn you for being so damn sexy." She whispered. He let go of her arms leaving her standing naked but for that beautiful little strip of lace that barely covered her heat.

The three women bustled about the room, Vittore repositioned himself on the chair and Cara stood naked, looking at herself and all that was going on in the room through the mirrors reflection.

Vittore was smiling too broadly damn him he knew she'd get into this predicament.

She scowled at him and mouthed, "Just wait!"

His eyes were alive with laughter as he sipped his champagne, watching Cara. Her not knowing whether to cover her breast or not; her arms kept going up then stopping. She was very uncomfortable and he found it very erotic. His Cara Bella, complex, childish, yet strong, how did God ever create something so perfect? He sipped and watched them dress her.

For over an hour she tried on cocktail dresses, gowns and evening suits. She was exhausted. Vittore sensed her need to rest and sent everyone from the room. She had on the cocktail dress she had tried on last. Vittore took a seat on the sofa and motioned her to sit with him.

She plopped in the cushion next to him and laid her head on his shoulder. "I'm tired! I've never been so exhausted. I've been trying to figure out the cost of these dresses but I can't find a price tag."

"You will not find one, Bella; couture dresses have no price tags." He kissed her head as it rested on his chest.

"Then how are you supposed to know which one to buy!"

"Cara, you buy the one that makes you beautiful. And depending on the event, the paparazzi, the notoriety of the person, you negotiate the price." He held her closer, resting his chin on her head, enjoying the feel of her in his arms.

"So is this a small event? You've only been planning it for a few days. It must just be a small dinner, right? So we'll have to pay pretty much full price." He could hear her mind working on guessing which dress would be the least affordable. He gave a slight shake to his head.

"It will be covered by the media and many notable people will be attending and it will actually be a large event. So do not worry about the cost, I think I can negotiate a good price, Mia Bella."

"Which one should I get? I've tried so many on, I can't remember!" her head fell hard on his chest. "I'm tired, you're exhausting be around, do you realize that?"

He laughed and held her head tight to his chest. "You do not need to worry Bella the dressers will determine which is best. After all, it is their reputation you will be wearing. They will return with their final choice, altered and then a final fitting. We have but another hour before they return and then we will go to lunch."

"What are we going to do for an hour?!" She was surprised they would be there that much longer. She lifted her head and looked at him. "Oh No! No!" she laughed trying to get away from him. "No! They walked in on us the last time, No!" She was still squirming.

"Ah but Bella I told them to knock next time." That damn grin, damn him!

"No they will think I am your concubine! No!" she was still struggling with him, laughing. "You are awful!" He let her loose, knowing she would not go far.

Cara jumped up from the sofa and ran to the center of the room. She was laughing and shaking her head. Then she took on the posture used by Bianca and her at the winery. She bent at the waist looked him in the eye and waiving her finger at him as she shook her head, no.

"Oh Bella." He said breathlessly as he launched himself from the sofa, catching her at the waist and pulling her into him. "You are a very bad girl, Bella." He laughed as he covered her mouth with his.

Vittore pushed her back against a wall pinning her with his chest and hips. He took her wrists in his hands and lifted them out to the side of her as if she were a sacrifice. He lowered his mouth to her neck and began kissing lower.

"Take off the dress, Vittore, I don't even like it and I don't want to buy it, take it off." He spun her fast and pushed her chest gently into the wall, with one hand he held her shoulder, his hips sinking into her soft rear and with his free hand he lowered the zipper very slowly.

"We must take care not to damage it, no, Bella?" She never knew a zipper could be undone this slowly. When it was fully unzipped he eased it from her shoulders and let it fall to the ground. He did not turn her back around, but began kissing the back of her neck, shoulders and down her spine.

Being pinned backwards between him and the wall was amazingly erotic. She placed both palms on the wall in front of her just above her shoulders.

His mouth continued to move around her back and with every lick she trembled. She felt his hand between her and his waist, she heard the quite sound of a zipper being lowered.

She turned her head slightly to see and she caught their reflection in the mirror. She saw as he released himself and step back holding her shoulder into the wall forcing her hips out slightly. She watched as his hand moved between her legs, she felt the pad of his thumb rub her, pressing her hard, feeling for the flow of warmth and it came. Cara gave a soft moan and pushed her hips back into him.

She watched as he entered her and she watched him watch her. As the motion increased she saw him draw air into his lungs. His eyes were smoldering.

She watched and she became aroused and tried to turn to take him into her mouth, but he held her, moving in and out, in an erratic rhythm that only heighted the pleasure.

Vittore was lost in the sensation of her warmth, her heat. As he concentrated on feeling her rub along his shaft, he drove harder, feeling the resistance within her give way to deeper thrusts. His breath held, he drove deeper and upward, causing Cara to moan loudly. He drove upward again and she released her sweet honey onto him. He drove again and she pushed back from the wall to meet his thrust.

She watched and was in ecstasy. She watched him release in a spasm of desire and she smiled.

Vittore withdrew and Cara turned around and lowered herself onto her knees in front of him. She was so tender, so soft, his head tilted back, enjoying the attention Cara gave. "Mia Bella, I do love you." He held her tight.

Moments later there was a small knock at the door and Vittore asked the sales ladies to enter. They had the gown of their choice for Cara on a hanger with a Versace bag covering it so Cara could not see. Vittore and one of the women had a very long conversation all during which Vittore nodded his head in approval. Finally they left with the dress and Cara stood dumbfounded.

"What was that all about? Are they bringing a different dress? What you didn't like what they choose?" She was standing naked in her lace panties, "Look I am not an exhibitionist and all this standing around naked is starting to get on my nerves. Versace or no, I want to get dressed!" She turned on Vittore her anger becoming apparent. He just smiled his wicked devil smile with those beautiful soft lips.

"You can get dressed Cara, we have made the purchase. They are sending your gown to the hotel and will have shoes sent to match, Faragamo I believe." He sipped more champagne.

"What do you mean I can get dressed? I thought I had to try it on again, if I can get dressed now why the hell was I standing naked in here waiting for them?!"

"You are naked, Cara, because I like you to be," a smile broke his lips as he held the flute up for another sip.

"You pervert!" She laughed throwing a pillow at him. He narrowly saved this champagne.

"Hurry, Cara, we will have lunch, then go to Cartier."

Her mouth dropped, "You have got to be kidding! Now you're in a hurry. And what planet do you live on anyway? Versace in the morning and Cartier in the afternoon. How the hell did you make all your money. I know, I know... watching!"

She tugged on her sweater and fastened the skirt around her waist. When she was done dressing she gave him a defiant look, "No more games! That was embarrassing! Not again, do you hear me?"

Vittore laughed loudly, "Si Bella I hear. No more games." He wrapped his arm around her waist and they walked out of Versace's.

"You do know I was kidding about going to Cartier, right? I was being a bit flippant with you." Cara had finished her lunch and they were getting up from the table.

"No Cara, it was a good suggestion, I have a ring being made that I need to pick up and a few other things I need to attend to. It will not take us long."

They spent another hour in Cartier, Vittore mostly in conversation with one person in a private room. Cara was bored and excused herself to roam around the store. She was spellbound by the quality of the gems. The finest and rarest only were for sale in houses like Cartier and Tiffany's and of course Winston's. But the settings were magnificent as well.

She was drawn to a yellow diamond that was about four

carets, beautiful oval cut as only an expert hand could. The top
was a broad table but the faceting underneath was extensive
and caused the ring to explode with brilliance. It was set
high and the gallery was a filigree carriage set off with white
diamonds that flowed gracefully down around the finger. It
was breathtaking.

The clerk asked if she would like to try it on, well at least
that is what Cara assumed she meant as she withdrew it from
the case and placed it before her. Cara had worked around
gems for the last ten years, and five of those at Tiffany's, but
she had never seen anything this beautiful. She asked for a
lope and when she examined it her knees went weak. Her
hand shook as she placed it on her finger.

She held it out to catch the play of light dance through the
stone. She couldn't stop twisting it making it play with the
light. She finally removed it from her hand and placed it back
on the velvet mat. The manager came over and said something
to the sales clerk and gave a weary glance towards Cara.

The sales lady said "Scusi" several times to him as she
picked up the stone and began polishing it vigorously.

*Gezzee even at Tiffany's we let the little people try on the
rings.*

These two were acting like she infected it. Pretty
intimidating place, made Tiffany's look like Sax!

She scoped the store looking for Vittore. He was outside
the room saying good bye to Dario, the man who had been
helping him, and carried a Cartier bag containing the ring
they had made for him. He looked up caught Cara's eyes made
a motion he would be with her in a minute, then shook the
man's hand and walked towards her. "Did you enjoy yourself
Cara?"

"I still am amazed how minerals can be polished to be so beautiful. They are a mystery." She looked at the bag, "Your ring?"

"Si, now that I have given Davide my ring, I have felt naked. Cartier has made a replica for me or should I say more for you Bella." He smiled brightly and she hit him in the chest.

"You deserve to feel naked after what you put me through! You are no gentleman, Vittore! Have I told you that?"

"Si, Cara, many times. Let us find a dress for Antinella and then we will return to the hotel and you can continue to scold me."

That devil grin, oh this man was trouble!

CHAPTER SEVENTEEN

They woke the next morning to cell phones ringing. Both Vittore's and Cara's went off simultaneously. They looked at each other and laughed. Cara shrugged her shoulders, "Guess it's going to be one of those days. Mine's probably Jenna."

Vittore flipped open the phone as he climbed out of bed, walking naked towards the balcony grabbing his silk robe along the way and slipping into it.

Everything he did was sexy, damn him!

Cara answered hers and could not have been angrier as she listened to the voice on the other end of the phone. "I don't have to answer to you Bryan! You are out of my life."

Her mouth dropped, "You want your ring back! I paid for the damn thing you weasel! Hell, no you can't have it back! I've sold the stone and used the money to pay for one hell of a trip."

What the hell did she care if she lied to this ass.

"Oh you better believe I did! You are screwed up Bryan! Don't ever call me again!" She raised her phone to throw it just as she caught Vittore's glance, he gave a little shake of his head. She smiled and shrugged her shoulders as she closed the phone.

Vittore's call took longer so Cara climbed out of bed and ordered breakfast, she could get used to living in a hotel. She would never have to cook and that would be just fine by her. She slipped into the shower while waiting for breakfast and for Vittore to get off the phone. She knew it was going to be a busy day.

She was standing under the hot water beating down on her head and neck when she felt Vittore slip in beside her. Cara wiped the water from her face and looked at him.

"Bryan?" He asked.

"Can you believe it? He wanted me to explain where I have been! He's been trying to get in touch with me for days. Decided since he had no idea where I was why return to Italy. Why didn't I see this, what the hell is wrong with me. Everyone else knew he was a jerk, what took me so long to see it?" She stopped and let water pour over her body. "I'm doing it again, rambling. I do it when I get mad, sorry."

"Si, Cara, I know." He picked up a sponge and poured soap on to it and began squeezing until it was mounded with bubbles. Then he began washing her back and shoulders, down the back of her body leisurely rubbing the sponge between her cheeks, than moving down her legs.

Cara stood facing the shower tiles, Vittore's caressing strokes felt so soothing and the hot water and bubbles were so sensual. "Does everything you do have to be perfect, feel perfect," She glanced down at him washing her feet, "look perfect?'

He smiled up at her, "Bella, you are the only one I know, that thinks I am perfect." He was crouched at her feet and reached up holding her hips, turned her so her back was against the tiles. He kissed the front of her thighs as he began washing them with long slow strokes, then squeezing the bubbles in to her soft triangle of fur. He stood and brought the sponge up her belly and around her breasts, moving in soft circles. Cara had closed her eyes, it felt delicious. He moved the sponge to her neck and across the tops of her shoulders. "I believe this is where I began."

Cara opened her eyes. She loved him. She knew it at that instant. She loved him. She didn't want to be apart, she wanted to share in all his joys and hardships. She wanted to ease his mind when he was troubled.

She kissed him softly tenderly, "I love you, Vittore." She laid her head on his shoulder. They remained in the shower letting the needle sharp water beat over their bodies while they held each other, barely moving, touching gently stroking each other's bodies.

"We should get out Cara." He kissed her head, "Come Cara, breakfast awaits us." He pulled her out of the shower and wrapped a big soft robe around her wet body and rubbed the cloth against her skin. "Does that feel good Cara?"

"Too good, you spoil me," She kissed his cheek, "Why do you spoil me Vittore?"

"I am in love with you, Cara. All I want to do is spoil you, Bella." He held her shoulders in his hands as he kissed her.

Vittore's morning was filled with last minute arrangements for the banquet and meetings with his lawyers about the mergers and the resolution on Cara's situation in Umbria. He had scheduled a luncheon with the men whom he was entrusting his companies with, to dine with him in the hotel's dining room at 1PM. There were several issues about transition of management that needed to be clarified. He apologized to Cara for being so busy, but informed her that Antinella and his family would be arriving by noon.

She spent her morning walking the streets of Roma being a tourist. She only had a few hours before Antinella and the Falco's arrived and as much as she wanted to see the sites of Roma, spending the last few hours she had in Italy with Vittore's family meant more. In a few short days she had fallen in love with Antinella and the rest of the Falco family. She justified her decision telling herself Roma had stood for hundreds of years and would be there when she returned. These people, she may never see again. And the thought of that made her very sad.

While traveling the streets of Roma she hunted for a gift for Antinella. The dress she and Vittore had selected for her was a sleeveless jewel necked white taffeta with brown polka dots and a cummerbund tied in the back with a big bow. It was dressy but still very little girl. The polka dots would distract from a necklace, but Cara wanted to buy her something jeweled as a gift of remembrance.

She scoured the shops along the Via del Corso and found a beautiful hair comb encrusted with white and chocolate pearls along with a few diamond chips to make the light play against the pearls. With care it was a gift that would last a lifetime. That thought pleased Cara.

She stopped back into Cartier to get a gift for Vittore. His kindness and generosity was something she could never repay. She thought of one piece of jewelry that would look great on him and from what she could tell he did not have. When they were at Cartier yesterday she saw it, now she needed to know if she could afford it!

When she entered Cartier the same doorman allowed her entry as yesterday and he smiled broadly in a welcome. Now she just prayed the manger that made her feel like she was contaminating his store was off for the day.

She walked straight to the case where yesterday she saw a collection of three open backed titanium bangles that were designed for a man's wrist. The surface of each was inlaid with Ivory, Onyx, and Amber but the design combination was different on each. And at certain points of the design it looked like threads of black gold were wrapped; like binding to hold the design stones in place.

As she stood examining the bracelets through the case she heard soft footsteps approach, it was the manager from yesterday.

Great!

She smiled pleasantly and asked if he spoke English.

"Si, a little." He was very cordial and pleasant today and seemed eager to help her.

"These bracelets, may I see them?"

"Si." He went to the other side of the case and opened the lock laying the three bracelets on a velvet mat. She examined each one carefully studying the craftsman ship and the quality of the stones. "What are these made of?" She pointed to the fine wire binding that was black, "Black gold?"

"Si." He bent closer to Cara and using his little finger pointed to each element and counted the metals and stones off, "Titanium, black gold, ivory, onyx, amber and red jade, very masculine, no?"

Not only very masculine, but very sexy and would look great on Vittore.

Like he needed anything else to make him look sexy.

She held the bracelets imagining them on his wrist. One would be too small, two seemed incomplete. She sighed loudly. She knew she needed to get all three. God this was going to be expensive.

She did a quick calculation of what she had left on her American Express. She hadn't spent one penny since she arrived in Roma and she knew there would not be a hotel bill. She hoped she had enough. Just then her eye caught her engagement ring.

A smile formed on her face, "Why not!" Not intending to; she said it out loud.

The manager said "If the Signorina wishes to discuss the purchase the bracelets," he bowed slightly and extended his hand toward a bank of rooms at the end of the shop, "please follow me."

He led her to the room where she and Vittore had met with Dario from Cartier yesterday. She waited for a short while and the door opened, "Signorina, it is good to see you so soon. I see something caught your eye when you were here yesterday with Signore Falco?"

She saw he held a matt of black velvet in one hand and a beautiful box in the other. She assumed he had the bracelets in the box.

"Yes," her head nodded to indicate the box he held, "I would like to purchase those bracelets for Signore Falco. I don't know if Vittore mentioned yesterday but I am a gemologist and work part-time at Tiffany's in New York City." She didn't mention as a clerk. "So I am familiar with a few options I may have in this purchase." She waited for him to reply.

"Si Signore Falcon did mention you worked at Tiffany's. Very fine house."

"Then you know the quality of stones is in line with that of Cartier?"

"Si."

She slipped off her engagement ring, "Then we may need to talk."

Butterflies where running rampant in her stomach, she was cashing in a ring that cost her $6,000, for a man she barely knew. "It is a ¾ carat, Tiffany brilliant cut E-flawless diamond." She placed it on the velvet matt.

The gentleman picked it up and examined it with his lope. He nodded in appreciation of its beauty. "Ah, Tiffany never compromises quality for size. It is magnificent Signorina. I am sure you know the price is for the stone not the setting?"

"Yes, I know." She knew the platinum setting had no value for Cartier, it would only be the stone they would be interesting in bartering. And even then she knew she would not get its full value. But better to barter it to get the bracelets for Vittore, then to throw the ring in a box to let it sit unworn. Then a thought hit her.

"I'd like the Platinum redesigned into a toe ring."

He raised his eyes and there was a little laughter in them, "I see. You want to walk on the platinum?"

"Yes, something like that." She would love knowing every time she took a step she'd be symbolically stepping on Bryan.

"It is a lot of platinum, too much for a toe ring. What else could we make for you?"

"How much do you think would be left and what would you suggest?"

"I think the Signorina would not want another finger ring, No?" She shook her head an emphatic no. "I see. Not to be indelicate, but does the Signorina have any body piercings?"

A shiver shot down Cara's spine and she flushed.

Ohmigod a belly ring! She had wanted to get one, but Bryan said he thought it was repulsive.

"No, but I'll get one! What about a belly ring?"

He smiled brightly and looked very quickly at Cara's stomach, "Si that would use the rest of it nicely. Scusi. I will have the stone appraised and work out a price of the bracelets and rings. May I get you some Champagne?"

Another world, "Grazia."

In one fell swoop she got rid of the ring, bought a gift for a man whose kindness she could never repay and has done a *Take that Bryan* with a toe ring and belly ring. Shivers went down her spine thinking of Vittore playing with her belly ring with his tongue. Damn him, he was right, she cannot stop thinking of having sex with him! Damn him!

Champagne was brought to Cara as she waited to hear if the diamond would cover the cost of the bracelets. After about a half of an hour not only did Dario return but he was accompanied by another gentleman, but much older.

"Signorina, this is our gemologist and he is the one appraising your stone. He found it breathtakingly beautiful and wanted to meet an American that understood beauty rather than carat weight."

"Cara McGuire," she extended her hand, "it is a pleasure

to meet you as well." She was tickled that this older man was so intrigued by the stone. It had taken over a year before a stone came into Tiffany's of this perfection. It was the right cut for the stone and though small gave a play of color that could be seen across the room.

Gino leaned over her hand and kissed her knuckles. He then turned to Dario discussed some additional details then left the room. Dario sat and looked a Cara, "We can offer $4,000 American dollars for the stone and that will pay for the cost of the bracelets and some of the cost of the design and construction of the toe and belly ring." He sat and awaited her decision.

"Great, do it!" Never had she had as much fun blowing $6,000 not even when she bought the ring! With that Dario left the room to make the bracelets ready for her to give to Vittore.

He returned with the Cartier signature red leather box and bag. She was so excited she couldn't wait to get home and give her gift to Vittore. Home, hum there was a Freudian slip.

CHAPTER EIGHTEEN

Cara stopped briefly into the Caffe Greco for a cappuccino and to relax before going back to Vittore's. She had been thinking about her trip, how incredible it has been. She looked at the Cartier bag holding the bracelets she bought for him. She thought about the whirlwind of emotion she had experienced since arriving in Italy; about how much she enjoyed making love to and just being with Vittore. In her heart she did not want to leave but she knew his was a life separate from hers and this could never be. She rose and strolled out into the Piazza di Spagna.

Vittore's family arrived while she was out. And the normal quiet of the apartment had the din of activity only a family can bring to a house. It was pleasant and Cara smiled when she heard every one's voices. Bianca scolding Antinella from the bedroom as she was trying to get her to stand still as they tried on Antinella's dress; Davide and Vittore were in his office talking and laughing and no doubt congratulating each other on their success.

Giovanni was sitting enjoying some wine and apparently had been all afternoon. "Ah Cara, you are beautiful! Come sit with me. Everyone is too busy to relax and drink wine with an old man. Come Cara, sit!"

"How can I refuse?" She leaned over gave him a kiss on

his cheek as she accepted a glass of wine. "This Sagrantino is amazing. You should be proud of your sons."

"Si, it is good they will make a success of Conti Vineyards, but my real pride comes in the men that they are, they are both good men."

Cara smiled and held her glass in a salute, "Si Giovanni, they are, good men."

They sat in comfortable silence for a few minutes then Cara asked, "Are you retired Giovanni?"

"A little, I slowed down once Vittore took over the running of the hotels. It is a good thing Vittore likes business, Davide has his heart set in the vineyard." Giovanni laughed, "Leave it to Vittore to design a plan to merge it all together."

Cara sat a little stunned the word "hotels" kept playing through her head. "How many hotels do you own?" She took a sip wondering if she will need the wine for strength.

"Me, Cara? I only own 5 they are all here in Italy, but Vittore owns," Giovanni began doing some calculations in his head, "it must be over 50 now. He has them all over Europe and America."

Cara choked on her wine and barely got out the word, "Fifty!" and without thinking she added, "Who is he, Hilton of Europe?"

Giovanni smiled and nodded his head, "Si, Cara the last article written on him did that comparison! But Vittore only has the finest boutique hotels. He knows he can make more money with lower quality hotels, but only wants his boutiques."

Cara sat there looking at her wine, what the hell is she doing! She doesn't know this guy at all! She knew he had money, but this was Money with a capital M. She had to get home and get back to reality! She glanced at the Cartier bag and chuckled.

You dope! What were you thinking!

"Cara?" Giovanni invaded her daydream, "Cara, are you doing well?"

"Oh sorry, I just drifted off, thinking about all I need to do before I go home. I am so happy I get to see you, Bianca and Antinella once again. I was so afraid when we said goodbye that would be it." She saw confusion in Giovanni's eyes.

"But Cara, you will be coming back soon to see Vittore, no?" His expression was very troubled. "I know my son, Cara. He has fallen in love with you. Do you not know that?"

"Giovanni," she chuckled a little, "it's beautiful to think one can fall in love so quickly. He will forget all about me in a few days."

"No, Cara, he will not." Giovanni placed his glass on the table in front of them, "He has not forgotten you in over a year, why would he forget you now when he has finally loved you?"

"What do you mean "not forgotten me in over a year"? We just met Giovanni on the flight over, I've only know Vittore for a little over a week!" She looked kindly at him knowing he was getting Vittore's conquests mixed up.

"No Cara, he has loved you in silence for over a year! The lawyer he sent over to do his merger was not a good man for you; Vittore had hoped you would see that."

Cara stopped her sip midway, a cold wave spread through her body; she had to make sure she was getting this right.

Damn this was all confusing, too much happening, she had to have misunderstood.

"Giovanni, what do you mean the lawyer he sent over? From the United States? He had a lawyer come over here to do merger assessments? How long was this lawyer here, Giovanni?"

"I met him Cara, not a very giving man. Vittore was right, you are a woman of passion, and it is not good to be married to a man who has none. But I guess to be a lawyer you need to be a little cold." He took a sip of wine and relaxed into the sofa. "Si, this man came from the States, he was here three months."

Cara nearly dropped her wine glass.

Just then Antinella ran into the room and rushed up to Cara and gave her a huge hug. She had her dress on and she twirled to show Cara how beautifully if fit.

Cara pulled her in and held her tight; it has all been a lie! He pulled me into his world on a lie! He introduced me to his family knowing I would fall in love with them. That bastard, she held Antinella tight and tears streamed down her face. What was she going to do?

Bianca came in and excitedly told Cara her gown had arrived from Versace and reminded them that they had to go to the salon in less than an hour. She was twittering about the room talking and Cara was numb. She couldn't listen, she shook with rage. She wanted to explode.

How dare he!

"Cara are you alright, you do not look well, Cara. Why are you shaking so? Vittore come quick it is Cara! Vittore!" Bianca pried Antinella away from Cara and held her hand patting it saying, "Cara what is wrong? Cara you shake so!"

Just then Vittore rushed into the room and was stopped cold by her glare. He saw his mother trying to sooth Cara, but her eyes told him there was a rage building and was about to explode. "Papa?"

"I do not know Vittore, I told her about the lawyer from America and how you love her and she began to shake." Cara rose off the sofa and stood in front of Vittore and slapped his face so hard it burned the palm of her hand.

"You liar! You lied to me from the moment we met! You are Bryan's client, you sent him here, you sent him home and you arranged this whole thing! Why! What made you think you had the right to mess with my life! Who the hell do you think you are?" She raised her hand to slap him again, but he grabbed her wrist.

"No Cara, you do not understand." The look on his face was one of pain and sorrow. He knew he had messed this up, but he had hoped he could tell her in a way she could understand. "Cara let me explain!"

She spun out of his grasp and quickly surveyed the room, they were all there looking at this fight, watching her fall apart, seeing another man betray her.

She turned to face Vittore again, "You bastard," she lowered her voice hoping Antinella could not here, her voice shook with rage, "you lying fucking bastard! Don't ever touch me again!"

She heard Davide give a low whistle, "Pissed is an understatement."

Cara turned to light on him, "What you knew he was playing with me!"

Vittore reached out to pull her into his arms. "Hell no! Hell no! I am so out of here!" She looked into his face, "How could you do this? How? I didn't think you were a bastard as well! But you're the worst! Tell the bellman to get my things delivered to my room."

She looked at everyone in the room and her heart broke, "I am so sorry you all saw this, but," she glared at Vittore again, "I am sorry. I have loved knowing all of you, but I have to go back home."

"Cara, no! Let me tell you what has happened! Cara, do not leave without hearing me, please Cara!"

She turned to him again and said one word, "No." and headed for the door, crying, shaking, terrified. And then she heard a voice she didn't know, "Fermati, Cara! Papa no! Far aspettare, Cara! Grazie, Papa, Grazie!"

She turned to see Antinella beating on Vittore's chest with her little fists, "Papa, Papa, no!" Vittore crouched to be level with Antinella's eyes, "Mia Piccoli," Tears streamed down his face and he pulled her in and held her tight.

Cara stood motionless, everyone in the room staring at Vittore and Antinella, crying. Bianca was lifting prayers to heaven, Davide was crying but pacing like an animal and Giovanni looked at Cara and simply said, "You cannot go Cara, you cannot go like this. It is an answer to prayer. You must listen to my son. Listen to Antinella, Cara. They both love you. You must find out the truth before you can make such a decision. Stay Cara!"

Vittore looked up at Cara as she stood at the door, hand

on the knob, tears of joy and anger pouring from her eyes. "Please Cara, do not go like this. Let me explain, please." He still held tight to Antinella as she cried on his shoulder murmuring words in Italian.

Cara removed her hand from the door handle and moved towards Vittore and Antinella. "Antinella?" She whispered softly, "Antinella, I will stay and listen. Tell her I will listen to what you have to say, but I swear if you give her false hopes and break her heart, too, I will scratch your eyes out Vittore! I swear!"

Vittore relayed the message and Antinella ran to Cara and held her tight around the waist. What was he doing, introducing this little girl to a hope based on a lie? She had been through enough. At is precise moment she never hated a man more in her life!

Vittore brought Antinella back into his arms as he knelt to hold her in whispered words to calm her. She spoke, for the first time since her parents' death she spoke and it was to make Cara stay. It made Vittore's heart break. He wanted her to know he would do everything in his power to make Cara understand and stay, but he had been unfair to her and she may not forgive what he had done. He asked her to let him try to talk to Cara, to please not lose her voice now that she had found it. He would do everything he could to make her stay.

Antinella took his face in both her little hands and made him look at her. She said she would not lose her voice. She loved him and trusted him. Her little eyes were so serious, her voice so sweet. Vittore choked back tears. He was an emotional wreck. She said he was her Papa and she loved him. He pulled her into his chest, buried his face in her little shoulder and cried.

Davide began gathering everyone to leave the room so Vittore could begin his explanation without everyone listening. Vittore gave his brother a nod of thanks. When the room was cleared, Vittore cautiously turned to Cara. He had felt her rage and he knew she had not calmed. Her eyes were burning with anger and hatred. He ran his hand through his hair.

"I need a drink." He poured himself a glass of wine and refilled Cara's glass.

She was still standing, not a muscle in her body was relaxed. She was coiled and ready to strike and he knew he had one chance and only one chance to make her understand or he would lose her forever.

Vittore paced running his hand through his hair trying to decide where and how to begin and as he paced he stole glances at Cara.

"Rocco's parents worked for Papa. His father was head of security and his mother was my mother's best friend, her companion, Davide's and my second mother. After Rocco's death I did business as usual. Soon, I became aware of the enormous responsibility Rocco had put in my trust, Antinella and the winery. Antinella was not responding to the doctors and it was suggested she needed a more stable home environment. Implying I was not a good family for her." He looked to see if any softening had occurred in her posture, it had not.

"I could not let her go live with another family so eighteen months ago I decided to make Conti Vineyards a successful winey. I asked Davide to come home and help. The vineyard I knew produced excellent grapes, but it needed some investments to make it truly successful."

"I love my business, Cara, it has allowed me to do many things. I had to become a good parent for Antinella. But how can I do this and still manage my hotels and the winery?" Vittore finally sat, even if Cara would not, he had to stop pacing. He placed his elbows on his knees and put his head in his hands, rubbing his temples.

"The only solution was to allow others to run my hotels and I oversee their management. It is no small thing for me to give up that much control." He smiled to himself knowing it took every nerve he had to do that, he glanced at Cara. Her eyes burned, he should not have talked about control.

"I had decided to purchase three hotels in America, in Phoenix, Chicago and Seattle, a few months before Rocco's death. The locations were ideal and the properties were in good shape, but would need extensive decorating to bring them to the standard I have for my properties. I needed to secure a sizable loan. So I hired a firm in New York to assist me with the contracts and loan arrangements. That firm was Reed, Thompson and Fulbright." He looked again at Cara, not a muscle had moved.

"They came highly recommended by my attorneys here in Roma as being excellent in acquisitions and mergers. I met with them about fifteen months ago, in January of last year." He paused and looked directly into Cara's eyes. They were still cold and unforgiving.

"That is when I first saw you Cara. You had come to the office to collect Bryan to go sledding in Central Park." He smiled and shook his head with a little laugh, "Cara, you were like a breath of fresh air standing on the other side of the conference room window! Bundled up like a Michelin Man. Too many pairs of pants, a coat so big you couldn't put your arms down." He looked at her and laughed, "Cara you did not care of your appearance, you were on your way to play. It stole my heart. With all that I had been through with Rocco and Antinella, I wanted to see someone have joy. In a world of so much which is false, you stood there real."

Cara dropped onto the sofa.

He was there that day! He was the appointment. The reason Bryan couldn't join Katherine and the kids in Central Park to play. It was after the appointment that day that she and Bryan had their biggest fight. He said she always embarrassed him, that the man he was meeting with was going to be his biggest client and she showed up looking ridiculous. He made her feel so awful that night after he got home. He said that his client abruptly canceled the meeting after seeing her and it took that entire evening to make things right.

Cara was staring at Vittore.

He was the reason everything went wrong over the past year with she and Bryan.

Vittore saw the realization in her face, "I saw him yelling at you Cara, treating you roughly. He made me very angry. And while he was in the hall berating you, I canceled the appointment. I did not like this man who would be working on my account. I walked out moments after you entered the elevator." He watched her expression to see if any of this was making a difference.

"When I exited the building, I saw you crossing Fifth Avenue to go into the park. I followed you Cara." He rose from his chair and began pacing again. "I needed to see something real, Cara, something alive and joyous. I thought I would see it in you and I did." He knelt before her not touching her but making her look at him. "I watched you play with your nieces and nephews in the snow. I watched the snowball fight where you got hit in the face and how you took revenge on your sister. I watched you laugh so hard Cara, it made me laugh! I watched you for hours while you played and finally took a carriage ride to The Plaza."

He took a chance at touching her. He held her chin and ran his thumb along her jaw, "Cara not many women can be as free as you are. I cherished that. The fact that Bryan did not, made me angry. I watched him stand you up at restaurants and ignore you when you were out together. Spend long needless hours at work when he had you waiting for him. He is a fool Cara. I knew that. I wanted him away from you so you could figure it out yourself." Cara's eyes went cold as she stared at him.

"I asked that he be sent to Europe to inventory my hotels to give you time to realize he was not a good man for you. Cara he was killing your spirit, he had no right."

She exploded, tearing her chin from his hand, "No right! You're the one who had no right! Who the hell do you think you are? My relationship with Bryan had nothing to do with you! It was none of your business, I did not ask for you to save me from him. I did not ask to be one of your projects. I did not ask you to watch me! Because you deemed it not a good match you decided to screw it up! You are the most arrogant man I have ever known!"

She tried to stand but he knelt too close for her to get up. "No Cara, it was not like that. I heard your friends and sister worry about you. I knew what he was doing. He thought that befriending me would draw us closer. He shared things with me, Cara, things that if you knew would break your heart. I cherished you and hated him. I wanted you to find someone who would love you, not use you. I did not know it would be me. I am so sorry, Cara."

Vittore rose to sit beside her on the sofa, he managed to take one of her hands in order to keep her seated. He had to finish this, whatever the outcome. "Cara, please look at me." He used his other hand to turn her face towards him. "He is the one who left Italy. It was Bryan I was speaking to in the lobby of the hotel when you arrived. I told him to remain, the paperwork could wait. I did not send him back, Cara, it was his choice. I was not playing a game. I did not know I loved you until the night at the fountain. I knew you would be broken hearted. I put you in a suite, ordered the dress and shoes, it was the only thing I could think of to do. I wanted you to know how special you are."

Tears came to her eyes, it was all Vittore. Bryan had nothing to do with any of it. So Bryan did stand her up in Italy. God she was a fool. Could she ever pick them? Her lips trembled as the tears streamed down her face, he wiped them away with the pad of his thumb.

Her voice shook she barely spoke above a whisper, "You knew he was seeing other women didn't you? I thought maybe he was, but you knew didn't you?"

It broke his heart. He did not want to take her down this path. She did not need to doubt herself. She did not deserve this, but he had been too untruthful with her and he would not deceive her again; even if it meant losing her. "Si, Cara. I am sorry, Bella. He thought he would impress me, he did not. Cara, I am not a playboy. This is why I have handled this all so badly. I have never been in love. I was not expecting to fall in love. It happened and I was in too far and did not know what to do."

"Cara, please believe me. I thought if you saw me, the real me, my family, my passion, you'd fall in love with me.

So when I told you who I was and how it intermingled with your life, you wouldn't be so mad. I did not mean for you to hear of it this way. After the banquet tonight I was going to tell you. Cara, I fell in love with you at the fountain the first night we walked the streets of Roma."

He sat silent, hoping she would say something that was not filled with anger and rage. His heart beat loud in his chest and he prayed she would forgive him.

"I don't know what to say. I don't know what I should feel. You never should have approached me on the plane, you knew who I was, that I'd be meeting Bryan. How were you going to explain all that?"

"That was my stupidest plan." He hung his head in embarrassment. "I thought if I flirted with you, made a connection pretend I did not know who you were; when Bryan introduced us later he would see in both our eyes that we had found each other attractive. He would begin to see you as other men do, beautiful and alive. It was stupid, Cara. Not my proudest moment." He lifted his eyes to see if she would at least smile over his stupidity.

Her body was beginning to relax just a little, "You did all this to keep me from marrying Bryan because you did not think he deserved me?" Her voice was low but rattled. "Is that what you are saying, Vittore?" She stared straight into his eyes challenging him to speak truthfully. "That you did not interfere? You just watched and decided to make Bryan jealous to jar him awake, but you fell in love with me along the way and wanted me to fall in love with you too?" She finally smiled, "Oh Vittore that is pathetic!"

"I know Bella, it was very stupid. What do we do now Cara? Can you forgive me long enough to let these emotions settle down so we can see clearly? Please Bella, do not go away angry, we may both regret if for the rest of our lives. Please stay and think about all this, Bella."

Cara was exhausted, her emotions had been challenged since she got to Roma and it wasn't slowing down. She thought about the last several days. She closed her eyes momentarily and sighed, "I will not go away angry, Vittore. But I am not promising I will stay either. I will promise to think about this mess. I need some time to sort this out in my head decide how culpable you are. I know I am going to have more questions, do I have your promise that you will answer me honestly?"

"Si Cara, no more deception, only the truth even if it means losing you Cara. I promise." His eyes were hopeful.

Cara wanted so badly to still be angry with him, but she couldn't. Bryan was an ass. It just took her too long to figure it out. Vittore did not move the chess pieces on this board, Bryan did. She knew in her heart Bryan was having an affair, that he really didn't love her. She was just too scared to break it off. Now the decision was made for her by Bryan himself.

Cara touched his cheek, "Let's get through tonight and see where everything stands in the morning." She rubbed his cheek gently, "I really didn't mean to hit you so hard. I am sorry."

She couldn't dismiss the last several days either. She knew she had deep feelings for this man. Now she had to determine if they are real or imagined. "If you still want me to join you tonight, I had better get ready. You are a difficult man to be around Vittore. You are emotionally exhausting."

She smiled and rose from the sofa going out to the balcony where the family had gathered. "Bianca, Antinella, let's go get pampered. And you little girl had better talk to me nonstop! Now that I've heard that sweet voice I want to hear it 24/7."

Antinella ran to her, "Did you and Papa make up?" Bianca translated.

"Let's just say we are working on it. Come let's go do what girls do best."

Bianca translated again then rose giving Cara a hug. "Men can be very stupid, Cara, especially if they are a Falco!" She shot a glare at Giovanni and shook her head. Cara could tell by Giovanni's posture he had received a hefty lecture from Bianca while she and Vittore spoke.

CHAPTER NINETEEN

The salon gave Cara a chance to think about the last several days and what Vittore had told her. Since she couldn't engage in conversation she had almost two hours to think of nothing but what she had just learned. Piecing the puzzle together, filling in the blanks. She decided Vittore didn't interfere but was just not forthright and he was stupid as hell.

Who did he think he was the rescuer of the world! What was more confusing were her feelings towards him. This morning she was positive she loved him, now she was leery, not knowing if any of it was a game. That she still needed time to work that out and it couldn't be done in a salon. She decided to enjoy the evening and the next few days.

If she wasn't deported, there was still that hanging over her head! God how did she get into such messes?

When the three ladies returned to the suite they had about ninty minutes before they needed to be downstairs at the banquet. Cara still had not seen the dress Versace had sent over and decided to not look at it until it was time to put it on. Just in case it was one of the ones she didn't like, then it would be too late to even worry about it. She wondered if this was why some famous people were photographed in some of the ugliest dresses she had ever seen.

Please don't let it be ugly!

She went into Antinella's bedroom and helped her get a bath without damaging her hair. Edwardo's assistant did a perfect style, bangs cut straight across; hair straightened and pulled back on the sides to form a little braid in the back. She knew the perfect place to put the hair comb she had for her, right at the top where the braiding began.

Cara held Antinella's hair away from her body as she scrubbed herself clean. Then when she was done, Cara wrapped her in a big fluffy robe hugging her close. "Your Papa is a very bad boy Antinella. It will take a lot for me to forgive him." She made a face knowing Antinella knew a little of what she said, "How can such a good man do such stupid things?"

Antinella began rattling off Italian so fast Cara could barely make out a word, "Whoa, Whoa, since you found your voice you are a little magpie. I have no idea what you said." She did her finger talking by her mouth and shrugged her shoulders.

Antinella laughed, "Tu no Italiano, mi no English. Noi parlare mimica," and she moved her hands to her mouth, smiling.

"Si," she thought she understood her. "Tu?" Cara asked again pointing to herself, "tu is me?" Antinella nodded, "mi," she pointed to Antinella, "mi is you? I speak no Italian, you speak no English, what is noi?"

Antinella took Cara's hands and extended the pointer fingers and pulled them together, "noi." She brought them together again, "noi"

"We! Noi is We! You and I!" Cara pointed between herself and Antinella.

"Si si!!"

"I speak no Italian, you speak no English and We? What is mimica?." Cara kept saying "We" and moving her hands near her mouth," We....I know, we still talk with our hands! Parlare mimica!!" She hugged Antinella, "You are a very good teacher, I have a lot to learn!"

Bianca poked her head into the bath to see how things were going and told Antinella and Cara she had laid out her clothes on the bed. "Cara, you may want to dress Antinella last, she has a habit of getting dirty very fast!"

She studied the two of them sitting on the floor of the bath, laughing. "Cara, I have no right to offer an opinion, but please think hard about forgiving Vittore for whatever he has done. He has never brought a woman to the villa to meet Antinella. I know my son, he would never expose her to a woman he did not love. He loves you Cara, and sometimes love makes us do stupid things." She smiled and left the bath.

Cara played that thought over in her head, Bianca was right. Vittore would never do anything that would hurt Antinella. As mad as she was with him, as much as she tried to convince herself she didn't know this man, she did know one thing for sure; he would never ever let Antinella get hurt.

She had a lot to think about.

Cara popped up off the floor, "Come with me Antinella, we have some presents to distribute." She ran into her bedroom and grabbed the two bags, one for Antinella and one for Vittore, then went in search of him with Antinella in tow. They found him on the balcony, sipping wine already in his tux. When he heard the laughter behind him he stood and turned to look at the two of them.

Cara's heart stopped, Vittore was breathtakingly handsome. "Wow!" It just came out, Cara blushed.

Vittore stood before her in a custom tailored suit that fit his chiseled body, accentuating his broad shoulders, long torso and thin hips. The weight of the fabric draped comfortably around him. His jacket was opened revealing a vest of black on black brocade. The white shirt had blue sapphire button covers and his cufflinks were huge sapphires encased in white gold.

Vittore laughed, "You are no longer mad at me Cara?"

"Ah, still deciding, but mad or not you look...wow, that's what you look! Wow!"

He put his glass on the table, "I am glad you approve. Now what has the two of you laughing?" He reached out and picked Antinella up into his arms. He held her on his hip and picked up his wine glass again enjoying the dark rich flavor.

Cara stood in front of the two of them and held out the two bags. "Despite being mad at you, you have been very kind to me and some sort of thank you is deserved."

"Cara, you did not need to do this. Cartier, it is very expensive no matter how small the gift. What have you done Cara?" He looked at her left hand and noticed she was not wearing her engagement ring. "Mia Bella, what have you done?"

"What I wanted to do! Open it! Antinella first!"

Antinella tore into her bag and produced a pink box wrapped with a satin ribbon with little hearts stamped all around it. Antinella squealed something in Italian and tore the present open to see resting inside a beautiful hair-comb covered in pearls and diamond chips. She couldn't wait to get out of Vittore's grasp to begin jumping up and down and hugging Cara and Vittore alternately. Then she ran off the balcony in search of Bianca.

"So I guess that leaves me?" Vittore carefully opened the bag and found the red leather box within. He peeked at Cara and smiled. Her eyes were full of excitement.

"Cara you are sure you want to do this? I am not sure you have forgiven me and if you do not then this is a very expensive gift."

"It is the right thing to do, no matter what. Open it! I want to see if you like it!"

"Mia Bella, you are very complicated" He opened the hinge of the box to reveal the three bracelets. "Cara, they are beautiful! Cara you are too generous!"

"Put them on, I have fantasized about how they would look on you." She held the box opened towards him so he could remove the bracelets and put them around his wrists. "I knew they would look perfect on you! Wow do they look good on you? How do you do it?"

"Bella, they are exquisite!" He hesitated only a moment and pulled her into his arms, kissing her, gently moving his tongue so tenderly around hers. He did not want to separate. He wanted to feel her body close to his. He wanted the fear of losing her to disappear. If he could only kiss her until she forgave him.

"Bella, I do not know what to say. They are perfect. You are perfect. Please Bella, forgive me. Think only of the past few days, not the past few hours. Please know I love you." He whispered the words inches from Cara's mouth his breath was like butterflies on her lips. He held her waist in close to his body as his other hand held the back of her neck, pulling her in as close to him as possible. "Mia Bella I love you!" he rested his forehead on the top of her head.

"I know Vittore, I know." She kissed his neck. "I know."

Bianca walked onto the balcony and smiled seeing them in an embrace, thinking there might be a chance for forgiveness. "Cara, I am sorry, but you need to dress! Hurry we only have 20 minutes!"

"Go Cara." He kissed her temple.

"You know I have not seen the dress. Do you know which one they sent?"

"Si Cara and you will be pleased, go put it on I want to see how beautiful you will make the dress."

Fifteen minutes later Cara walked out on to the balcony where everyone had gathered to enjoy each other's company before the banquet. Davide saw Cara first and gave a long low whistle. Vittore spun around knowing Cara had entered the balcony.

Giovanni said, "Mama Mia"

Vittore stood staring at her, she was beautiful. The Versace gown was yellow chiffon. The strapless gowns' bodice was hand embroidered with hundreds of natural colored seed pearls forming no pattern but dense and brilliant it their color. A small asymmetrical bow was tied under the bodice and from it floating gracefully to the floor were layers of chiffon. Cara wore a small gold chain at her neckline and single diamond pave bangle bracelet.

Her auburn hair was in a bun that sat low on her neck so it was soft and had a loose feel as if it would fall out at any moment. The look was sophisticated and sexy.

"Oh Cara, Versace should pay you to wear this dress! Mia Bella you are exquisite." All Vittore could do was stare, she was beautiful. He was lost in her beauty, time stood still, all he wanted to do was feast his eyes on her. No one spoke it was silent.

Cara twirled, "I cannot believe this is the dress they sent, it was the one I wanted. It is the most beautiful dress I have ever worn."

"No Cara you are the most beautiful woman that will ever wear this dress. No one can make it as beautiful as it is on you, Bella, no one."

Antinella came in close to Vittore and motioned him low to whisper something in his ear. "Si piccolo. I almost forgot." Vittore reached inside his jacket pocket and produced a red leather ring box.

Cara's eyes went wide with fear.

"Cara, it is the right thing to do, no matter what." He used her words. Her hand shook as she took the box from his hand. She just stared at it closed between her fingers. She couldn't move. She was frozen.

Vittore held the box gently in her hands, "Here you seem to not know how to get started." They were the words he said in the dressing room at Versace. She trembled in anticipation.

He lifted the hinge and inside sat the yellow diamond she had admired at Cartier. "Ohmigod, Vittore, no. You can't." It was a whisper.

"But I can Cara and I did and I will forever, if you will allow me." He searched her eyes for understanding. "For now it is a gift, I hope later it is more. Do not panic, no questions are being asked right now, no promises to be made. Wear the ring with your beautiful gown tonight and enjoy, Cara, enjoy."

He slipped the ring on her finger and kissed her hand and softly swirled the tip of his tongue between her middle and ring finger, looked into her eyes and smiled. Her knees went weak just as he wrapped his hand around her waist. "It is good I know your weaknesses Cara, no?"

The banquet was a media frenzy. Cara had no idea Vittore was so well know, so famous.

But she was the focus of the reporters.

Who was she? Vittore had never been seen in public with a woman before! He was considered the most eligible bachelor in Italy. Who was this American woman?

The only thing that saved Cara's sanity is she had no idea she was the center of attention.

Vittore was never far from her side and if the paparazzi got too aggressive he was there to gently move her out of their way. In the dining room it was calmer. No media was allowed, this was in essence a business dinner and press releases had been prepared before hand to pass out.

Since the entire dinner was in Italian she had to rely on the Falco's to keep her informed. Vittore basically was announcing his decision to promote others within his company to manage the hotels, while he and his brother focus on Conti Vineyards. He would still have controlling interest, he was not selling his company, just stepping back to assist in the development of the winery.

The evening was magical. They danced, laughed and joked with his family. Made polite conversation with so many people she couldn't count. It was a whirl of fantasy.

Bianca, Giovanni and Antinella had returned to the suite hours ago and the dinner was finally wrapping up at 2AM.

She and Vittore were having their last dance. It was a slow and easy tempo. He held her gently in his arms, pulling her hips in as close as possible. He kissed her shoulder, "You are beautiful, Cara Bella, exquisitely beautiful."

"Vittore, when you spoke to your attorneys today what did they say about me? Am I being deported?"

"No, Cara. The police in Montefalco have decided they are not going to press charges." He held her close and kissed the top of her ear. "After Niccolo was arrested they went to his home and discovered information on the Mafia's drug trafficking in Umbria. This information led to the arrest of a Mafia Don they had been seeking but unable implicate until now. So the police are happy that the incident at Conti Vineyards happened. They might even name a day in your honor."

"They are not. God, you must think I am the most gullible person alive!" She laughed thrilled she would not be deported nor arrested.

"So you stalked me for a year? How did you stay hidden? And please do not tell me you hired a detective!" She smiled and looked into his face.

Vittore lowered his eyes.

"Vittore, you hired a detective to watch me! To watch Bryan! Oh Vittore, I should be so mad at you, what were you thinking!" Cara rested her forehead on his chest as they danced.

"I have so many things to apologize for Cara. I really did not know I would have the chance to love you. I thought my love would be in my heart forever, but never realized. Then when Bryan told me you were flying to Italy, I flew to New York City and booked the same flight to return to Roma as you were on."

"I only knew a week before I left that I was coming to Roma."

"I caught the first available flight to New York City and arrived a day before to catch the flight back to Roma that you were on. I negotiated with two of the first class passengers to buy their seats."

"Oh Vittore, do you mean the seat being available next to you wasn't an accident?"

"No it wasn't."

"How did you know little Bethie would have a temper tantrum and I'd end up in first class?"

"I am good Cara, but that I couldn't even plan. No my plan was to have the purser quietly move you up to first class using some excuse. I figured you wouldn't object too much given a chance to travel first class rather than coach. But Bethie relieved me of trying to come up with a believable lie."

Cara rested her head on Vittore's shoulder as they danced. "Vittore if this wasn't so pathetic it would be funny. What were you thinking?!"

"All I thought is I would have a chance to be alone with you. It was not my intention to come between you and Bryan, I just didn't want him to hurt you. Until that first night we spent on the streets of Roma, I had no thought of having a woman in my life. Up until then all my focus was on reorganizing my company, moving back to Montefalco, managing the winery and taking care of Antinella. I had accepted that I would be a single parent and was content with my decision." Vittore gently lifted her chin and looked into her eyes, "Then I saw you flirting with Paulo at the bar, you smiling and laughing. You were beautiful, joyful. Oh Cara, I love your joy!"

Cara followed his lead around the dance floor for a few more songs and finally asked if he would mind if she went up to bed.

As they made their way to the lobby, she caught sight of Davide dancing with a beautiful dark haired Italian beauty. Cara thought the amber ring. She went flush, was it really only twelve days ago, so much had happened!

They entered the private elevator and half way up Cara pressed the stop button. "I have been giving today a lot of thought, Vittore, and I have made a decision." She waited for his reply, it was slow in coming, she knew he was afraid of what she was about to say.

"Cara, please do not make a fast decision, let your temper calm. Please Cara, for both our sakes." He pleaded with her.

"You have not been entirely honest with me Vittore. But, I do not think you did anything to interfere with my relationship with Bryan. I think your desire to make all things right in the world got the best of your good judgment. So I have decided not to remain mad at you, but this cannot go unpunished Vittore," she whispered as she undid the buttons of his shirt and lowered her hand to his waist. "You are going to be punished." Her fingers curled around him stroking slowly as she kissed his chest.

Vittore pressed the stop button so the elevator could continue its assent. "Mia bella, I have no doubts."

When the doors opened, Cara took hold of his shirt tails

and walked backwards into his bedroom pulling him along. They never broke eye contact, she had a very mischievous smile on her face, he, his devil smile.

They both wanted to make up, to no longer have this tension between them. When they entered the bedroom Cara dropped the shirt tails and began kissing his chest, sliding his shirt and jacket off his shoulders.

He stood bare-chested in front of her, smiling waiting. His hair was tied back and fastened with an ornate medallion. She reached up and undid the fastener and let his hair fall forward. She pushed him back on the bed and made him sit down. Lifting first one leg then the other, she removed his shoes and socks. He reached out to touch her.

"No Vittore, I will tell you when." She had him stand as she reached down and unfastened the waistband of this trousers and easing them down his legs, kissing his thighs as she removed them, tossing them aside. He never wore anything besides his trousers and she did no more than run the tip of her nose up his hard shaft as she stood.

Vittore's deep guttural moan was ragged and needy. He tried to hold her head near him, but she eased her way up to kiss his lips. "No Vittore, I will tell you when." She turned her back to him and as she removed the pins that held her hair in place, he unzipped the gown and let if fall to the floor. She turned to face him.

"Oh Cara," he stepped forward. The vision before him was heaven. Cara wore a cream lace strapless bustier, garter belt, thong and hose. Vittore shook with desire. He wanted her now. But she put a palm on his chest and said once again, "No Vittore I will tell you when." And she pushed him back onto the bed.

She laid him back on the bed and stood in between his legs, working her tongue up his body pausing, teasing, until she was leaning over his entire torso kissing his chest, neck and nibbling his earlobe. She kept climbing until her breasts were within inches of his mouth. He attempted to capture one, but again, she made him wait. She climbed over his shoulders brushing her heat over his face, not allowing him to taste its sweetness. She knelt at the head of the bed and beckoned him forward with her forefinger. He placed his head on the pillow. Vittore moaned, "Cara Bella, I like the way you punish me."

Vittore's lust was building. He reached out a hand to pull her near and she inched back and shook her head no. She straddled his stomach, leaning forward she ran her hands up his arms stretching them over his head and off to the sides, stretching herself open in front of him.

Cara reached down between the mattress and headboard and brought out a silk cord she had secured there early that morning and slipped a noose over his wrist gently then she took his other wrist and secured it with a tie fastened to the other side. She then rose sitting on his belly and looked down on him smiling.

He reached to stroke her face and noticed the restraints, "Cara?"

"I told you I was going to punish you Vittore." She began feathering kisses down his neck across his chest over his belly along his hip. Her hair dipped softly and played with his growing arousal sending shivers across his body. He fought against the restraints. "Cara, please!"

"No, this is your punishment. You must lie there and be silent." Cara lifted her head and gave him a wicked smile.

"Cara you drive me mad! This is too much."

"That's the plan." She rose and tied a silk scarf over his eyes. "All you are going to be able to do is feel Vittore. No touching, no seeing." He felt a pull on his lower lip, "And no talking or I will tie another scarf around that soft perfect mouth."

He groaned, "Oh Cara, you do not know what you are doing."

She whispered in his ear, "Oh yes I do." She stroked his lips with her tongue and placed her opened mouth over his and whispered, "Vittore, I will not warn you again, Shsssh." Then she licked the roof of his mouth. He released a loud painful moan as he continued to struggle against the restraints.

Vittore felt her weight shift as she sat again on his belly. Her fingers feathered over the inside of his arms trailing the touch across his shoulders, around his clavicle, down his chest stopping to twirl gently around his nipples.

She leaned forward and licked; nipping, lapping, swirling her tongue over his chest. Her warm hands following behind each lick trailing lower.

Vittore was struggling against the restraints in an attempt of stop his body from shaking with desire. Not being able to see or touch Cara heightened his senses. The perfume on her filled his lungs. The softness of her hair as it cascaded over his body. Vittore moaned, "Cara!"

He heard a soft, "Hush my love." He moaned.

Cara moved to his side continuing her journey down his body, lingering at the top of his thigh, kissing where the leg merged with his pelvis allowing him to brush gently against her cheek. Cara trailed her kisses down his leg, feeling the taunt muscles ripple under his skin as she kissed and nipped her way to his foot, licked his instep then transferred her attention to his other leg working her way up towards his hips.

"Cara," He could barely talk. His body never felt so alive, he trembled with desire, "stop, please. This is torture, please!"

Cara slithered up his body like a cat on the prowl. She captured his mouth with hers and whispered, "Hush."

Vittore fought harder against the silk cords and Cara noticed his wrists were chaffing. She lingered long enough to kiss the wounds and administer tender kisses to his pulse. It was like lightning struck. Vittore had to touch her. The submissiveness and helplessness was driving him mad. He had to break the ties, he fought against them.

She crawled down his body, using her tongue to arouse points on his body she knew would bring him pleasure. She lingered as she moved slower hearing his breath ragged. Cara played at the base of his steel before plunging the heat into her mouth. All Vittore could feel was the warmth and slickness play over him. He was sure he would not survive.

Rather than continuing to fight Vittore relaxed and allowed Cara to possess his body. She moved like silk over him and it was delicious. He lay still, all senses peaked, he lost his breath he had never felt anything so wonderful. He couldn't see her or touch her and it was the most sensual experience of his life. He moaned very quietly, he did not want her to bind his mouth. He wanted to scream her name, but he knew he had to obey her wishes.

He felt her straddle his hip, and she slowly encircled him, soft, wet and hot. She began moving leisurely on top of him resting her fingertips softly on his chest. Her movements were slow and deliberate. She knew how to move her hips to heighten her pleasure and his.

Vittore was going mad; he fought hard against the restraints. Cara leaned forward and kissed his neck.

His hips bucked against her. He was in a frenzy. He had to touch her, see her, to take control of her. He had to do this now!

"Hush my love. You're being forgiven. Be quiet and let me show you how much I love you Vittore. I am yours to love forever, Vittore." Her movements were so gentle, languid, but the more she moved her hips the harder he fought to touch her.

"Cara, you have punished me long enough, release me so I can see your face when you tell me you love me. Bella it is all I have wanted to hear, but now I want to see you say the words, I want to know it is not a trick." He felt a length of silk tickle over his lips. "Cara no! No!"

The binding of the silk tightened around his wrists. He didn't care if he broke the wood of the headboard. He had to get loose, to rip this blind fold off to see her face. A rage deep inside was building, he knew in a few moments he would be out of control. Cara leaned her breasts just above his face and he felt the silk release.

A loud roar escaped his lungs and he rose throwing the blindfold aside and rolling Cara onto her back, hovering over her. His eyes were dark and clouded, his skin was on fire. His arousal was in need of release.

"Cara, I love you. I have never loved like this. Please let me hear your words, see your mouth form them."

"I love you." She paused and searched his eyes, "I never want to be apart, I want to share a life with you, Vittore, until we are old. I have never wanted anything more in the world." Her words were but a whisper, but they rang loud and joyfully in Vittore's ears.

He lightly kissed her lips, "Cara I am glad you are no longer angry with me. I think if you ever punish me again I will die. Please Cara, never do this again." He slowly slid into her and felt her body shiver in anticipation. "Promise me Cara, never again." He moved slowly deeply his eyes were hooded as he watched her face.

She lay enjoying the sensation of him, "I promise Vittore, never again." Her head rolled in ecstasy.

"You are lying to me Bella."

She smiled broadly, "Yes I am, Vittore." His hips moved into her, "Oh I am definitely lying to you!"

POSTSCRIPT

Many of my readers were interested in the background history and locations I included in Vittore's Secret. I'd like to briefly address a few questions that have been posed to me.

There is a town called Montefalco nestled in the mountains outside Assisi Umbria which produces the local wine of Sagrantino.

Montelfalco does boast that is the birthplace of 8 saints and they do feel they are blessed with a rich wine harvest every year due to that fact.

The information about the Amber room is factual. It was made in Germany in 1710 and given to the Peter the Great in 1716. When the Nazi's invaded Russia during WWII the room was disassembled and removed by the German's, never to be seen again. However, there is no indication the amber from that room ever became jewelry.

Also the opera, *Christmas Eve's* opening performance by Rimsky-Korsakov at the Imperial Mariinsky Theatre was attended by newly married couple, the Czar Nicholas II and Czarina Alix. Alix had not yet changed her name and although there was much distain for her Germany heritage, there was no attempt on her life, at least not at the Mariinsky Theatre.

The Murgese horse is an Italian treasure and is unique

to the country. It is a gentle and obedient horse that is used largely for cross country riding.

The hotel St. George, though English in its name is exactly as described, with the exception of the salon but the spa is very much a part of the hotel. It is located on the Tiber River directly across from the Vatican.

The Autostrada does wind its way beside the ancient road of Flaminia passing the town of Narnia. And I do not know if Italy's Narnia is the inspiration for C.S. Lewis but as magical as the area is, it very well could have been.

The fountain at the bottom of the Spanish Steps was a creation of the Bernini and it is a representation of a boat.

Umbria has recently seen an increase of drug trafficking and has been diligent in doing all that is possible to keep the mafia out of its region.

Caffe Greco, the Spanish Steps and the area being a fashion district filled with designer shops do exist and is a very busy tourist district.

And yes, theft is the bane of all tourists, even in Italy. So if you visit be mindful of how you carry and where you place your purse and other valuables. You may not be as lucky as Cara to have a gorgeous Adonis to protect you. If only, huh?

Finally thank you for selecting my book. I have several other projects in the que, so check my tweets occasionally to keep posted on the updates.

Follow me on Tweeter: http://twitter.com/CiprianiKelly also www.blogspot.com/kellyciprian